A SECOND SHOCK . . .

The storm poured everything it had at the desert complex, slashing at the buildings with a frenzy of sound, light, and rain that left Al momentarily deaf and blind.

"Admiral Calavicci!" Gooshie cried, stepping back from the console and raising his hands to shield his eyes against the flash of electricity that sparked across the controls, making them surge with an array of color as every sensor and dial went red-line. The lights overhead dimmed to almost black, then flared brighter than before. "Get out of there *now!*"

He didn't have to say it more than once. Al swung about and managed a single racing step toward the exit when the world around him suddenly screamed with light so brilliant that he was blinded. A ripple of sensation that wasn't exactly pain or quite pleasure shot through his body, exciting every nerve and raising every hair . . .

. . . then the Accelerator, Philip Payne, Gooshie, Ziggy, and everything he knew as familiar were gone, replaced by darkness and pandemonium.

QUANTUM LEAP

OUT OF TIME. OUT OF BODY.
OUT OF CONTROL.

QUANTUM LEAP Novels from Ace Books

QUANTUM LEAP: THE NOVEL
TOO CLOSE FOR COMFORT
THE WALL
PRELUDE
KNIGHTS OF THE MORNINGSTAR
SEARCH AND RESCUE

QUANTUM LEAP

SEARCH AND RESCUE

A NOVEL BY

MELISSA CRANDALL

BASED ON THE UNIVERSAL TELEVISION
SERIES *QUANTUM LEAP*
CREATED BY DONALD P. BELLISARIO

ACE BOOKS, NEW YORK

Quantum Leap: Search and Rescue,
a novel by Melissa Crandall, based on the
Universal television series QUANTUM LEAP,
created by Donald P. Bellisario.

This book is an Ace original edition,
and has never been previously published.

QUANTUM LEAP: SEARCH AND RESCUE

An Ace Book / published by arrangement with
MCA Publishing Rights, a Division of MCA, Inc.

PRINTING HISTORY
Ace edition / December 1994

ISBN: 0-441-00122-X

ACE®
Ace Books are published by The Berkley Publishing Group,
200 Madison Avenue, New York, NY 10016.
ACE and the "A" design are trademarks
belonging to Charter Communications, Inc.

PRINTED IN THE UNITED STATES OF AMERICA

10 9 8 7 6 5 4 3 2 1

To JoAnn Baasch, Sharona,
and Risë Shamansky.

But mostly it's for Edward Everett, Jr., with love.
He knows why.

ACKNOWLEDGMENTS

The author gratefully acknowledges the following individuals for their willingness to assist in the preparation of this manuscript:

Pam Spurlock; the Canadian Consulate General; the Canada Map Office; Kristin Rooke and Wendy Carofano, for answering late-night medical questions; LaVerne Barnes, Manager of Media Relations for the Ministry of Tourism and Ministry Responsible for Culture, Province of British Columbia; the Parks and Outdoor Recreation Division of Clearwater, British Columbia; Jim and Gabrielle of Richmor Aviation at the Saratoga County Airport, Saratoga Springs, New York; and, most especially, Ellen Hodgson, Zone Clerk of Wells Grey Zone, British Columbia Parks, Clearwater, British Columbia.

CHAPTER
ONE

With a cheshire cat grin affixed as firmly to his features as the ever-present cigar was to his person, Al Calavicci ascended the basement stairs of the Quantum Leap complex at a jaunty pace. The long-cut, peacock-hued suit jacket flapped gaudily around his thighs, the metallic-threaded material of pants and jacket rippling under the overhead lights in coruscations of violent, tear-inducing blue, green, magenta, and purple as he fairly danced up the steps like a psychedelic Fred Astaire.

All things considered, life was good. Sure, his best friend was trapped somewhere in time. But other than that, life was very good indeed. With the past several years serving as a comparison, he had long ago realized that, compared to those at other organizations, the work conditions at Quantum Leap were certainly a whole lot more pleasant than any he'd ever experienced in a previous career.

Just think of it: the entire complex was astringently clean. His co-workers were brilliant, erudite professionals whom he had come to genuinely care for a great deal (except for Gooshie, of course, though he supposed he could find the largesse to forgive even that little dweeb for the bad blood between them regarding Tina. There was no arguing that

1

the man was brilliant). There wasn't a deficient pair of legs in the bunch (again, except for Gooshie, although it wasn't as though Al had ever looked at the computer programmer's legs with any interest. What a thought!). The food was better than average, a fact to which he could sincerely attest, having recently come from his evening's repast of steak and baked potato in the basement cafeteria. (No day-old egg salad on two slabs of cardboard for Mama Calavicci's baby boy!) He felt safe and secure from the bouts of paranoia that had haunted him for so long after his return from Vietnam. Here in the middle of the desert, there wasn't much chance that someone would break down the door and make him a POW all over again.

Best of all, he got to make his own hours (a condition he had voluntarily, and somewhat stringently, curtailed since Sam got himself caught in whatever it was that made him Leap from life to life like a cattle-prodded rabbit). Despite the stiffness of his self-imposed schedule, Al still managed to finagle a free hour here and there in between Sam's Leaps to catch a little shut-eye or (and this, of course, was what had put the shit-eating grin on his face) catch a little afternoon delight with his beautiful, winsome, adoring, loving, legs-to-her-ears, and stacked-to-the-rafters-like-a-brick-barn Tina. God! Just thinking about the woman made it difficult to walk!

Using both hands, Al pressed the horizontal release-bar on the orange door at the top of the stairs and stepped into the white-walled corridor beyond. Out of a mostly unconscious habit long ingrained by his years in the service, Al gave each direction a thorough look-see. There was no one in the brightly lit hallway and the offices to his right were dark, their doors closed and locked, the staff long since gone home to dinner and the evening's entertainment, then bed, and of course . . .

He shook his head with tolerant amusement. "Get your mind out of the boudoir, Calavicci, and back on the Project, where it belongs. You've had your fun." He leered, his ever-present good spirits coming to the fore as they nearly always did. "For now." A deft movement of his tongue smoothly switched his cigar from one cheek to the other. Sighing with blissful indulgence, he turned left and headed down the longer leg of the corridor toward the central hub of the Quantum Leap complex, where the Imaging Chamber, the Accelerator, and Ziggy were housed.

A few minutes' brisk walk brought him to his destination. The wide, blue, electronically secured sliding doors leading into the main laboratory were security-locked against easy ingress. Too much was at stake—particularly now that Sam, for all intents and purposes, was missing—to risk the intrusion of curious eyes. Al didn't have a clue as to how he was going to deal with the money people when they began sniffing around, asking probing questions and demanding progress reports on the advancement of Dr. Beckett's theory of the link between quantum physics and time travel. He knew he hadn't a prayer that it would be *if* they asked. With investors, it was *always* a case of *when*. He only hoped the powers-that-be would let Sam be back home by then so *he* could deal with it. He was the boss, after all, though lately Al had become uncomfortably aware of the role that a "sidekick" really played in life . . . particularly when the chips were down and the head honcho (unwillingly, in this case) had taken a powder.

Blowing a thick blue cloud of cigar smoke over his head, Al withdrew from his jacket pocket a white plastic card embossed with his picture, name, and Social Security number. His Project access code number was punched through the plastic in a series of seemingly random holes. Al slipped the card into the slot beside the door, over which was a row of three lights. The first in the row came on, glowing bright red. Al tapped out the access code number on the finger pad beneath the slot and the light switched to the second bulb, shining a brilliant blue. Al then punched in his personally chosen code word (S-E-X, much to Sam's patient chagrin), and the final light lit up in emerald green. He heard the lock click deep inside the door and Ziggy's voice greeted him before the two panels had even slid apart.

"You're a scoundrel and a rogue, Admiral Calavicci," the decidedly feminine voice remarked in a tone that was awfully

3

amused sounding for a machine that wasn't supposed to be capable of emotions.

"And you're a girl after my own heart, Zig," he returned routinely. "Now if we could only make you a body to go with that voice, you'd own my soul."

"Who would want it?" she responded. "Having witnessed the vigorous performance you inflict upon the female human form, I think I'll pass if it's all the same to you."

Al stopped short, the door shooshing silently closed behind him, and glared up and around the room, knowing full well that Ziggy could see him from almost every possible angle. "You've been spying on me again, haven't you?" he demanded impatiently. He received silence by way of a reply and made a face. "Oh, jeez, can't a guy have a little privacy once in a while?"

"There is not enough privacy in the world for you," Ziggy replied. "I checked. And, Admiral Calavicci, what does it mean when Tina says—"

"Later!" he snapped, cutting her off, and strode toward the center of the room where Gooshie, in his habitual and nearly paranoically clean white lab coat, worked diligently behind the main console. *Ziggy's only a machine,* Al kept reminding himself. So why the feeling that she was having a belly laugh right now at his expense? He suppressed a chuckle. Women. You had to love 'em.

"Hey, Gooshie!" he called. "You got a fix on Sam yet?"

"Not quite, Admiral," the short, dark-haired programmer replied. His face was a lot more unhappy than it had any right to be, if everything were normal. His thick-fingered hands toyed with the dials in front of him and he chewed on his bottom lip in a manner Al found disconcerting.

" 'Not quite'?" Al reiterated testily, his pace slowing. "What the hell does that mean?" He glanced into the Accelerator. Sam's familiar form lay stretched out on the floor where the last inhabitant had left it upon fleeing back to her own skin. One hand rested atop his stomach and his head was tilted slightly to one side, the graying forelock falling across his closed eyes. From here, his chest rising and falling with the pace of his slow, even breathing, the physicist looked

4

peacefully asleep. In point of fact, that was probably close to the actual case, but with one pertinent exception—the lights were on at the Beckett household, but no one was home.

Al's molars ground hard on the cigar. He puffed an agitated cloud of smoke toward the ceiling and ignored Ziggy when she began to fake a cough. Damn it, but he'd be glad when Sam took up residence again where he belonged! He wanted to hear *Sam's* voice coming out of that body instead of the anguished cry of someone frightened right down to their soul. He wanted to see his friend looking back at him out of those eyes instead of some terrified stranger. He wanted Sam's laughter and company. He wanted to shake Sam's hand and know it was the physicist feeling the contact.

Al crammed one hand into a jacket pocket, pulling it all awry in a manner that would have earned him a rap up side the head with a wooden spoon when he was a youngster. "What's going on, Gooshie?" Al asked more quietly, knowing the other man got flustered when he was out of sorts. One hand on his hip, he jabbed the cigar toward Sam's prone body. "Ziggy told me Sam had Leaped. She *interrupted* me when I was very, *very* busy to tell me that," he added threateningly. "I was up to my eyebrows in, uh, work, and you know how I hate being bothered when I'm working."

If the programmer picked up on the innuendo, he gave no sign. He shook his head confusedly and raised mournful eyes from the panel before him. "I'm sorry, Admiral Calavicci. Dr. Beckett *has* Leaped . . . I think. At least that's what Ziggy says."

"Unlike humans, *I'm* never wrong," the computer replied frostily from whatever part of her wasn't absorbed in trying to solve the current difficulty. Her voice came from the speaker closest to Al, as though she were standing beside him for support.

Real or imagined, the gesture warmed Al's heart. "Down, girl," Al soothed as Gooshie winced and whispered a heartfelt apology to the computer for even *alluding* that she might make an error. He directed his next question at both of them. "If Sam's Leaped, then what's the problem?"

5

"This storm is the problem," the programmer replied promptly, casting a brief glance toward the room's windows, set high in the wall near the ceiling. The long, horizontal frames and the wire meshing between the plates of unbreakable glass were briefly illuminated in a flash of lightning that lit the entire night sky and gave an eerie, bluish cast to everything in the room. Moments later, the floor trembled faintly beneath their feet as thunder roared its deafening response.

Al squinted in the flashbulb-like glare, blinking away the spots before his eyes. Oh, yeah. The storm. Deep within the Project's basement, the incessant howling of thunder had been reduced to rumbles so mild he barely paid attention to them. Besides, his mind (as well as other portions of his anatomy) had been busy elsewhere. Coming upstairs afterward, he'd thought he heard something, but hadn't paid it much mind.

Now he realized just how severe a storm it was. Wind buffeted the complex, howling in the gutters, the sound deadened only by the building's thick structure. Rain battered and slashed against the complex with the fierce intensity only Nature at her best can unleash. Thunder rolled and lightning cracked again, brightly enough to make both men wince and lift a hand to shield their eyes against the glare.

Gooshie's hands strayed back to the console and the readout dials. "According to the local weather service, Admiral, a storm of this magnitude hasn't visited this area for two decades. The high winds and intense electrical surges are playing havoc with the machinery, making it difficult for Ziggy to get a fix on Dr. Beckett or bring through whoever he's Leaped into." His sad, slightly molelike dark eyes sought Al's. "Technically speaking, for safety's sake we should probably shut down until the storm is over, but—"

Angered by the suggestion, Al went right up into the programmer's face, their noses almost touching. Gooshie's words had sent a bullet of fear through his spine. "Read my lips, Gooshie. We are *not* shutting down!"

"As I was about to say," the other man continued quietly, unperturbed by Al's threatening stance or tone, "if we shut down, there's a chance we might never find Dr. Beckett again."

"There is a seventy-five percentile probability of that occurring if we effect a shutdown of the current system at this time," Ziggy told them helpfully.

"Shut up!" Al snapped, and worried the soggy stump of his cigar with his teeth as he thought over their options. He didn't ask either of them for further extrapolation. The unspoken consequences reverberated in the high-ceilinged chamber like one of Quasimodo's bells in Notre Dame and sent a bone-numbing chill through Al's body. He didn't like the odds at all.

When he spoke, his voice was very, very quiet and very, very determined. "Listen to me, both of you. We are not, repeat, *not,* shutting down the system. Not under any circumstances. I don't care how bad this storm or the odds get. Is that clear?"

"*I* wouldn't do it even if you ordered me to," Ziggy replied smugly. "I'm not leaving Dr. Beckett out there on his own."

The Navy man smiled slightly at the computer's staunch support of his friend and mentor and pursed his lips at one of her monitors. "I love you, Zig."

"I'll bet you say that to all the girls," she replied primly.

"But I only mean it with you, darlin'." His head came up determinedly, eyes fixed on the Accelerator and the still body within. "Gooshie, if the person Sam's Leaped into doesn't put in an appearance soon, what are our chances of locating Sam on his own?"

The programmer paused a moment to consider. "Our best bet, Admiral, would be to do a rapid scan run-through of every year from Dr. Beckett's birth to the present day with you in the Imaging Chamber to facilitate contact."

"That sounds puke inducing," Al muttered unenthusiastically, but ready to do it if need be. "And what do we do if he's Leaped *out* of his lifetime again, like when he went back to the Civil War?"

Gooshie's dark gaze was level, his expression serious. "We take our best shot and pray like hell."

Al appreciated the man's honesty even if he didn't particularly like that response. None of this was Gooshie's fault. "Okay," he agreed simply. "Let's hope it doesn't come to that.

7

You and Ziggy keep trying to get a clear lock on Sam's coordinates and bring through his recipient. If it doesn't happen in"—he glanced at the lime-and-tangerine-colored watch on his left wrist—"ten minutes, I'll get into the Imaging Chamber and we'll see what we can find out."

"Ten minutes isn't very long, Admiral," the programmer warned.

"It's all I'm willing to give, Goosh," Al replied seriously. "We don't want Sam lost any longer than absolutely necessary."

The other man nodded sharply, evidently glad to have someone take the reins and issue the orders. "Yes, sir." He patted the side of the console. "You heard the man, Ziggy. Let's get to work and find Dr. Beckett."

"*I* haven't stopped working," she reminded him tersely. "And keep your hands to yourself."

Al stepped to the rear to give them a little privacy in which to concentrate and converse in the confusing computer parlance that Gooshie spoke more fluently than he did English. He paced a tight ellipse along one of the short ends of the room, the smoldering cigar forgotten in his hand and one eye always on the wide windows of the Accelerator and the somnolent body of his friend.

What if this was it? What if this was how Project Quantum Leap ended? What if whatever or whoever it was that had hold of Sam decided to keep him or get rid of him permanently without sending him home? What if . . . ?

Frustrated and angered by the dead-end whirl of his thoughts, Al slammed his fist into the open palm of his other hand and narrowly missed burning himself on the ruddy ember of the cigar's end. It wasn't going to end like that! It couldn't!

He'd never liked stories with sad endings, and there had been too many sad endings in his life. He wasn't going to let this be one of them. His relationship, his *friendship,* with Sam Beckett wasn't going to fizzle out on the whim of some unseen something-or-other. Not if he had anything to say about it, anyway. And, given enough impetus, Al Calavicci could find a whole *lot* to say about it.

He glanced at his watch. The allotted time had nearly run its course. Another few minutes without results and he'd have to get into the Imaging Chamber and endure whatever it was Gooshie had in mind in order to find Sam. His stomach did a funny little jig at the thought and he quelled it with a stern reprimand. He'd do whatever needed doing if it was for Sam. Al didn't feel that generous about anyone else he knew. He would die for Sam Beckett, without once ever looking back.

But he really hoped it wouldn't come to that.

Another look at his watch. Two minutes to go. Overhead, thunder roared and lightning cracked deafeningly. Rain lashed viciously at the windows and the overhead lights flickered ominously, browning down, then coming back up to full illumination.

"Admiral!" Gooshie's call was a cry of triumph.

Al spun around, coattails flying out behind him as he whirled. "You found him!"

The programmer had another of those unfunny funny looks on his face. "Well, not precisely, sir . . ."

"*Gooshie* . . ." Al's dark brows beetled together above his eyes and he lifted a fist threateningly as he strode toward the programmer. "I'm gonna give you such a *hit* if you don't start talking in English!"

"We're still having trouble locking onto Dr. Beckett's present position in time," Gooshie hurriedly explained, one eye on Al's fist and the other on his fingers as they flew over the console. "But his counterpart is coming through . . . *Now!*"

Al turned as a flare of brilliant, rainbow-hued light filled the Accelerator. Dropping his all-but-expired cigar into a nearby ashtray, he hurried forward as the luminescence faded back to normal lighting.

Initially, Sam had made strict rules regarding the handling of anyone who came through the Accelerator from another time. Chief among those was no physical contact between the visitor and the Project scientists. Questions could be asked, as needed, through the intercom system, and that was it. But theory and Sam's best intentions had proven useless against reality. Sometimes physical contact was necessary to ensure the well-being of the visitor, and Al had found that seeing

9

and touching another human did wonders when it came to reassurance.

Now he wanted answers to Sam's whereabouts and the individual inside the chamber was the only one who could give them. He didn't have to clear the procedure with anyone. Until Sam's return, he was the boss (dammit).

Dogging open the door latch, he stepped inside and moved slowly toward the body sprawled on the floor. Sam (or, rather, whoever it was now inside Sam) groggily propped himself up on one elbow and put a hand to his forehead with a groan. "Gawd, do I have a headache!"

"I'll bet you do." Al spoke gently, halting several paces away from the newcomer. He was all too familiar with how easily one of the unsuspecting visitors could be frightened by a too-hurried greeting or overenthusiastic response. It was hard enough to suddenly find themselves transported away from everything familiar and into a situation and body that was unrecognizable and over which they had little control. Most of them screamed at first. Al really hoped this person wouldn't. It never failed to cut him right to the bone. "Welcome."

Slowly, Sam's head came up and the person inside gave Al the most thorough going-over from crown to heel that the Navy man had ever had. Even inspection in the service hadn't been like this. "Oh, bloody hell," the stranger said after a moment. The voice was Sam's, but the inflection was such that Al instantly suspected their new visitor was British. "I've been abducted by the ruddy Martians."

Al smiled slightly and gestured with one hand. "Well, not precisely."

The man inside Sam's skin eyed him skeptically. " 'Not precisely,' he says. That's bleeding reassuring." He looked around, eyeing the specially constructed four walls and ceiling that comprised the chamber. "You could flipping well use a new interior decorator, that much is certain." The circular motion of his head as he looked around obviously made him dizzy, for he abruptly sagged to one side. His head dropped down into his palm and he went a little green around the gills.

"Take it easy, friend," Al soothed, knowing it had to be meager comfort considering the circumstances. "Sometimes

10

there's a little disorientation. You'll be okay."

"One minute I'm driving down Canada's Yellowhead Highway," the man muttered, head still in his hands, and swallowed convulsively. Al frenziedly motioned behind his back for Gooshie to bring a bucket, a bowl, some anti-nausea medication, anything, but one glance over his shoulder showed him the programmer was too busy at the console to be of any help. "The next thing I know, there's this bright flash of light and I'm . . ." He stopped and angled his head, peering up at Al out of one eye, the other obscured by a lock of Sam's hair. "Wait a bleeding minute. Where's Eric?" Moving his head slowly to avoid further nausea, he looked in all directions, finally centering back on Al. "What have you done with him?"

"Eric's okay," Al reassured him, hoping it was the truth and praying he wouldn't get asked any more questions he couldn't truthfully answer.

"The hell he is." The man struggled to rise and succeeded in getting as far as his knees before vertigo overwhelmed him and he gagged. Sometimes people had this reaction to a Leap. Al felt badly for him, but there wasn't much he could do. It was one of those things that just had to wear off. "He's got leukemia," the visitor panted, going green all over again. "The bloody fool shouldn't be out here at all, but Lynnie's plane . . ." He gave up speaking in favor of trying to relieve his borrowed stomach of its last meal. He did a pretty good job of it, too.

Used to this, Al stepped around the pool of vomit and placed a supportive hand around one arm. "Take your time and don't try to rush things," he suggested. "You're safe here. What's your name?"

"Who wants to know?" the other man gasped, arms wavering like the legs of a newborn calf.

Much as he admired the man's pluck, if he hadn't been sick, Al just might have hit him. (Well, not really, but the thought was there.) The last thing he needed right now was a hard-nose. Not that Al could exactly blame him. This *was* pretty weird. If their positions were reversed, and he was the one suddenly transported far from everything near and dear to him, he'd probably be a hard-nose, too. "My name's Calavicci. I run things around here." Okay, so maybe that wasn't precisely the truth, but the boss wasn't exactly *in* at the moment, either.

The man nodded. "Fair's fair. I'm Dr. Philip Payne." He leaned back away from the mess he'd made on the formerly clean floor. "Where am I?"

It was the question Al hated most. "Ah . . . I'm not authorized to tell you that unless absolutely necessary."

"I see," the visitor replied dryly and licked his lips. "Then I guess anything else you want from me isn't absolutely necessary, either." He arched a saturnine eyebrow.

Al sighed. This was going to be one of those headache-producing Leaps. He just knew it. "Actually, it *is*. We need to know—"

"We can talk about your needs after Eric's taken care of." Payne's tone brooked no argument. "He's my patient and I don't think you understand how grave a situation this is, Mr. Calavicci. The stubborn son of a bitch needs to have someone keep an eye on him or he'll drive himself into the ground. He and Lyndell . . ." His throat worked convulsively again, nausea striking a third time, and he hurriedly lay down. Bloodshot eyes stared up at Al where he knelt beside the visitor. "Look, friend. I don't know why I'm here, but this is—" The man's eyes rolled up in his head and he fainted.

Al growled low in his throat with frustration. He was going nowhere fast. He started climbing to his feet, intent on finding someone with a mop and pail to clean up the mess on the floor, but was cut off in midmotion by a cacaphony of thunder and lightning that made everything previous seem like a child's sparkler on the Fourth of July. The sky opened up as though cracked from within by the noise, and the storm poured everything it had at the desert complex, slashing at the buildings with a frenzy of sound, light, and rain that left Al momentarily deaf and blind.

"*Admiral Calavicci!*" Gooshie cried, stepping back from the console and raising his hands to shield his eyes against the flash of electricity that sparked across the controls, making them surge with an array of color as every sensor and dial

12

went red-line. The lights overhead dimmed to almost black, then flared brighter than before. "Get out of there *now*!"

He didn't have to say it more than once. Al swung about and managed a single racing step toward the exit when the world around him suddenly screamed with light so brilliant that he was blinded. A ripple of sensation that wasn't exactly pain or quite pleasure shot through his body, exciting every nerve and raising every hair . . .

. . . then the Accelerator, Philip Payne, Gooshie, Ziggy, and everything he knew as familiar were gone, replaced by darkness and pandemonium. People screamed all around him in panic and fear. Acrid smoke tainted the air, bringing tears to his eyes. He tried to stand and realized he was belted into a seat. His fingers clawed at the restraint, frenziedly seeking release.

The unexpected touch of a human hand on his nearly made Al jump out of his skin. His head snapped to the right, toward the face of the pale, dark-haired girl seated beside him. She smiled bleakly, her eyes a dark smudge in the poor lighting. Her fingers burrowed between his and she squeezed his hand hard enough to hurt. "What a way to go, huh, Gordon?" she asked, her voice tight with tears.

Al's eyes tracked past her to the window on her right. They were in an airplane and it was going down *fast*. If the trees rising rapidly from below were any indication, they were in for something markedly less than a soft, three-point landing.

He clenched his fingers hard around hers and shut his eyes tightly against the impending crash. "Oh, boy."

CHAPTER
TWO

Al rose out of unconsciousness by barely perceptible degrees, like an air bubble turgidly ascending to the undisturbed surface of a cold, deep lake. It was so alluring in the blackness and the blankness, wrapped in darkness with every sense circumvented, that he really didn't want to leave. Here nothing bothered him or caused him distress. Here there was no world . . . no desert . . . no complex . . . no Project . . . no Sam. . . .

Sam!

Recollection made Al reach for consciousness with a will, struggling to regain it and fighting hard to hold on to it once it was won. His eyes fluttered open and he found himself staring at an unrecognizable riveted ceiling. The metal swayed, but it was his own head playing tricks and not some genuine danger. The image doubled dizzyingly and his eyes slammed shut again as vertigo kicked in with a vengeance and made his head swim. The sour-sweet taste of nausea teased him threateningly, but never manifested itself. That was all to Al's liking. Puking had never been a favorite pastime.

A stray thought surfaced. Where the hell was he? He had to think for a while before disorientation subsided enough to let memory supply scattered fragments of information about the moments just prior to the crash. The airplane went in fast and hard. Someone in the cockpit was swearing loudly, urging the plane to keep her nose up. After that was blackness, though one particular thought stood out with immense, important clarity, practically strobing with intensity: he was *alive*. Nothing felt broken, for which he was profoundly grateful. Pain was something else he wasn't particularly fond of.

Eyes closed against the dizziness still lurking at the front of his brain, Al moved his hands slowly, groping across his lap and down either side of the seat in search of the handlink that must be somewhere in the vicinity. The equipment, his umbilical cord to Ziggy, had become an annoyingly vital and integral part of his wardrobe ensemble ever since Sam made his first . . .

Oh, hell.

If his eyes weren't already closed, they would have shut now in an agony of sudden realization. Thoughts of reaching the contrary computer via handlink to discover what was going on evaporated like dew in the desert as precocious memory filled in another bit of the past.

Al stifled a groan behind clenched teeth. He'd been Leaped again, dammit. That meant Sam had the handlink and would be the happy hologram appearing through the Imaging Chamber's glowing blue-white portal.

Speaking of that, where the hell *was* Sam, anyway? Al had no idea how long he'd been unconscious, but some sort of inner clockworking told him enough time had passed that Sam should be appearing soon to tell him where he was and what Ziggy thought he had to do to get out of it and, he hoped, return home. Al didn't relish the idea of cooling his heels in the past any longer than he had to.

Then again, there was probably a good reason for the delay. After all, Sam was home for the first time in years. There were a lot of things waiting for his personal attention, besides reacquainting himself with Donna (and didn't Al envy him *that* experience!). There was the Project, and friendships to renew. There were current events and gains in science, many of which touched upon Sam's theories, and all of which he should be made aware.

15

Now that Al thought about it, a hell of a lot had happened in the years since Sam first stepped into the Accelerator and went *poof*. There was a lot of catching up to do.

The image of Sam back home where he so desperately longed to be made Al glowingly warm for a moment until he remembered it also meant *he* was the one now stuck in time. Spending eternity like this hadn't been a pleasant consideration when it was Sam doing the Leaping. It was even less alluring now that he was occupying his friend's place.

Another thought saved him some further angst. Sooner or later, all things being equal and Sam being so much *Sam,* the self-sacrificing physicist would find a way to bring Al safely home, even if it meant consigning himself to once more being trapped by whatever (or *whomever*) had brought them to this impasse.

Al swore softly under his breath. At this point in life, there were only two things he really wanted. Most people would have guessed a good woman and an even better cigar, but those schmoes didn't know the real Al Calavicci, the man hidden behind the brusque exterior and flashy clothing, the lecherous leers and the know-it-all attitude, the man buried beneath anger and pain at a depth only Sam Beckett had been willing to plumb.

What Al wanted most in life was this: to see Sam safely back inside his own skin, and the opportunity to meet whoever was responsible for this entire mess in the first place and knock the interfering son-of-a-bitch on his pompous ass.

Some things in life just weren't fair.

"That's old news," he muttered, and was startled by the unanticipated baritone of his voice . . . or, rather, the voice that was his for the duration of the Leap. Something wasn't right. He frowned and listened closely as he slowly repeated the phrase. If he'd changed places with Sam, as he assumed until an instant ago, he should be speaking in the soft tenor tones of the Brit who appeared in the Accelerator just prior to Al's leap. But the voice that was now his own had a soft, almost midwestern drawl to it. What the hell was going on?

Maybe his ear had been fooled when Philip Payne spoke back at the Project. After all, there was a lot going on and Al *did* actually hear Sam's voice and only made an inference that the accent should be British. He'd obviously been mistaken, that's all.

Except that "all" was a lie and Al knew it. He'd met enough Brits in the armed forces to know the rhythmic inflection of their speech, even if the voice wasn't precisely British in accent. Nobody in the world said "bloody" and "ruddy" the way an Englishman did. No, he'd swear Sam had definitely Leaped into the Brit who then transferred into the scientist's body on the Accelerator floor.

But if that was true, then whose skin had Al Leaped into? And where the hell was he? Could it mean that Sam was here, too, as one of the other passengers?

Twiddling thumbs and waiting patiently for rescue had never been the Calavicci way. It was time to quit speculating on circumstances and find out what was really what. Cautiously, Al experimentally slit open one eye first, and then the other and trained them on the ceiling. No vertigo or nausea assailed him this time, tipping vision or stomach. So far, so good. He wasn't ready for breakfast, mind you, but at least he didn't appear in immediate danger of bringing up his socks and a pair of loafers to boot.

He snorted mirthlessly at the inadvertent pun and blinked at the ceiling, listening. It was very quiet. Except for the fact that he'd heard himself speak, he could almost have been convinced he'd been struck deaf in the accident. Faintly, he heard twittering birdsong, the swirling swish and sigh of wind whipping through tree boughs, and the methodic tick of cooling metal. He breathed deeply through his nose and was relieved to detect no gas fumes. It's always reassuring to know you aren't in immediate danger of incineration. He remembered his ears ringing with the panicked cries of the other passengers, as well as the peculiar metallic screaming of the airplane, pieces of it shearing away from the main body as it plowed through trees and crashed into the earth.

Al took a deep, slow breath and silently ordered his nerves to steady. First on the agenda was discovering if his borrowed body functioned along what he considered normal parameters. He desperately didn't want to find out he was paralyzed anywhere crucial, which meant anywhere at all.

He knew his hands and arms could move. Gingerly, he tried his toes, then his legs. Everything moved with an obedient, albeit stiff, reluctance. He turned his head from side to side and a sharp twinge of pain along his upper spine warned him to move very slowly. He had a nice case of whiplash. Carefully, mindful of the pain, he craned his neck to get a good look at himself from the feet up.

A sigh whooshed out of him and he grinned with profound relief. He was a *guy*! The baritone voice had given it away, but confirming it with his own two eyes (sort of) made it wonderfully real. Having unmercifully ribbed Sam on numerous occasions about Leaping into women (in a way Al Calavicci had never dreamed possible), he'd been afraid Fate, who had a sense of humor even more perverse than his own, would deal him a similar blow. But somehow he'd managed to get on somebody's good side, and for that Al was more grateful than he could express.

Not that he had anything against women, of course. On the contrary, he was an enormous fan of the female segment of the human species. In Al's estimation, women were God's gift to the world, and he held them in the highest possible esteem and admiration. It was just that with everything else on his plate right now, dealing with being a woman and learning everything *that* was all about would have been just one hassle too many. He had plenty to concentrate on as it was.

Heavy-duty hiking boots encased Al's happily wiggling toes. Worn jeans faded at the knees covered his legs, and a green-and-brown plaid flannel shirt encased what would turn into a respectable beer-gut if this guy he was inside of wasn't more careful about his future alcohol consumption. Over the shirt he wore a brown goose-down vest, unzipped.

Blood spotted the front of his shirt. He touched it with fingers larger and thicker than his own, and rubbed them together. The blood was tacky, well on its way to being dried. He felt his face gingerly and discovered blood crusted on his upper

18

lip. Careful prodding proved inconclusive, though the entire area was sore to the touch. Whatever had happened must have occurred during impact, but his nose and teeth weren't broken. He wiped his fingers clean on the front of the already-soiled shirt and watched the motion of the hands with fascination. They were callused and very capable looking. A workman's hands, skilled in trade. Without knowing why, Al sensed he would have liked this guy, whoever he was. What had the girl called him? Gordon?

Thought of the girl brought a warm flush of shame to Al's face. Concerned with his own welfare, he hadn't even considered hers or that of the other passengers beginning to stir in the rear of the airplane. Someone was crying quietly. Another spoke in a low voice, but whether it was to himself or to the crying individual, Al couldn't say. Carefully, he turned his head to the right and studied the profile of the girl sitting beside him.

Her head was tipped forward, short, straight dark hair half obscuring her elfin features. Looking at her more closely now, he guessed her age to be actually in the early thirties, which made her far more than the girl he'd first assumed, though he'd known some women whose personalities never let them get out of the "girl" category, and some young girls who were born mature women. This woman was breathing regularly and deeply, which was a good sign. Her mouth was open slightly and a line of drool was suspended from her parted lips and hung halfway to the camera cradled loosely in her lap by one limp hand. A pair of round-framed horn-rim glasses also lay in her lap, but whether they'd been put there on purpose for safety's sake or had fallen there in the crash was impossible to guess. Dark brows and lashes were in stark contrast to her washed-out skin. She wore brightly hued hiking sneakers, jeans, a heavy red sweater, and a canvas photographer's vest with one pocket crammed full of 35mm film canisters. A laminated tag printed with thick black letters read PRESS and was pinned over the vest's left breast. Beneath the single bold word on the tag, in smaller letters, was printed Lyndell Freeman and, under that, National Geographic.

Al pursed his lips in a soundless whistle. This young lady had some friends in high places if she worked for the prestigious scientific magazine. That tiny bit of information raised all sorts of intriguing questions about their present circumstances and who they all might be. Unfortunately, most of those questions would go unanswered until Sam came through the Imaging Chamber. And what the hell was taking him so long? Ziggy should have a fix on him by now.

Don't forget the storm, his mind prompted, and he stilled momentarily. Oh, yeah. The storm. The storm was probably the reason why he Leaped. Assuredly, it was the cause of Ziggy being unable to lock onto Sam. And if she couldn't lock onto Sam, what made Al think she had any hope of locking onto *him* until the storm abated?

If then. Great. Just what he wanted to think about.

His eyes tracked past Lyndell's bent shoulders to the window beyond and the obstructed view outside the aircraft. He couldn't see much except for a few trees, jagged heaps of rock, and a covering of snow all awash in the early light of day. His faint reflection stared back at him in wide-eyed consideration. Dark eyes, a heavy thatch of dark hair that looked perpetually uncombed, heavy-set features, broad shoulders. Not a handsome man by any account, but the face was pleasant to look at. Again, Al had the feeling he would like this man if they ever met face-to-face. There was something inherently trustworthy and competent in the rough-hewn countenance.

A quiet moan brought Al's attention back to the woman beside him. Lyndell stirred, her head moving in tiny questing motions like a newborn kitten's in search of mother's nurturing teat. Her left hand flexed weakly on the worn arm of the seat.

Gently Al reached across to carefully tilt her head back against the seat. She winced and he froze with one big hand cupping the back of her neck like a protective cushion. "Lyndell?" he asked, trying out her name for the first time, confident that they were on a first-name basis. "Are you okay?"

Her eyes opened as her left hand rose and slowly wiped the drool off her chin. "Gross," she murmured, and cleaned her fingers against the seat arm. She swallowed with some difficulty. "It hurts."

"Your neck?" Fear chilled him. Had she broken her spine?

She shook her head. It was just a tiny side-to-side motion, but it stilled Al's fears. "My leg," she replied quietly. The fingers of her right hand crabbing gently against that thigh. Before he could ask anything else, her dark eyes tracked searchingly to his face and she squinted. "You're all fuzzy, Gordon. Where are my glasses?"

"Right here." He retrieved them from her lap and gently fitted them atop her nose, adjusting the bows over her ears.

"Thanks." She blinked woozily, the heavy frames accenting rather than detracting from features suddenly touched by amazement. "My God, Gordie. We made it." She said it as though it were the last thing she'd expected. She tried to turn in the seat and stopped, grimacing fiercely at some undefined pain. "Where are the others? Are they okay?"

"I don't know. I woke up just before you did." Movement at the back of the craft alerted him to someone's approach. That someone swiftly brushed past them up the aisle without stopping to check on their condition. Al's surge of annoyance changed to compassion as the stranger hurriedly threw open the passenger door on the starboard side of the plane. It slammed loudly against the side of the aircraft and the man lurched outside upon an inrush of cold air. Moments later came the retching sounds of someone being noisily sick.

"Gideon, I think," Lyndell replied tiredly to no question he'd voiced. "At least we know he's alive. One down and four to go." She shivered suddenly. "I'm cold." She crossed her arms over her chest, but it didn't seem to help. The tremors intensified. Her teeth chattered clatteringly against one another and her hands shook as they balled into fists and jammed under her armpits for warmth.

"You're okay," Al assured her, having seen the symptoms before, surprised that he wasn't in the same condition. "It's just a combination of shock and the door being open. You'll be all right. Here." He undid his seat belt and stood.

A glance back showed him the airplane was smaller than he thought when he first made the Leap, seating no more than ten

21

passengers. There was a baggage area to the rear and possibly storage space under the floor as well. He and Lyndell were in the second row of seats that were on the left of the plane's entrance. A man was sitting two rows behind them on the other side and another man and woman were sitting in the last row on the same side as he and Lyndell. The first man sprawled back in his seat, staring sightlessly at the ceiling. His neck was bent at such an angle that his fate wasn't difficult to guess. The woman was crying quietly, her face in her hands, and shaking her head with an almost mechanical, metronomic rhythm. Her companion's bleak eyes rose and met Al's over the backs of the intervening seats. His head dipped in a brief nod of recognition and his face lit momentarily with a wan smile before he turned back to the woman and resumed speaking in a low, reassuring tone. Al was immensely grateful that Lyndell didn't seem to be the hysterical type. He never knew what to say to that sort of woman.

Shrugging out of his down vest, he draped it across Lyndell's chest and tucked it in around her shoulders. "That'll help you conserve some body heat until we get out of here and get a fire started." He smiled in what he hoped was a reassuring manner. He didn't like flying blind, but it made him feel good when she tried to return the smile.

"Thank you, Gordie, but take back your vest." She plucked at it ineffectually. "My coat's here somewhere. You'll freeze your ass off."

"I have a lot of ass to freeze, so let me worry about that, okay? Let's take a look at that leg."

Her smile turned into a grimace of pain at just the thought. "Just do what needs doing, Gordon, and get me the hell out of here," she ordered.

Al liked her tough-girl style. It reminded him of himself. "Right away, ma'am." Balancing with one hand against the back of the seat in front of her, he bent to inspect the damage. The fuselage had dented inward against Lyndell's right leg, trapping the limb between it and the seat in front of her. No blood stained her clothing, which was a good sign. With any luck, the leg was just bruised instead of broken.

Right, Al. And maybe this is all a dream.

He reached out and she flinched, but he shook his head. "Don't worry, I'm not going to touch it." He pointed. "Can you move your toes?"

Pain printed its image on her face as she tried. "No," she said, her voice high pitched with the fear that struck her eyes and made them look stark and huge.

"Easy," he soothed, and rested a big hand on her shoulder. "Don't automatically assume the worst."

She nodded fractionally and tried to obey, taking a deep breath and releasing it slowly. "It's a habit of mine."

"Well, cut it out. Try moving the leg itself this time, Lyndell, but take it slowly."

"Simple enough for you to say, Huckstep." Clutching the camera in her lap with her left hand, she crossed her right hand over her body and clamped the fingers around his wrist where his hand squeezed her shoulder. Eyes steady on his face, she tried lifting the injured limb. It raised off the seat maybe half-an-inch, but Al saw what the attempt cost her, and felt it as her fingers spasmed around his wrist with enough force to painfully grind the bones together. She grunted with effort, sweat popping out across her forehead and cheeks. Her skin turned waxy with pain and her freckles stood out as though they'd been drawn onto her face with a Magic Marker.

"Hey!" he cautioned. "Take it easy! I'm not asking you to run a marathon."

"Damn good thing," she panted, head pressed tightly against the headrest as she relaxed her efforts. Her lips were as pale as liverwurst. "I'm going nowhere fast." She glanced ruefully at her leg and made as if to pat it, but didn't. "Something in here is trashed," she announced with a matter-of-factness in direct contrast to her fear. Her head toggled back and forth with the same oddly mechanical, repetitive movement Al had witnessed in the other woman. The sight of it on Lyndell chilled him. "This is not happening," she said adamantly. "We did not just crash in the middle of goddamned British Columbia. I did *not* do something terrible to my leg and it is *not* March and damned *cold* out there."

A voice from the front of the craft cut her off, interrupting the roll of Al's thoughts as he tried to assimilate that bit of

23

information. *British Columbia?* "You guys okay?"

Al turned around. A short, stocky man stood in the open arch between the main body of the airplane and the cockpit with his weight resting on the hands braced on either side of the doorway. He looked as washed out and watery as the rest of them, but he was mobile and obviously unhurt. His straight reddish hair was thin over the crown of his head, exposing a riot of coppery freckles like those sprinkled liberally across his nose and on the forearms bared beneath the rolled sleeves of his khaki shirt. An embroidered ellipse over the left pocket read Dan Dodds, Pilot. A faded red baseball cap dangled from the fingers of his right hand. Al read the upside-down words Cromie Aviation printed across the front in white.

"I'm okay," Al replied. "But Lyndell's hurt. Her leg's trapped. She thinks something's broken." He glanced down when her hand stole inside his like a small animal seeking shelter and curled up beneath the warmth of his fingers.

"It's really starting to hurt bad, Gordie," she whispered, her expression bleak and tears threatening. She was trying so hard to be brave against all the fear and pain.

His heart went out to her. He squeezed her fingers gently, then bent and kissed her on top of the head. "Okay, sweetheart. We'll take care of it as soon as we can," he promised without the faintest idea how he was going to keep that vow.

Dodds grimaced ruefully, then rubbed one hand over his face. Sighing, he tabbed the cap securely onto the back of his head. "You're several up on Big Baby, Lynnie. In the vernacular, our landing gear has shit the bed, not to mention our wings and various other important bits and pieces. I'm surprised the sorry old hulk held together as well as she did."

"Amen, brother," she responded fervently.

"I'll second that." Blue eyes sorrowful, he patted the wall with one hand in something that almost seemed like an apology, then jerked his head toward the exit. "Gideon's outside. He brought up a lot of stuff, mostly that huge lunch we told him not to eat in Vancouver, but there's no blood in his vomit. It's just shock reaction, I think." His mouth quirked. "Can't imagine what he'd have to be shocked about." He raised his head to sight past them to the others in the rear. "Mr. Bassey?

24

Are you and Mr. Bachellor and Ms. Marlowe all right?"

Al glanced back as two of the remaining passengers joined their little group. The woman, older than Lyndell by probably thirty years or more, was small and plump with a head of wildly curled white-blonde hair and green eyes streaked with tear-run mascara. She wore tailored tan slacks and a matching suit jacket with a tan wool coat thrown over her shoulders and contrasting pumps on her feet. In shock and seemingly barely able to function on her own, she was being propelled from behind by her companion, a tall and skinny individual with sun-lightened brown hair, brown eyes, a healthy outdoorsman's tan, and dressed all in perfectly faded denim.

"Bob's dead," he announced quietly with a brief, pain-filled glance toward that side of the airplane. His hand tightened around the woman's arm when she moaned bleakly at his news, though she must have already known it. His Australian accent was as tangy on the ear as a gin and tonic was on the tongue. For an instant Al's heart soared, so certain was he that *this* was the man into whom Sam had Leaped . . . except the accents were nothing alike, and this fellow's name was Bassey, while the man in the accelerator had called himself Payne.

Despite the accident, Bassey looked ready to trek the outback with nothing more than an umbrella and a Thermos of margaritas. "I'm okay and so's Faye." He patted her shoulder soundly.

"Oh, my God . . . oh, my God . . . oh, my God . . ." The older woman's voice was a faint litany and Al wondered if that was all she'd been saying since waking at the crash site. Her hands trembled uncontrollably.

"Well," the Aussie amended. "She's mostly okay. Just a bit shook up, right, ducks?" He gently prodded her toward Dodds. "Get her a breath of fresh air, eh, Danny?"

Dodds's head dipped in a quick nod. "I think you're right about that." Gently, almost solicitously, he took Faye's arm and urged her toward the open hatch. "Come on, Ms. Marlowe. Let's get you outside, okay? You'll feel better after some fresh air. . . ." If he said anything more, it was lost as they stepped out of the airplane.

CHAPTER
THREE

Bassey leaned both bony elbows on the back of Al's vacated seat and surveyed the two remaining passengers with compassionate eyes. He jerked his chin toward the hatch through which Dan and Faye had exited. "Poor old walley's had a bit of a go. I don't think she's used to the odd rough and tumble." He raised a sandy-colored eyebrow. "Bit of a bind you're in, Lyndell."

"Tell me something I don't know, Hugh," she grated from between clenched teeth.

Her acerbic tone didn't phase him in the least. He looked at Al and gave a brief tock of the head toward the offending bit of fuselage. "Well, mate, we'll need to find something to pry that framework out a bit if we're to free her leg."

"It would probably be easier to take the seats out instead," Al suggested, eyeing the cabin's interior.

"*If* there are wrenches aboard that'll fit those bolts," Bassey countered pragmatically.

"Stop talking like I'm not here," Lyndell interrupted. "I happen to be very much attached to this leg and I intend to keep it that way for a long time." She swiped a shaking hand across her damp forehead and dropped the brave facade. "So just do something, guys, will you?" she pleaded. "Because if you think I'm staying trapped in here until help arrives, you're out of your minds."

Al gave her a fleeting smile meant to reassure and swatted Bassey on the shoulder. "You heard the lady. Let's get started." He turned away, not wanting her to see his worry. If her injury proved to be major, they would be in deeper trouble than they already were. The prognosis was not good for packing a severely injured person out of the wilds of British Columbia when he hadn't a clue where they were within that vast stretch of Canada, or when or where their ETA was. And how could he ask without the risk of looking like a total idiot? The others already knew he was lucid, so feigning amnesia was out of the question.

More problems. Just what he needed. Well, Mama Calavicci always used to tell him that God never threw anything at you that you couldn't handle, but Al was beginning to wonder if maybe God hadn't screwed up his paperwork and given Al someone else's problems in addition to his own.

"We'd best check the outside first," Bassey recommended. He stepped back to retrieve a dark green down jacket off his seat and slid his arms into it as he talked. "If we're going to have to pry, we'll want to check if there's anything up against the fuselage that needs shifting before we get started. No sense in pushing against the unmovable."

"Good idea," Al agreed. With another brief glance at Lyndell, he stepped up to the open hatch. The chill breeze hit him fully then and cleared away, like a naked leap into the cold Atlantic, whatever post-accident muzziness lingered in his brain. He wished fleetingly for his vest or the coat he assumed was somewhere inside, but right now Lyndell needed the vest more than he did, and he didn't want to take the time to look for his coat. For now, he would just make do.

A jump to the ground found him knee-deep in a mound of snow. A moment later, Hugh Bassey landed lightly behind him. Any remarks either of them might have made to the other passengers grouped in a sorry huddle near the wrecked front of the airplane were stilled by the sight around them.

It was a battle over which would win their attention first, the majestic scenery or the wreck of devastation. It was a miracle that most of them had survived. Dodds had done his best to find an open space in which to land, but the narrow slice of valley was so small it could hardly be called that, and the surrounding forest had done its damage.

Reading the damage to the land, it was easy to guess what the sight had been like as the plane fell from the sky and entered the stand of trees to the west. Shattered portions of the aircraft lay strewn behind them across the valley and flung into the woods. The landing gear and propeller had snapped off and gone in opposite directions. The wings had been sheared away from the main body, leaving behind ugly, ragged stubs like bloodless, unattended war wounds as they went tumbling end over end, gouging out hunks of frozen earth. Behind the remainder of the fuselage lay a wide swath of impact-blasted trees broken off halfway up their trunks, with their heavy crowns strewn every which way. The sharp, Christmasy smell of resin hung sharply in the cold air, twinging Al's nose with its antiseptic tang.

As for the scenery, it was majestic and was made more so by their survival of the crash. Heavy, old-growth forest, a mix of mostly firs and the like, surrounded the small clearing. Mountains rose all around, sides white with snow and summits hidden from sight by a slow-moving swirl of mist and thick low-hanging clouds. They enclosed the little valley in what, under better circumstances, would have seemed a protective embrace, but now seemed sinister and dangerous. Getting out, if they could, wasn't going to be easy.

The ground beneath the snow was rocky and sharp edged against the soles of Al's boots. Great masses of stone were upthrust here and there through the forest floor. The entire area was covered with a layer of snow a foot deep or better. It was not fresh snow, light and fluffy as Al remembered snowfalls from his childhood, but old and softened by thaw. Parts of it had a crusty, rotten, yellowish cast to it. The air was heavy with chilly humidity and a smell that promised more snow to come. One glance at the clouds overhead was all it took for Al to decide that it probably wouldn't be long in arriving. As though confirming this, a teasing flake tumbled out of the sky and danced right in front of his eyes before skittering away

28

on the steady breeze. Great. So much for surveillance planes being able to hunt them out.

If anyone even knew they were missing.

"Is everyone else all right?" Al asked quietly for lack of anything else to say in the wake of shock over their miraculous survival. His breath rose like smoke in the cold air as he turned toward the others, wondering why no one replied. He stopped short and a cold shiver that had nothing to do with the weather shuddered up his spine. The looks on their faces were identical and familiar from a time in his life that he would have preferred to forget and knew he never would. That same look of dependence was directed toward him in Vietnam by the other POWs held in the Viet Cong internment camp. Now that look was focused on Gordon Huckstep and the heavy-set man had all of Al's sympathy (and a lot of his envy, since Al and not Gordon would have to deal with this). For whatever reason, be it the whim of Lady Fate or some special talent he possessed that others instinctively recognized, Gordon had obviously and unreservedly been declared the team leader. Not only was he the center of everyone's attention, now he was the center of everyone's *universe*.

Al quelled a sigh and repeated his question. The others responded then, nodding silently, all except for the pale, unfamiliar face that must belong to Gideon. The fox-faced man with the full head of wavy brown hair leaned against the side of the airplane, obviously favoring one leg. He still looked a little green around the gills and the red-and-black check of his lumberjack coat didn't do anything to improve his appearance.

Al gestured. "Is it broken?" he asked, expecting the worst.

Gideon pursed his thin lips ruefully and shrugged bony shoulders. "No. I think I pulled a groin muscle."

Comparatively, that was as worrisome as a hang-nail. In Al's opinion, Gideon should be grateful for getting off so lightly. Evidently the other man didn't think so, if the sour expression on his face was any way to judge. "Can you get around on it?"

Gideon hesitated fractionally. "After a fashion," was the guarded and somewhat surly reply.

29

Al nodded. He had this joker pegged and wished him anywhere on the planet except stranded with them in British Columbia. Sam always chided him for his snap judgments about people, but how many times had they been proven correct? He was grateful, at least, that the guy didn't attempt any pseudo-macho, Joe Wilderness bull dinky. "Okay, just take special care with it. If it's herniated, you don't need to make it worse."

Gideon snorted contemptuously, but whether or not it was directed at Al was hard to say. He gave their surroundings a baleful once-over. "I don't think things *could* get much worse."

"Really?" Al snapped sharply before the others succumbed to the same doom-and-gloom outlook. Gideon's attitude pissed him off. There was always a party-pooper in every crowd, just as there was always at least one worse-case scenario to every situation. It didn't take a Rhodes scholar to come up with several for their present circumstances. "We could all be dead instead of just . . ." His mind raced and snagged the name. "Bob."

"Which is what I'm going to be if I have to stay in here much longer," Lyndell called from inside the airplane.

Her sarcastic, singsong tone made a couple of the men smile slightly. "Point well taken, Lynnie," Hugh called back to her. "Rest easy. The cavalry's on its way."

"Tell them to hurry the hell up."

Bassey looked at Al, the smile sliding from his face as though it had never been. "We need to take care of Bob. There's no sense keeping him in sight." He grimaced slightly, eyes pained. "'S not exactly good for morale."

Dan slapped his hands together, drawing their attention, and shifted away from the huddle of Gideon and Faye. "We'll all feel better with something constructive to do."

"That's a charmingly Pollyanna attitude," Gideon sneered.

"Can it *now*," Al ordered tersely. "Listen to me, all of you." He scoped them with the most serious expression he could muster. He knew what it looked like on his own face and wondered briefly how Gordon's appeared. He hoped it was as effective. "Don't fall apart on me, folks. We're down, but

30

we're not beaten. We have a lot to be thankful for." Four sets of eyes regarded him, one all but blank, one derisive, one speculative, and one full of utter faith. He looked away, uncomfortable under such steady scrutiny, and couldn't think of another thing to say that would help the situation. He didn't want to start sounding like the Pollyanna Gideon had accused Dan of being. "Let's check the outside damage," he muttered, eyes averted, and moved away.

With Bassey and Dodds in tow, Al paced the length of the ruptured aircraft to the area in front of Lyndell's seat. Her face looked pinched with fear as she watched them through the window, but Al was too busy inspecting the damage to pay her much mind.

It was readily obvious that there was no way to pry her leg free. The airplane lay canted against the side of a big boulder that had dented the fuselage and trapped Lyndell's leg.

Hands on his hips, Al stared at the damage. "Your suggestion was a good one, Hugh, but it's out of the question unless you can think of a way to move that rock."

The Australian snorted. "Thanks all the same, mate, but I'm not Arnold-bloody-Schwarzenegger."

"Then let's hope we can get rid of the seats." He looked at Dan. "I don't suppose there's a wrench set somewhere inside the plane?" he asked hopefully.

"There's more than that inside the plane," Dodds replied, a cryptic twist to his mouth. Gesturing with one arm, he led them back toward the open hatch.

Faye Marlowe stumbled along behind like an automaton, ready to follow them inside until Gideon, gingerly testing his weight against the painful groin muscle, tugged on her arm to stop her. "Stay here, Faye. You can't do anything."

Maybe not, Al thought blackly. *But at least she's trying.* He bit down on the bitterness, tasting bile on the back of his tongue. He'd better school his emotions or he'd be worthless as well.

"Gordon's right, you know," Hugh said from behind as the three men climbed into the plane. He pitched his voice to assure Gideon and Faye heard his motion of support for their new leader. It was his eyes that expressed such utter faith in Gordon's abilities and Al fervently hoped the lanky Australian wouldn't be proven wrong. "We *are* lucky and it doesn't take much imagination to figure out how. That the plane didn't blow is a major miracle to my mind. I wonder how the radio made out?"

"I tried getting off a may-day as we came down, but I don't know if it got through," Dodds replied unhappily as he moved down the narrow center aisle. They each smiled gamely, and all three averted their eyes from Bob Bachellor's stiffening corpse. As Al passed, he grabbed someone's jacket from the seat beside the dead passenger and draped it over the body to conceal as much as possible.

"I tried the radio again when I woke up after the crash," Dan continued. "But it's dead. Even if it weren't, I don't think it would matter much in this valley. The mountainsides are too steep around us to let a signal escape."

"Where are we, anyway, Danny?" Lyndell asked quietly. Al wanted to hug her. Every new piece of information helped his situation *and* theirs. And the more questions answered, the easier it would be to pass himself off as Gordon Huckstep.

Dodds glanced back at the pained, unhappy woman as he bent to shift some debris away from the door which opened into the cargo area. "We're west of the Columbias. I know, because I saw the ice fields before we started losing altitude. I figure we're either in or west of Wells Grey Provincial Park. If I remember the last reading correctly, we're about one hundred miles southeast of Prince George."

"How long since we missed our ETA?" Hugh questioned.

The pilot didn't even glance at the enormous watch strapped around his meaty left wrist. "Five hours."

"Then someone should already be looking for us."

Dan shrugged. "Maybe. Maybe not. Someone will eventually notice the missed ETA and make some inquiries, but before they consider the possibility of a crash they'll first check airports between here and Vancouver and between Vancouver and Monteray to see if we had trouble on the way and landed somewhere else." He snorted. "Well, we sure had trouble and we certainly landed somewhere else." Turning his broad back to them, he reached for the compartment's angled pull and paused. His hand dropped to his side and he bent his head, cap bill almost touching the fuselage. "I'm sorry." He spoke toward the floor, his voice so quiet that Al, who stood directly behind him, had to strain to hear. "I blame myself for this. Somehow something must have gotten past me when we refueled in Vancouver. I just didn't . . ." His stooped shoulders gave a single heave as he sighed heavily.

Al laid a hand on the pilot's arm, drawing his attention. Dodds's pale-lashed eyes were haggard with self-imposed guilt and doubt. "Dan, you should be congratulating yourself. We'd all be dead if it weren't for you. I'll lay odds not one man in fifty could successfully bring down a plane in these surroundings without loss of life. I'm sorry Bob died, but it's hardly your fault." He glanced anxiously at the others.

Hugh was the first to speak. "Gordon's right, Dan. Thank you. Because of you, the rest of us are alive."

Lyndell took up the litany, her voice pain filled but sincere. "We're a team," she added stoutly and managed a smile.

Let Gideon take this Pollyanna stuff and cram it in his pipe and smoke it, Al thought. All that mattered to him was that it worked. "And we have to function like a team if we're to survive," he finished sternly, eyeing each of them in turn and hoping the two waiting outside heard him. "That means no self-doubt and no recriminations, okay, Dan?"

Hugh and Lyndell nodded enthusiastic encouragement and Dan joined in after a moment. "Okay," he said quietly.

"Okay," Al agreed, praying he still remembered all the survival techniques learned in the Navy and during his stint in the hellhole called 'Nam. "Now—"

"Now," Lyndell interrupted. "I'm going to chew off my leg at the knee if you don't hurry up!"

Her barbed remark broke the solemn moment. Dan raised his head and smiled gratefully. "Thanks, Gordon." Grasping the handle again, he swung it up in a smooth quarter-turn arc and opened the door inward. The three men crowded into the tiny opening. The cargo hold's murky interior was a jumble of suitcases, taped boxes, and . . .

"Campin' equipment?" Hugh barked with surprise. "Who's the psychic?"

"Me, after a fashion," Dan admitted shyly as he stepped into the bay. "Once I dropped you all off in Prince George for the environmental conference, I was going to take a little camping trip into the interior for the week until it was time to pick you up for the return trip. I guess my itinerary got a little ahead of itself." He shrugged lightly and Al was glad to see that he evidently wasn't going to dwell on misfortunes. "It's mostly one-man stuff, but it can't hurt to use it. I've an ax and a bunch of other things."

"The hell you say," Lyndell protested as the rangy Australian pushed past the pilot and started handing bundles back through the open doorway. "Are any of you qualified to do that kind of surgery?"

Al shook his head. "Not in this lifetime." The inadvertent pun almost sent him into a fit of giggles. *I guess I'm a little shell-shocked,* he thought. *It just took a while to set in.*

"Too bad," Hugh quipped. "I could fancy a good bit of roast."

"Roast this, you cannibal," Lyndell shot back, and flipped him a gesture that widened their eyes.

"And I thought you were just an innocent young thing," Bassey said reproachfully.

"Never," she vowed stoutly.

Dan smiled and accepted the leather-covered ax Hugh poked through the hatchway. "Never fear, Lyn. I won't let him carve you into steaks." He put the sharp-bladed implement aside across one of the seats. "Hey, Hugh, hand me that gray case."

"This one?" He slapped the side of an expensive suitcase.

The pilot shook his head. "No, the smaller one to your right. The hardshell case. That's it. Thanks." He balanced the briefcase-sized container in both hands. "Come out of there for now, Hugh. We'll get the rest of the stuff later. Right now, we have work to do." Leaving the rest of the equipment in an untidy pile to either side of the open door, the three men returned to Lyndell's side to scope out the situation.

CHAPTER
FOUR

"What's that?" Al asked curiously as Dan lay the case on the floor. His eyes widened with appreciation when the pilot snapped the catches open and popped the lid to reveal a small and extremely formidable-looking tool kit. A corner of his mouth quirked wryly. "Are you always prepared for everything?"

"That's one of the reasons I get paid," Dan countered seriously. "Old John Cromie would bite the head off any pilot not carrying a good tool kit at all times, and rightly so."

"Remind me to buy the man a drink when we get back."

"Make that several," Hugh agreed. "We get out of this and I promise to personally take Mr. Cromie pub crawling until he's too blighted to stand."

"I second that." Al eyed the row of seats, ignoring for the moment Lyndell's wan expression. "No offense, Dan, but you and I aren't going to fit down in between these seats." He patted his stomach in demonstration and winced inside. Al Calavicci was never out of shape in his life and it stung him to be so heavy now, even if this was someone else's body. He was used to maneuvering in tight places, figuratively and literally, and wasn't certain Gordon

Huckstep's body would give him what he needed when he needed it. "This will have to be Hugh's job."

"No offense taken, Gordon," the pilot agreed, and gave his own round girth a slight pat. "You're only citing the obvious."

"Right-ho, then, mates," the Aussie said ardently. "Hugh 'Beanpole' Bassey to the rescue. What is it you want me to do?" The Australian's enthusiasm was almost annoying. Much as Al appreciated the other man's strong show of support, he almost wished Hugh would act at least a little worried about their situation. On the other hand, his buoying confidence would almost assuredly come in handy somewhere down the line, if only to keep up Al's spirits.

Al bent down and pointed at the floor. "We'll need a wrench to fit the bolts holding these seats to the floor."

Dodds perused the tools for a moment. "Ummm . . . ah! Here we go." He passed the tool to Bassey, who tossed it once or twice in his hand, a pensive expression pursing his lips for a moment.

"Hugh," Al continued. "Squeeze down in the aisle and loosen the bolts on these three seats." He indicated first his recently vacated seat beside Lyndell, then the one directly in front of it, and, finally, the seat in front of the trapped woman. "Take them out in that order, so the three of us will have room to maneuver and so Dan and I can get close to Lyndell. I want to support her leg when the last seat gets taken out, because I don't think she can hold it up herself, and I don't want the sudden release slamming it onto the deck."

"Make that two votes for no slamming," Lyndell fervently agreed. Her knuckles were white where they clutched the seat arms.

"It's unanimous," Hugh agreed. "No slamming." Kneeling in the main aisle, he set about freeing the first seat while Dan waited patiently to lift it out of their way.

Al felt Lyndell's frightened gaze on his face and looked up to give her a quick, tight smile of encouragement. "Can you feel anything, Lyn? Is your leg bleeding?"

36

"I don't think so," she answered in a tiny voice, her eyes flicking between him and the bent hump of Bassey's back as he worked. "It hurts so much, it's kind of hard to say for sure."

"I know, kid. Hang in there. We're working on it." Her eyes held his, pouring all her hope into him just as the others had done. Oh, well. He might as well relax and go with the flow. There wasn't much chance of it changing. "Your leg may hurt worse once the pressure's off. There may be some bleeding. If you feel like screaming, just do it."

She nodded rigidly. "Rest assured that I won't try to hold in my emotions."

"Okay." Dan lifted the first seat free and shoved it out of the way, placing it atop seats in the opposite row. Bassey inched around on his hands and knees like a hunched-up praying mantis and began tackling the second seat, grunting as he worked at a particularly stubborn bolt.

What Al must ask next he hated doing in front of Lyndell, but he wanted an answer now in case he needed to improvise. "Dan, I don't suppose you have any medication among all your camping equipment?"

The pilot gave him an odd look. "Come on, Gordon, you know I'm a seasoned camper. I never travel without my magic kit."

Al didn't have a clue what to make of that cryptic remark, but hoped it meant something stronger than aspirin. "Sorry," he said lamely, covering his gaffe. "I guess my thoughts are elsewhere."

"Surprise, surprise," Dan remarked sympathetically.

Bassey sat back on his heels and rubbed a forearm across his face, blotting sweat onto the sleeve of his coat. "That's the second one, mates. Lift away."

With the second seat gone and put aside, they had more room in which to work. Sprawled on his side under Lyndell's slender legs, Bassey worked diligently at the final two bolts securing the last seat to the floor. He grunted, shifted for better leverage, then grunted again. Abruptly, he ducked back up from beneath her legs. Sitting with his knees bent and his arms loose around them, he let fly a string of vitriolic profanities, the likes of which would have made a longshoreman blush. In the stunned silence that followed, he raised his head with a look on his face that could have set water to boiling. "That last blighter won't come free," he announced. "I think the threads are stripped."

The pronouncement was made so mildly, after the spate of swearing they'd just heard, that Al almost laughed. Unfortunately, there was nothing to laugh about.

Lyndell's voice was strident and scared. "I meant it, Gordie! If you think I'm staying in here until—"

"Shut up, Lyndell." His voice was soft but sharp, and she instantly obeyed, staring at him with a wide-eyed expression of surprise. "I know you're frightened, but you're not helping matters any." He bent down beside Hugh to take a closer look at the problem. "Can we pivot the seat on the bolt that's stuck? Just swing it around a little?" He looked from Hugh to Dan.

Dodds shrugged. "We can try."

"There's not much room to maneuver," Bassey cautioned.

"We don't need much room," Al pointed out. "Just enough to inch the leg up and lift it clear."

Bassey sighed and slid the wrench into his coat pocket as he stood. "Then let's do it and get her the hell out of here."

He and Dan positioned themselves on either side of the uncooperative piece of furniture, Dan gripping the armrests in front and Hugh straddling Lyndell's left leg to firmly grasp the back. Meanwhile, Al squeezed in between Dan and the wall and slid his hand along the narrow space between the seat and the fuselage until he reached Lyndell's foot. Shoving his arm a little farther, he cupped his palm under her heel as a brace. "Lyn?"

"Yes?" Her voice was tightly controlled. He peeked at her through the tiny space. Her fingers were spread clawlike, digging into the armrests.

"Can you feel my hand under your foot?" He moved his fingers slightly to give her a point of reference if she needed one.

She grunted sharply with pain. "Yes."

He hated hurting her, but now was not the time to apologize. "When Hugh and Dan shift the seat, I'm going to lift your leg free. I know you have a little mobility on your own, so you're going to have to help."

"Stop talking about it and just *do* it!" she demanded stridently. Sweat had broken out on her forehead and upper lip.

Al nodded at the others. "Do it," he ordered flatly.

They grabbed the seat and pushed with all their strength, faces flushing with exertion. The shift sideways wasn't much because of the interference of the inner wall, but Al felt his hand slip further up Lyndell's ankle as her foot dropped toward his palm. Grasping her ankle firmly, and sorry for the pain he must be inflicting, he pushed upward. The leg rose . . . and stopped, still pinned. "Lift it, Lyndell!" he grunted, almost on his face, and shifted for better purchase.

"I *am*!" she yelled back.

"I don't think the seat's going to move any farther," Dan commented, pushing harder and trying anyway.

Al ignored him. "Lift it!" he ordered Lyndell. "It's not going to come free unless you help!"

"I can't, Gordon!" she cried. "It hurts too much!"

"*Bend the knee and lift your goddamn leg!*" Al roared like the admiral he was, not knowing if she could. Lyndell pressed back in her seat, shrieking like she was being murdered. The foot abruptly slid free of his hand and was gone.

Al scrambled to his feet and slammed his head hard against the low ceiling. Blinking away tears of pain, he shoved Dan and Hugh aside and circled the troublesome seat to throw himself onto his knees beside Lyndell.

If she'd been pale before, now she was as gray as library paste. Sweat stood out in thick beads on her forehead and cheeks and soaked the sweater's turtleneck. She'd bitten her bottom lip, leaving a lurid slash of blood against her skin. Her arms, still rigid on the rests, pressed her hard into the seat, and her head was thrown back with her face tilted toward the ceiling. She panted hard, her breathing ragged, but the leg was free. Knee bent, she held it aloft with the heel balanced gingerly atop her other leg like she didn't know where to put it.

"Lyn . . . ?"

"It hurts," she gasped. "Ohmigod, Gordie, it hurts." She began sobbing quietly, her whole body shaking with the force of her tears.

While Al was a cold customer to fake emotionality, he could never stand to see a woman cry genuine tears. It turned him all mushy inside. He slid his arms around and under Lyndell and lifted her as gently as if she were a confection made of silk and glass. "It's okay, sweetheart. The worst is over," he soothed, silently praying that he was telling the truth and knowing it was probably a lie. "Let's get out of here."

Hugh and Dan preceded them out the hatch. The Australian took Lyndell while Al climbed down but, feeling somewhat proprietary about the young woman, Al reclaimed her as soon as his feet hit the snow. Her head lolled alarmingly against his shoulder. "Lyndell?" he asked anxiously, peering down into her face.

"Hmmm . . . ?" she inquired, eyelids opening just a fraction to show the rolled-back pupils before closing again. She sounded almost sleepy.

"Shock," Dan pronounced simply, and was gone again into the airplane.

Al looked around, hardly feeling the weight of the slight woman in his arms. Gideon still stood against the shattered nose of the craft, shoulders hunched against the cold, arms crossed over his chest. A narrow circular area was worn in the snow by Faye's busy feet as she paced nearby. Her eyes stared blankly ahead and she moved with a rigid monotony that Al didn't like. Neither had done anything productive in the others' absence, though Al wasn't certain what he had expected. Gather firewood, maybe, but the older woman was obviously still too shell-shocked to function at a decent level. As for the caustic Gideon, his pulled groin muscle was undoubtedly painful. Still, Al couldn't help wishing they'd shown a little initiative in improving their situation. The *attempt* would have meant a great deal to him and the general morale, even if they hadn't actually accomplished anything.

Gideon saw him looking, and what crossed his face fell just short of being a sneer. "Is she dead?"

"No!" Al snapped angrily, shifting Lyndell's weight in his arms. She moaned quietly in response, but did not open her eyes. "What the hell is the matter with you?"

He shrugged his shoulders in a way that made Al want to hit him. "Just asking."

"Just—!"

"She's hurting right now, but she'll be right as rain soon." That was Dan, returning from the craft's interior and cutting Al off before he could escalate the stupid remark into an argument. The pilot carried a leather pouch about the size of a trade paperback novel, with a zipper running around three sides.

"What's that?" Hugh asked curiously, taking a step nearer to get a closer look.

"My magic kit," Dodds replied simply, and slid the zipper around. It made a quiet little buzzing sound in the cold air. The pouch interior was segmented into efficient little holders and compartments. Among the things inside were a needle and various weights of thread, including surgical silk, collapsible scissors, an oral thermometer, matches in a waterproof container, a tourniquet, bandages of various kinds, a vial of antivenin, a syringe, and several small bottles. Al's eyes slid over the neatly labeled containers: antacid, aspirin, Tylenol with codeine, ampicillin, betadine, Demerol, Benedril, and . . .

"Morphine?" His eyebrows rose. "What are you, a black marketeer?"

"No, just a very prepared camper." His eyes met Al's and his expression suddenly grew guarded and concerned. "Don't look at me that way, Gordon. You've known me long enough to know I don't use recreational drugs. I know how to correctly administer this stuff."

"I'm not saying you don't," Al countered, certain of no such thing. "It's just that some of this stuff isn't exactly over-the-counter medication."

"That's true." When that obviously didn't suffice as an answer, Dan sighed irritably. "I thought you trusted me more than this, Gordon. I have a friend who's a doctor, okay? He knows I do a lot of solitary wilderness camping. With his help, this is just one of the ways I try to guarantee I'll make it out if something unexpected occurs." His bland eyes flashed unexpected annoyance. "Does that satisfy your curiosity? You don't need to be suspicious. I know what I'm doing and I'd never do anything to hurt Lyndell or anyone else. Now, if you don't mind, why don't you let me take care of her?"

Uncomfortable as he was with the situation, Al still knew when to pull in his horns. He'd obviously made a major goof in questioning Dodds and hoped it had only bruised his friendship with the pilot and not undermined it entirely. Dan was obviously competent in many areas and seemingly on Gordon's side. Al didn't want to lose that. He would need all the help he could get.

Trying hard not to jostle the woman in his arms, he bent and carefully settled her into the airplane's open hatchway. The movement roused her from the shocky half-faint into which she'd fallen, and her broken leg jerked spasmodically. Gasping, Lyndell sat up straight, eyes wide with pain. For a moment, Al was convinced she didn't see any of them and wasn't aware of anything but the agony in her leg. The moment passed and she sagged back with a moan. He caught her before she hit her head on the hatch rim and gently eased her back to lay flat on the floor.

Bending over her, he pushed damp hair back from her forehead. "Don't worry, sweetheart," he soothed. "We're going to take care of it. Dan's got some stuff that'll make it stop hurting."

Gideon shuffled nearer, favoring one side. "Slit the jeans and get a close look at her leg. You'll want to know what you're dealing with." When Al looked quizzical, surprised the man had offered something approaching cooperative, constructive advice, Gideon shrugged one shoulder self-deprecatingly. "I may be a zoologist, but I know something about human anatomy. Pills alone aren't going to do it. You have to assess the damage and splint it if necessary."

"Pills sound good to *me*," Lyndell put in muzzily, and blinked up at him. "Prop me up in the right line."

"You're already in first place," Hugh assured her. "Lucky for you, it's first come, first served."

42

The edge of Lyndell's mouth curved in a weak smile. "When does the show start?"

"Any minute," Dan told her without looking up, his fingers ticking over the small vials. "Are you allergic to any drugs, Lyn?"

"Not even aspirin, Danny," she replied. She struggled to sit up. When Al tried to gently push her back, she grabbed onto his arm and bodily hauled herself upright, leaning close to him and tucking her head into the hollow of his shoulder.

"You sure?" Hugh asked uncertainly, obviously a little concerned about Dan's impromptu pharmacopia and Lyndell's current ability to be the judge of anything.

Her gaze steadied on him. "I want the pain to go away almost more than anything, Hugh, but not enough to risk killing myself. I'm sure. As far as I know, I'm not allergic to any damn thing."

"Your word's good enough for me." Dan popped the lid on the bottle marked TYLENOL WITH CODEINE and spilled two pills into his work-roughened palm. "Can you take 'em dry or do you want us to melt you some snow?"

"I'll take them with a glass of sand if you want. Just make it stop hurting." Her hand shook as she scooped the pills from his hand and into her mouth, and swallowed hard a couple of times. "Ugh. They're gross, Danny, but I'm grateful." She shut her eyes and sank back against Al.

He glanced around at Gideon and motioned with his head toward Lyndell's leg. "It was your idea. Do you want to take a look? You seem to be the most qualified."

An unreadable smile briefly touched the zoologist's features. "Thank you." Moving slowly and with some assistance from Hugh Bassey, Gideon knelt. In the background, Faye Marlowe stopped her repetitive pacing and stood quietly, her face blank of emotion, but her eyes really *watching* them. Al hoped it was a sign the woman was coming out of shock.

"Lyndell?" Gideon's tone was cool and smoothly professional.

Her eyes remained closed, but her eyebrows rose fractionally. "What?"

43

"I'd prefer to wait until the pills kick in, but we need to see how badly damaged your leg is and the sooner the better. I just want you to be prepared for any additional pain I might inadvertently cause."

"It already hurts, Gideon. What difference does a little more make?"

"I'll work as quickly as I can," he promised. He swiftly untied her laces and eased them loose around the tongue to give the boot more mobility. Grasping the heel with one hand and the toe with the other, he slid the boot off her foot in one brisk, practiced motion.

Lyn grunted and pressed her head hard against the cushioning support of Al's shoulder, but never said a word. Her fingers dug sharply into his arm. He endured the pain, watching Gideon and wishing he knew more about medicine. Sam should be the one here, not him! What could he possibly do to help these people?

Lyndell's gray wool sock was unsoiled by blood, but tight around the enormous swelling of her foot and ankle. Hugh whistled at the sight, but Gideon nodded calmly as though he dealt with this kind of stuff every day. "I think we definitely have a break here. Of course, nothing's conclusive without an X ray."

"Got one of those in your magic kit, Dan?" Hugh asked in an effort to keep things light.

"Sorry, left it at home," the pilot replied, his eyes on Gideon's careful movements. "Do you need a jackknife?" he asked, hand poised over his back pocket.

"I've got one." The zoologist fished into the back pocket of his black jeans and pulled out a circular keychain to which was attached a red Swiss army knife with enough blades to allow its owner to successfully take over any major nation on the face of the planet. Prying out the largest blade, he neatly sliced the sock from top to toe and let it drop away from her foot and into the snow. Before the others got more than a glimpse of the damage, he took the leg of Lyndell's jeans between two fingers, sawed through the thick hem, and cut upward, opening it to the knee. The denim parted with a rough tearing noise and Al winced as he got his first good look at what had happened to Lyndell Freeman.

44

CHAPTER
FIVE

Her knee and part of the calf were a single huge bruise, a mottled display of blooming indigo, rose, bilious green, and smarmy yellow. Gideon prodded the upper half of her leg with practiced fingers, his face pinched down to a frown of concentration. Lyndell whimpered, her eyes closed, but the zoologist ignored her, nodding with apparent satisfaction before glancing up at the others. "Femur's intact. Let's take a look at the knee." Fingers manipulated the injured area. Lyndell's eyes squeezed tighter, but tears inched their way free to escape down her cheeks.

"Patella is intact and reasonably mobile." Gideon's voice had fallen into that singsong cadence most physicians seemed to adopt when thinking aloud or dictating. "Tibia and fibula are sound." He paused at her ankle, feeling carefully, and his brow wrinkled. "Oh, my." He looked up. "Here's the problem." He massaged the area to show them. Hugely swollen, her foot and ankle made the rest of her leg look monochrome by comparison. The foot dangled at an odd angle, obviously disconnected.

Gideon placed his palm under the loose limb and shifted it slightly. Lyndell vented a sharp cry of pain and promptly passed out. "Now the medication has a chance to work without fighting against her adrenaline," he said, making Al wonder if he'd done it for just that purpose. His fingers moved gently over the injured appendage and he whistled low. "Tarsus is busted. Can't say how badly, but I don't like the way this grinds together under my fingers."

Al swallowed hard, hardly noticing when Dan moved away and climbed back into the airplane via the cockpit hatch.

Gideon's fingers traveled Lyndell's foot. "Metatarsus feels okay, though it's kind of hard to tell around the swelling. I recommend packing snow around this to get the swelling down and splint it securely so she doesn't move it any more than absolutely necessary."

Dan reappeared behind Al and Lyndell, balanced in the main hatchway. "Here," he said to Hugh, and tossed a handful of vomit bags in the Aussie's direction. "I heard him from inside. Fill 'em with snow. As it melts, we'll just replace them."

"Good show, Dan," Hugh nodded. Popping open the first bag, he bent like a crane and began scooping snow into it with a sweep of one long-fingered hand. Folding the top shut, he handed it to Gideon, who placed it against Lyndell's ankle with the ruined sock in between as a buffer.

"We need to put her someplace where she'll be comfortable," Gideon opined. "And make a splint."

"Put her back in the plane for now," Dan said, almost before the words left the zoologist's mouth. "I'll take care of the splint." He disappeared back inside the aircraft only long enough to retrieve the ax. Jumping from the cockpit hatch, he stalked toward a nearby stand of trees, the set of his shoulders rigid.

"Does he blame himself for this?" Gideon asked, indicating the whole crash area as Al shifted the somnolent Lyndell farther back into the aircraft and pillowed her head on one of the removable seat cushions. He glanced at Al for confirmation and, when he got it, pursed his lips in thought.

It was Hugh who commented, turning to hand Gideon another bag of snow. "It's all karky nonsense, of course, but how do we convince him of that?" He took a long look around at the tall mountains and enclosing trees, and smiled slightly. "What say, Gordon? Gideon and Dan appear to have this end of things under control. Why don't the rest of us gather as much wood as we can?" His eyes flicked toward Faye and Al instinctively knew he wasn't including the woman in his "we". "I'd think the cold would be our greatest threat right now and it's a good idea to have a stockpile to burn rather than making lots of trips and using up our energy. Besides, I don't care for the look of that sky."

Al didn't know what kind of experience the Australian might have had with snow, but was grateful someone else had remarked on the lowering clouds. The air felt cooler than before and there was no doubt in his mind that it would snow. The questions were only "when" and "how much?"

Faye looked skyward in the first real notice she'd taken of their surroundings. "But if we get more snow . . . ," she began fearfully, her voice rising.

"Faye." Al brusquely cut her off. Her eyes shot guiltily to his face and she looked as though she expected to be beaten. "Snow is a possibility we have to consider for safety's sake. We need to be warm. Besides, an airplane might spot a fire. It can't hurt and it will definitely help. We'll consider our other options later, okay?"

She nodded jerkily. "All right, Gordon. Whatever you say." Turning, she stumbled off. Her well-tailored slacks were already damp to the knees and her shoes wobbled on terrain they'd never been made for as she struggled through the snow, following Dan's broken trail toward the trees.

Whatever you say. If only it were so easy.

"I'll go give ducks a hand," Hugh offered. "Keep her out of mischief and such. She's not exactly dressed for this sortie." He started after her with a hail to wait up. She jerked to a halt and then followed along behind as he stamped down the path to ease her progress.

Watching them, Al didn't immediately realize he'd been spoken to. When Gideon uttered his borrowed name a second

47

time, he snapped out of his reverie. "I'm sorry. What did you say?"

"I said, that goes for you, too."

"What goes for me, too?"

The zoologist sighed and flapped his hands as if he were shooing chickens. "Go. Vamoose. Get gone. This is under control. Go make yourself useful."

"But Lyndell . . ."

"Lyndell," Gideon interrupted, "is as okay as she's going to be for now."

He didn't want to leave her, but he also didn't have a good reason not to. Dodds and . . . he realized he didn't know Gideon's last name . . . were on top of things. He couldn't just hover over Lyndell all day. He had as much responsibility as the others (and maybe more) to assure their continued safety. "Okay." He rose slowly, his butt cold and sore from sitting on the edge of the hatch for so long, and turned away, his eyes scouting ahead for likely piles of wood.

"Gordon?"

He glanced over his shoulder. "What?"

Gideon plucked Al's down vest from around Lyndell and held it out. "Take this. It's getting colder."

"She'll need it."

"No, she won't. She's got a coat inside. I'll make sure she stays warm. You need the protection until you get back, and afterward as well." He tried a glower. "Doctor's orders."

"You're not a doctor," Al groused, but obediently (if unwillingly) took his vest and slipped it around his formidable girth, zipping it shut and stuffing his hands into the pockets. He hated to admit Gideon's being right, but he *did* feel better with a second layer of clothing.

"No, I'm not," the zoologist agreed. "But I'm the closest thing we have. Now get lost."

There wasn't anything more to say. Lyndell's eyes were closed and her chest rose and fell with her even breathing. The drug had obviously begun to do its work, aided by unconsciousness, and Al was grateful for that. Shifting to settle the vest more comfortably around his shoulders, and wondering if he had a coat and gloves somewhere inside, he

48

started in a direction different from the others. He needed solitude and time to think, to clear his head and consider all the possibilities.

Picking up pieces of wood as he moved through the snowy wilderness, he let his mind wander. His first responsibility was to the other survivors. Dan and Hugh were enormous assets and he was profoundly grateful for their presence. He would have felt the same about Lyndell had she not been injured, yet couldn't deny a special feeling for the girl that must be a bleed-over from the emotions of the real Gordon Huckstep. It wasn't love, precisely, at least not romantic love. It felt more like a long, deeply cherished friendship.

He wasn't certain whether or not he'd codified an opinion on either Faye or Gideon. Right now, Faye was a handicap unless they could shake her out of her lethargy and get her back to acting like a normal human being. As for Gideon . . . he was the wild card in all this. He was certainly capable, but seemed used to being catered to. There was no clue to how he'd behave in the coming hours. Or days.

How long they could survive out here was the real question and the real problem. They *might* be able to travel, even with Lyndell in her present condition, if they fashioned a travois, but in which direction should they head? What if it began snowing? And didn't all the rule books say that when stranded in the wilderness a person should stay put as long as viably possible? When did "viably possible" turn into "get the hell out"?

At least he knew one thing with absolute certainty. None of these people was Sam. The discrepancies between Hugh's name and accent aside, he'd seen Sam in too many other skins not to recognize him instinctively. If Sam were here, lurking inside one of these other people, Al was confident that he would know it. So, where *was* Sam? Come to think of it, where the hell was Ziggy? There had been plenty of time for Gooshie to locate his coordinates and zero in on him.

"What gives?" Al muttered, and suffered a sudden, painful craving for a cigar and the hustle-bustle of civilization. He'd seen enough trees and mountains in just this one day to last him a lifetime.

To the right, a tangled windfall of wood and dead brush looked like an excellent cache of fire fuel. Stepping carefully, Al entered the crackling concealment of the interlaced branches and abruptly realized he needed to relieve himself almost desperately. The initial worries put momentarily at bay, the earlier tensions finally took their toll in this most basic of ways. The call of nature was insistent and demanded to be attended to *now* or Al would be one unhappy (and extremely damp) camper.

Tossing down the few bits of wood he'd gathered, he hurriedly undid his zipper and relaxed. Ah! Some things were even better than sex.

He listened to the world around him while he waited out the process. A few birds piped. Occasionally, there sounded the higher-toned screech of some sort of bird of prey, but every time he looked up, he didn't see anything. Wind droned in the treetops, alternately moaning and whispering, but a preparatory hush was beginning to settle over the land. Something was coming.

A mosquitolike buzzing caught his ear and his head whipped around in search of the source. He didn't want any nervy little insect munching hungrily on *his* privates. He froze suddenly with only his eyes tracking back and forth. According to Lyndell, it was March and they were in British Columbia. There shouldn't be a mosquito for several hundred miles, so what *was* it?

The sound grew, rising from an insect's whine to a pitch sharp and annoying as a dentist's drill. He thought hard, trying to figure it out, and his eyes abruptly widened as he discovered the source. It came . . . from inside his *head?!*

It unexpectedly dropped in pitch and resolved into a tiny voice. Al bit back the desire to vent hysterical laughter. *Dan and Lyn are wrong,* he thought. *We're not in Canada, we're in Ireland. And the leprechauns have arrived.* The voice rose to a comfortable volume and he realized, with a start, what he was hearing. Or, rather, *whom* he was hearing, for he knew Ziggy's voice as well as he knew his own.

"Thank God," Al muttered, and zipped up fast. He had never felt the need to talk to that cantankerous machine so strongly as right now. A thought made him pause. How could he talk to her without the handlink?

"Ziggy?" he whispered, afraid of being overheard if one of his fellow passengers had wandered close. He glanced around, hoping to see the white rectangle of the Imaging Chamber door appear in place of all this nature. It didn't, but Ziggy's voice cleared.

". . . will attempt to locate you both as soon as is viable, and effect a rescue at that time. Until then, carry on with my hypothesis and good luck."

What the hell? "Ziggy—" Her voice cut him off and he listened hard to what she said. It proved to be an earful.

"Repeating. Dr. Beckett and Admiral Calavicci. Due to interference from an intense electrical storm, you have both Leaped. The storm's continued influence makes it impossible at this time to specifically locate either of you and attempt a rescue. However, your hosts have willingly provided their approximate coordinates previous to the Leap and I am broadcasting on a wide beam in the hope one or both of you will hear me. I modified the basic premise of the handlink and am attempting to contact you both via this new system. Unfortunately, I have no way of determining my success as I cannot hear you. If you read me, please note the following information, some of which was provided by your hosts:

"It is March 30, 1986. Admiral, you are twenty-nine-year-old Gordon Huckstep, a geology doctoral student. Your party was en route to an environmental conference in Prince George, British Columbia, Canada, when the aircraft malfunctioned and crashed."

"Big deal," Al groused. "Now I know my age. Tell me something I can use, Zig."

Her voice continued dispassionately. "Your companions are thirty-six-year-old Gideon Daignault, a zoologist; forty-five-year-old Daniel Dodds, the pilot; sixty-two-year-old Faye Marlowe, an environmental lobbyist; thirty-seven-year-old Robert Bachellor, an environmental activist; forty-two-year-old Hugh Bassey, a free-lance nature photographer; and thirty-year-old Lyndell Freeman, a photographer."

"Come on, come on . . ."

"It is Lyndell Freeman with whom I believe you must be most concerned, as I will explain momentarily. Dr. Beckett, you have Leaped into a forty-year-old physician named Philip Payne . . ."

Al listened with half an ear to Sam's share of the information, then the remainder of Ziggy's pertinent data, but his attention was drawn skyward. Slowly, he tilted back his head and cursed very quietly under his breath. There was no mistaking it. It was starting to snow. Just a few flakes at first, beautiful in their delicacy. The wind suddenly picked up, and the flakes twirled around him, swirling a dusty curtain of snow into his eyes as they began falling more quickly. In the distance behind him he heard someone voice a loud hail, calling them back to the crash site before they lost their way in the rising storm.

Bending to retrieve his dropped armload of wood and gather a few more stray pieces, Al turned and started back toward the inward-wending straggle of people hurrying back to the airplane. His boots crunched against old snow as he continued listening to Ziggy's message. All too soon her voice faded and vanished, though he tried hard to hang on to it, not wanting to let her go, not wanting to be left alone with all these strangers. He already had so much to worry about and now she'd laid before him the real reason for this Leap! Who did she think he was . . . *Sam?*

Head bent against the mounting wind and his hair full of snow, Al raised his eyes only long enough to check his progress and correct his trajectory. The others had already returned to the aircraft. They huddled around the open side hatch, arms raised, waving him in.

The sight unexpectedly warmed him. He wasn't with strangers, he was with friends. Sure, they were Gordon Huckstep's friends, but that didn't seem to make much difference right now. At least there were people who cared if he lived or died. Did Sam have it so lucky? How was he doing, anyway, with his half of the task? Did he even know Al was out here or that Ziggy was trying to reach them?

He shook his head. He had to believe that. He had to believe

Sam knew everything he did and that somehow they would find each other across the vastness of Canada's wilderness.

Further speculation on the convoluted mess of this Leap and the well-being of his friend were drowned in another wave of snow as he stepped into the circle of his waiting friends.

CHAPTER

SIX

"Oh, boy," wasn't precisely the expletive flitting through Sam Beckett's mind just after Leaping into his new host, but it was the only one his overdeveloped sense of propriety would let him utter aloud.

Through the years, since control of his life was first wrested from his hands, Sam had become quite adept in dealing with the vastly different post-Leap situations in which he found himself. Never knowing who (or, in the case of one Leap, *what*) he was going to end up as, had honed his improvisational abilities to a fine edge.

Despite this, he always experienced something of a knee-jerk reaction—a phenomenon along the lines of an emotional and psychical, as well as physical, twitch—to each new locale. This time was no different. Finding himself unexpectedly behind the wheel of a moving vehicle made him momentarily overcompensate his steering, swerving the vehicle slightly from one side to the other on the dark, blessedly vacant, headlight-illuminated road.

"Oh, boy, what?" someone mumbled from the passenger seat.

Sam snuck a glance sideways. It was difficult to discern details in the somewhat necrotic glow of the dashboard's green lights and harder still to make out features with the upper half of his passenger's face obscured by the furred frame of a parka hood pulled low. All he saw was the bulk of arms crossed over the chest, a faint thrust of unbearded square chin, and a wisp of white-blond hair. Whoever this might be was male by the voice and sounded more than half-asleep.

"Nothing," Sam said lightly, surprised to hear a British accent emerge from his throat. Inspiration struck with movement at the side of the road and the brief illumination of green eyes at the limit of his headlights before the unidentifiable animal bounded away into the night. "Something ran in front of us, that's all. I nearly hit it."

"You get a good look at it?"

"Uh . . . no. I guess I wasn't paying attention." Sam gave an uncertain laugh. "I don't think it was Bigfoot, though."

The man grunted noncommittally, evidently unamused. "It was probably a deer." He shifted slightly and Sam suddenly felt eyes upon him, though the shadows precluded any certainty. Would this man be able to tell that his former companion had taken an abrupt hiatus and left an utter stranger in his place? "Are you tired, Philip? Do you want me to take over for a while?"

Despite his offer, the man's body posture spoke otherwise, whispering fatigue. That suited Sam. If his passenger stayed asleep, or at least incommunicado for a while, it would give him a chance to scope out his situation without too many interruptions.

"No," the scientist quickly assured him. "That's all right, I'm fine. Thanks, though. You . . . uh . . . you try to catch some shut-eye."

"Suit yourself." Sam felt the man's regard slip away, and caught a fleeting glimpse of a gaunt, high-cheekboned face. "We wouldn't have this long drive at all if that stupid airport in McBride had let us land." Leaving that intriguing remark hanging in the air with no possible way Sam could reply that wouldn't sound stupid or out of place, the man shifted sideways in his seat to face away from the Leaper. The safety belt pulled taut across his chest and left shoulder as he tucked his head into the slight indentation between the upholstered seat and the headrest. In a few moments he was breathing deeply and regularly, but whether or not he was actually asleep, Sam couldn't say. It didn't matter as long as it gave him time to figure out where he was and what he was doing here.

One eye always on the stretch of open road winding barrenly ahead in case something really *did* dash out in front of them, he gave the vehicle's interior a cursory look. It was a four-wheel-drive truck with bucket seats in front, a bench seat in the center, and an open area at the back. A blue down coat lay across the bench seat and the back held what looked like backpacks and camping equipment. Sam couldn't tell for certain without turning on the interior light and he wasn't about to do that and risk disturbing his passenger. The heat was on medium, blowing a steady stream of warm air across their feet and up against the windshield. Despite the degree of interior warmth, Sam's passenger stayed bundled to the chin in his gray insulated coat, arms tightly folded across his chest as though conserving body heat.

The truck's ignition keys were tagged by a bird-shaped keychain bearing the name and stylized raven logo of Rooke Rent-A-Car. In smaller letters below that was the name "Christopher J. Rooke, Prop." and an address in . . . He tilted his head slightly and reached to turn the key chain to better catch the dashboard's faint light across its surface. Prince George, British Columbia.

British Columbia, *Canada?!*

Of course, British Columbia, Canada, you moron, he thought with a sigh, dropping the chain to let it dangle freely and clang gently against the other three keys on the ring. *How many other British Columbias do you know?*

So why was he in British Columbia? And where was he supposed to be driving *to* across that vast stretch of Canada? And where the hell were Al and Ziggy?

He glanced out the window, not that there was much to see in the darkness, and clicked on the high-beams to get a slightly better look at their surroundings. High banks of dirt-flecked snow bordered both sides of the paved but undivided two-lane highway. The top layer looked fresh and new. A layer of mixed snow and ice crunched under the tires as the truck moved along. It might have made the going difficult for a lesser vehicle, but the truck took it all in four-wheeled stride, humming along at a reasonably swift clip. Beyond the phalanx of his headlights there was nothing to see but the night.

Angling his head to peer at the sky through the windshield brought no success, either. Both moon and stars were blotted out by heavy cloud cover. A lack of natural or artificial light made for a darkness as deep and absolute as that at the bottom of the Marianas Trench.

He cracked his window and let a slender thread of cold air into the truck's warm interior. With it came a feeling of age, a sense of immensity so incomparably deep and profound and certain that Sam instantly knew they were in mountainous terrain. Which mountains could only be left to speculation for now. There were probably more mountain ranges in British Columbia than he had fingers.

Two signs, one slightly larger than the other, appeared at the distant limit of the headlights and Sam read them with eager eyes as the truck drew closer. The larger of the two read Valemount 140 km. The other was a small, logo'ed shield reading Yellowhead Highway South, Rt. 16. Well, he now knew where he was (sort of), but he still hadn't a clue of their final destination. And he couldn't ask without looking stupid. There wasn't even a map at hand to give him a hint.

His eyes flicked to the rearview mirror for a quick, habitual glance and stayed, fascinated as always to find himself looking out from behind someone else's eyes, wearing their skin like an unfamiliar, scratchy set of new clothes that didn't quite fit the way they were supposed to.

Sun-lightened blond hair was parted on the left and worn slightly longer than Sam's own, the ends brushing his shirt collar. It had silvered at the temples, but this heightened rather than detracted from the rest of the face. Heavy-lidded blue eyes looked back from behind gold rimmed aviator-style glasses. Sam tipped his head forward to peer over the frames. Yup, they were prescription. This fellow was badly nearsighted.

His features were craggy and not what the fashion plates would call classically handsome. Prominent, sunburned cheekbones were chiseled sharply like Abraham Lincoln's. The aristocratic prow of a nose hearkened back to an age when Romans invaded Britain and spread their blood among the native populations. The generous mouth looked capable of humor or severity. A healthy portion of wrinkles around the eyes and the corners of his mouth hinted at much time spent worrying or laughing, or perhaps a hearty helping of both.

Pulling himself away from the compulsion of the reflected image, Sam looked down. His new body was longer than his own and extremely slender, honed down to bone, muscle, and tendon, with a tensile strength like that of fine wire. He wore expensive hiking boots, dark corduroys, and a dark blue chamois shirt under a sweater patterned in autumnal colors.

"Cool." He nodded approvingly. It was always nice to like the face and body he'd Leaped into. "But who am I?" He asked the question quietly, not wanting his passenger to hear him make such an unusual statement, nor did he want the man to catch him perusing his own driver's license. He didn't expect an answer to his question, so he was startled when he got one.

"Dr. Beckett—"

Sam nearly Leaped out of his skin. His head snapped from one side to the other, seeking whoever had called him by name. By his *own* name. No one was there, of course, other than his passenger, who remained still and silent like before and seemingly unaware of his agitation. That meant the name came from only one of two sources . . . and Al only called him Dr. Beckett when he was being sarcastic.

"Ziggy?" Sam queried cautiously in a hoarse whisper. "Al, are you here somewhere?" He looked into the rearview mirror. No familiar Italian countenance brandishing the handlink like a rapier leered at him from the backseat . . . or from the front seat . . . or even from the engine block, for that matter. "Al?" he hissed, looking around surreptitiously, knowing that sometimes his friend liked to shake him up by appearing half-in/half-out of the floor or ceiling. There was no sign of the ebullient Sicilian anywhere.

For some strange reason, he still heard Ziggy as though she were sitting at the back of his brain, but he hadn't been paying much attention while he searched expectantly for Al.

He listened intently, trying to pick out individual words.

So distracted was Sam by this conundrum that he didn't notice the deer until it was too late. Perhaps because of the easier going the open area provided, a slender doe had decided to take her evening's constitutional up the center of the road and right into the oncoming beam of Sam's headlights as the truck rounded a curve. She froze, pinned by the bright halogens, her eyes reflecting back the same eerie green as the dashboard lights.

For a heartbeat, staring at her with as much surprise as she undoubtedly felt at being trapped under that harsh glare, Sam could have sworn he saw his face reflected in the dark orbs of her eyes. Then his foot slammed the brakes hard and he cranked the wheel over to the right, forgetting in his desire to save the deer injury that the road was covered with a hard-packed layer of snow and ice. The truck's heavy tires dug in with a grinding grunt, trying their best, but the most valiant tires in the world aren't a damn bit of good when ice grabs hold of them. The vehicle did two blindingly swift three-sixties with Sam clinging white-knuckled to the wheel. The slewing rear bumper collided with the deer on the first pass and sent her sprawling through the air and into the left snowbank.

"What the hell was *that?!*" Sam's passenger came bolt upright against his restraints and swept his hood back with one fine-boned, large-knuckled hand.

From the corner of his eyes, Sam glimpsed gnawed-down features as he stared through the windshield at the truck hood and swore under his breath, over and over again, an old Italian oath Al taught him after a particularly harrowing Leap. He threw the gearshift into park a lot harder than necessary and his shaking fingers dug at his seat belt. He fumbled twice with the catch before finally wrenching it free so hard it smacked back against the door. "I hit a deer," he snapped desperately. He flicked up the lock on his door and quickly got out. Cold air bit through the warm wool of his sweater, stung his bare skin, and crisped the hair inside his nostrils. Snow squealed coldly under his boots and he slipped slightly on the icy road as he hurried around the truck to survey the damage.

The rear bumper was dented and the left taillight had shattered into a million pieces. Slivers of red plastic were sprayed across the road in a wide arc, mixed with the larger and luridly brighter spray of blood from the slaughtered deer. The blood steamed in the cold, sending up tendrils matching those escaping from Sam's mouth as he breathed heavily.

"Dammit," Sam moaned with despair, heartsick, and took a useless step closer to the snowbank. Exposed by the headlights, the deer sprawled in the snow with her hindquarters atop the chest-high mound and her head hung low over the side. Her chest cavity was pulped. Blood pooled on the ground beneath her parted jaws, steaming strongly and staining the air with a gamey, meaty odor. Her blocky front teeth parted in a silent cry of surprised agony, and her large, dark eyes, no longer reflecting anything, stared sightlessly at Sam's feet. "Son of a bitch." He ran his hands over his face and tugged his hair in frustration.

The crunching whine of steps announced his passenger, but Sam didn't turn around, so caught was he by the sight of the deer. One moment she was vibrantly alive and the next lifeless, her spark fled into the night forever. The two men stared at the animal for a few silent moments, their breath clouding the frigid air with man-made cumulus, then Sam's passenger sighed resignedly and rested his hand on the Leaper's shoulder. "Don't let it get to you, Philip. It's not that big a deal."

Sam turned and the hand dropped away, taking its impression of thin wastedness back into the darkness of the other man's pocket. He knew he was overreacting, but the somewhat flip attitude made him angry, assuredly far angrier than he should be, except that he hated to have anything die by his hand. "Not that big a deal?" he questioned, his chest tight with emotion. "What would you call it?"

The man shrugged lazily, the nylon material of his coat making a mild shushing sound. Sam saw him more clearly in the wash of illumination from the headlights. His blue eyes were a shade or two darker than Sam's and his shaggy hair, cut in a style reminiscent of rock star Rod Stewart, might once have been blond, but had paled to white, stark and brittle looking. It framed his face, accentuating the hollowness around his eyes, cheeks, and at the base of his throat. His features were sharp and pointed, very Nordic looking, and pared to the bone with not as much meat under the flesh as there should have been. This was not a healthy thinness, like the body Sam now wore, and he would unreservedly have bet every degree he held that there was something physically wrong with this man.

The stranger's calm eyes never left the deer. He studied the corpse with a coolly clinical style for several moments before finally speaking. "Things die, Philip," he said impassively. "Plants, animals . . . people." He turned and headed back toward the truck. "They just die. There's no explanation. There's no rhyme or reason. There's no lottery and there's no fairness to it. It's just the way of the world. And who ever said the world was fair?" His words were heavy with caustic bitterness, tainting his tone like the smell of the blood dyeing the snow. It lingered on the back of Sam's tongue like a real taste, like the acrid scent of marigolds. He desperately wanted to ask what he meant, innately sensing that he needed this clue to help solve the mystery of his appearance in this time and place. But he couldn't risk arousing suspicion. Even if he could, he wasn't certain how to phrase the question. He didn't even know the fellow's name, for Pete's sake, though he obviously knew this Philip fellow well enough to call him by his first name.

Sam swung an arm at the deer, confusion warring with his sorrow over the animal's death. "What do we do with her? Shouldn't we move her or something?"

"Where to?" The tone was still brittle with anger toward something Sam didn't yet understand. "The cathedral in the wood?" He shook his head and bestowed what could only be called a pitying look. "There's nothing you can do. You can't *undo* it. You can't bring her back to life." He shrugged. "Leave her where she is. She's just a hunk of meat. The scavengers will take care of it." He paused with his foot on the running board. "They always do," he added quietly as he hefted himself into the driver's seat and paused with his hand on the door, ready to pull it closed. "I'll take over driving for a while," he continued as though nothing more had occurred than that they'd stopped to take a leak alongside the road. "You look a little shagged out. You were probably half-asleep at the wheel without knowing it." He slammed the door and jerked his head in admonishment for Sam to get a move-on. He glanced fleetingly at the odometer, then frowned and glared at Sam through the windshield as the Leaper rounded the truck, got in the other side, and shut the door. "Christ, Philip, you've driven well over a hundred kilometers! I thought we made a deal when we left Prince George to trade off at decent intervals so we didn't get overtired."

Sam shrugged, leaning forward to hold his hands above the dashboard heat vent, then busied himself with latching his seat belt. "I, ah, I lost track of time and I didn't want to wake you."

For a moment, Sam thought the man's expression softened slightly, but then it was gone and replaced by the earlier unexplained hostility. "Just remember you invited yourself along on this gig. I don't need anyone taking care of me. I'm doing fine on my own." He slammed the gearshift into drive and they took off again at a faster clip than Sam would have cautiously recommended, but he wisely decided maybe now was not a good time to remind his companion of such a thing.

I don't think you're fine at all, he thought, staring straight ahead and watching the gaunt older man out of the corner of his eyes. Knowing by the set of the other man's jaw that conversation was out of the question for now, he crossed his arms and settled back in the seat. "You mind if I catch some sleep?" he asked lightly.

"Don't stay awake on my account." The man clicked on the radio, tuning it to the distant scratchiness of a rock and roll station.

Sam held back a frustrated sigh and closed his eyes, determined to catch some sleep while he could and until he discovered . . .

Ziggy!

He schooled himself not to outwardly react, not to betray what he felt to the truck's new driver lest that lead to questions he couldn't field. Despair ached inside him like an open

62

wound. Ziggy had been here (though where, precisely, was something Sam had yet to figure out). She had been here, speaking to him, and then he'd hit the deer and forgotten all about her. Now she was gone. He listened hard, but there was nothing to hear beyond the crunch of snow beneath their spinning tires and the whine of a rising wind around the fast-moving vehicle.

"Shit."

Sam's eyebrows rose and he slit one eye cautiously. "Hmmmm?" he questioned, making himself sound sleepier than he felt.

"Nothing. It's snowing again." The man's palms angrily pummeled the steering wheel. "Dammit!"

Sam closed his eye again, sincerely hoping this crazy man didn't put them neck deep in a snowbank somewhere. He didn't need any more excitement in his life.

The warmth of the interior combined with the lulling movement of the truck and his own mental exhaustion worked their wonders on Sam Beckett. He was almost asleep, balanced precariously on the thin razor-edge between wakefulness and the abyss, when Ziggy's voice returned and jolted him awake. Eyes still closed, he fought to keep his breathing regular as he listened to the growing sound of her voice. One eye opened slightly to check the driver. It took only a second to realize the stranger wasn't hearing a thing. Somehow, it was all in Sam's head, but he hadn't a clue how Ziggy was accomplishing it.

He listened closely as she explained what Al needed to know. Despair warred in two directions and Sam's heart was torn by which was worse—the storm's continued interference blotting them from Ziggy's surveillance or the news that Al had Leaped as well. The brash Navy man was Sam's one true lifeline to the project and his real life. That lifeline was now severed, perhaps forever. What must poor Al be going through right now? He wasn't as familiar with this sort of thing as was Sam.

Ziggy supplied the barest outline that history afforded. Sam prayed Al had survived the crash uninjured and began listening even more closely when Ziggy again called him by name.

"Dr. Beckett, you have Leaped into a forty-year-old physician named Philip Payne. At his insistence, he has accompanied his patient and longtime friend, geologist Eric Freeman, to British Columbia to aid the search for Lyndell Freeman's downed aircraft. You should be made aware that, within the past year, Eric Freeman was diagnosed with leukemia."

Sam's eyes widened reflexively. He snapped them shut and stifled a groan, turning it into a sleep-induced mumble so as not to arouse Freeman's curiosity. No wonder the man looked so god-awful. Sam was no expert on leukemia, but if looks were any indication, this man didn't have long to live.

Ziggy's voice continued. "Dr. Freeman's illness has caused a rift in the close relationship he shares with his daughter. He is bitter over his illness and feels cheated by life. He has withdrawn from Lyndell in a misguided attempt to spare her, and himself, more pain than necessary. She, in turn, is increasingly angry over her inability to reach her father and his seeming determination to drive her from his life.

"In the original history, Lyndell and the others died of the combined effects of hypothermia and starvation before the rescue party located them. Dr. Freeman blamed himself and committed suicide shortly thereafter. I postulate a ninety-eight-percent probability that you have both been Leaped to this time to keep the downed party alive and to effect a reconciliation between the Freemans. Your hosts, though confused, have been most cooperative in our attempts to gain you the greatest amount of information, considering I have no assurance of reaching you via this system. In any event, the staff and I will attempt to locate you both as soon as is viable, and effect a rescue. Until then, carry on with my hypothesis, and good luck."

Sam desperately wanted an aspirin. Perhaps an entire bottle. His temples throbbed, but he refrained from rubbing them. His mind raced scattergun over the information Ziggy had given him and he felt a wave of despair rise up inside. How could he hope to rescue people he couldn't even locate, especially in a wild area the size of Canada's British Columbia and at the tail end of winter besides? Al was no slouch, but he wasn't used to Leaping. How could he survive under these conditions?

That's all you want, Ziggy? Sam thought. *Why not just have me build the Empire State Building out of ice cubes?* His lips tightened into a thin line and he took a deep breath. *I need help on this one,* he prayed silently, winging his thoughts toward whoever had been controlling the strings of his life these many years. *I can't do this one alone and neither can Al. You've got to help us. Please. Send me a sign or something that you're going to help us out.*

Whether it was a sign or not, he never knew, but shortly thereafter his headache faded and he slid gratefully into the welcoming arms of a deep sleep.

CHAPTER SEVEN

Sam was dreaming.

It was the real him in the dream and not Philip Payne, though he wore Philip's clothing. It was good seeing himself as he really was, or at least as he remembered being.

He was hunting for Al but, like Little Bo Peep searching for her lost sheep in the children's nursery rhyme, he didn't know where to find him. There were no features to this landscape by which to discern direction or judge progress. All around him was nothing but a heavy mist the oppressive color of a rainy day. Areas of the fog appeared backlit by distant, faint illumination. It shredded to gauzy filaments at his approach and closed in around him from behind. He hardly felt its brushing touch as he stumbled along blindly, hands out before him in the hopes of touching something that would give him a clue to his location or the whereabouts of his dearest friend.

Sounds reached him through the cloying fog, dampened by the enveloping mist in such a way that it was impossible to gauge distance, direction, or source. Sensing he had been searching for a very long time without resting and without success, Sam paused now to listen. As soon as he stopped, the sounds faded away to oddly spaced murmurings all but lost in the whispering hush of the mist.

"Al!" His voice bounced back from the cottony wall of fog. The echo sounded flat, unreal, and nothing at all like his normal speaking voice. "Al, are you out here?" He listened again, straining his hearing to the limit in search of any little sound that might tell him in which direction to turn. Direction! That was a laugh! When he turned in a circle, searching, he had no real assurance he ended up facing the way he'd begun. Nothing responded to his call except the soft murmuring movement of the fog as it eddied slowly around him like a film of motor oil floating on the still waters of a lake.

He found it impossible to stay in one place. There was a compulsion in him to keep moving, to keep searching. He started forward again at a trot, his hands stretched out in front of him to ward off an unexpected approach or to save himself from collision with unanticipated obstacles hidden in the fog. At this point he would have loved to touch something, anything, just to gain some sort of perspective out of these blank surroundings.

Something crunched crisply under his next several steps, startling him. He stumbled to a halt and knelt to cautiously feel around him. The ground was cold and crystalline to his touch. Something melted against his bare fingers and through the knees of his pants, chilling his skin. Snow!

His breath fogged the air as he cupped his palms together, raised a handful of the fluffy white flakes to his face, and inhaled a deep lungful of the sharp, almost bitingly metallic wilderness scent of the snow. It smelled clean and fresh, and reminded him of mornings as a child and going to do farm chores with the white flakes falling softly onto his upturned face, or waiting for the school bus while surreptitiously packing together a snowball to throw at his brother's back when he wasn't looking. The odor reminded him of Thanksgivings, Christmas Eves, and his mom's hot chocolate simmering on the back burner of the stove. The snow had the scent of all outdoors as Pop and he brought in the tree and set it into its stand along the living room wall near the fireplace.

Sam blinked hard, surprised to find himself near tears from the poignant reverie. Guilt burned hotly in his breast and flamed his cheeks with shame. How could he lose himself in memories of the past when Al needed him? What kind of friend was he that he could be so easily distracted from the task at hand?

Sam wiped his eyes and raised his head to realize that the quality of the light had changed while he mulled over remembrances of times past. The mist had lightened around him and lost its dull gunmetal gray in favor of a brighter hue. He still couldn't see beyond the impenetrable veil of smoke, but the additional light lifted his spirits and piqued his curiosity.

More intriguing scents reached him through the paleness beyond the circle of mist and snow. They were real smells, too, not just the leftover remnants of his ruminations about the past. He really smelled pine now. It was a comforting, sharp, and pleasantly biting odor, reminding him of the time when he had a cold and Mom rubbed some Vicks onto his chest.

Sam shook his head hard. "Stop it," he sternly ordered himself. What was happening? Why was it so easy to lose himself in thoughts of the past when he had a major problem in the present? What was wrong with him? Why couldn't he keep his mind on finding Al?

He squeezed his eyes shut for a moment, then opened them and stared sternly ahead into nothing, marshaling his wandering thoughts. No more confusion. It was time to find a way to make his surroundings work for him, rather than against him.

What brought Sam back to the present more than his own will and sense of purpose was the sound of footsteps crunching faintly through the snow. Whoever walked here with him undoubtedly was as lost as he, hidden by the white swirl that blotted out the surroundings.

"Al?" he called, hope rising like a wave. "Is someone there? Follow my voice." The steps paused. He imagined the other lost soul listening, considering the timbre of his voice and weighing the advantages and disadvantages of meeting a stranger in a bank of fog. Evidently he passed muster, for the steps resumed and turned in his direction. Closer, they had a strange double-step cadence that rang oddly in Sam's ears. They crushed the snow noisily, crunching through the thin layer of crust.

"Al, is that you? It's me, Sam!" He started out to meet the newcomer, then stopped, afraid of going off course in the dense fog and missing the person altogether. He didn't want that to happen. It would be wonderful having some company, someone to talk to, even if it turned out to not be Al.

"Al? I'm here, buddy. I—" The words died aborning, trapped in the cage of Sam's lungs like captured animals. Coherent words fled his mind in a rush of primal emotion as the creature stepped out of the fog and halted before him.

The bull elk was monstrous in its bulk and majesty. Never in his life had Sam seen anything this huge up close. The animal's proximity left him feeling very small, just as he did when he stood outside the Project at night, staring up at the panorama of stars and contemplating the importance of mankind in the grand scheme of things. The tiny portion of his scientific mind that functioned imperturbably even under the most dire of circumstances told him there was no way this side of heaven that an elk could be this big. Nevertheless, there it stood, towering magnificently over him like a conquering king demanding homage, complete with a crowning rack of antlers. Sam quelled the sudden, strange desire to sink down onto one knee and bow his head, but it was a near thing.

The animal calmly stared at him down the long, slender planes of its dark-marked face. Totally unafraid, its expression seemed to convey an almost disdainful compassion for this puny human it had happened upon. Dark eyes hunted Sam's features, flicking from place to place, studying him intently. Sam knew it was waiting for him to speak.

Sam shook his head in exasperation. That was nonsense, of course. The elk's dark orbs caught his gaze and held him. The steady, unfrightened regard quelled the negative motion of Sam's head and the Leaper swallowed hard. Yes, it was nonsense, except . . .

Except he got the feeling that this was all far from nonsense. Why was the elk watching him so attentively? What was it looking for? What could Sam hope to say to a wild animal as foreign to him as one of Al's cigars?

Al. He could tell it about Al.

"I'm looking for my friend, Al Calavicci," Sam began, his voice quietly polite, at once feeling eminently stupid about and utterly compelled toward this course of action. "He's around here somewhere, I think. I have to find him. He may be hurt and—" Words froze in his throat as the elk moved. It took a single step toward him, one dark foreleg stretched forward as if it might bow at any moment. Its muzzle moved fractionally toward Sam, then tilted slightly upward as the elk extended its long, statcly neck as far as it would reach. The barrel of its rib cage widened like a bellows as it took a deep breath. There was an anticipatory pause and then the air carilloned with the animal's belling call. Its lips formed a black ellipse as it cried, and Sam caught a glimpse of its teeth, so much like those of the doe killed in the road. Steam from the elk's hot breath tendriled around its face and antlers as three times it sent out its eerie, ringing cry. The mist caught the call and, instead of holding it captive as it had Sam's voice, sent it spinning in every direction, echoing and reverberating off things Sam could not see.

When the last echo died away, the elk snorted loudly through its wet, shining nostrils and pawed the ground once, slicing a line through the pure whiteness of the snow underfoot. It looked away, its eyesight running along the same trajectory as the mark in the snow, then looked pointedly back at Sam.

"What?" Sam whispered, wanting to understand. But the elk was gone, turning and lunging away from him in a sudden single bound to vanish between the curtains of mist. In the instant between two heartbeats, it was as though the animal had never been there at all.

A breeze caressed Sam's cheeks, making them cold, and he understood he'd been crying without even realizing it. He blinked rapidly a couple of times and ran a forearm across his face, confused and awed by what had just occurred. The breeze rose, freshening and bringing with it more smells he could not identify. It tugged his clothing and riffled through his hair, coaxing him on. Sighing deeply, Sam faced into the wind and continued searching.

If he shifted in his sleep, twisting uncomfortably within the constraints of his seat belt and murmuring under his breath, it was not enough to wake him from the dream, and he never knew that Eric Freeman favored him with a long, speculative look as they drove into the night toward their unknown destination.

The wind continued tugging at him and the dream mist began swirling and roiling in great cumulus billows. Occasionally the fog broke apart for a moment and through the jagged holes Sam glimpsed rocks and trees and sometimes more snow. Other times, the soaring vastness of mountain peaks towered over him and then vanished behind another wall of cloud.

A porcine grunting alerted him to his next visitor just before the thick-waisted black bear waddled swayingly out of a stand of trees. Besides sounding like a pig, it was sort of built like one. Its eyes were small and myopic as a mole's, and the nose was shaped like a plow. Its thick fur was a rusty cinnamon in color, as sometimes occurred despite its moniker. It was definitely an *Ursus americanus*.

Sam recalled the time many years before when his uncle A. J. went on a deep-woods hunt for bear and, as A. J. put it in his prideful drawl, "bagged one." Sam, being only about seven or eight at the time, was allowed by his squeamish mother to see only the flat remainder of the carcass, empty of meat and devoid of personality, the eyes lusterless as dusty attic marbles and the glossy black fur dull and stiff under his curious fingers. The indignity and crime of the animal's death made him very sad. As soon as he could get away without anyone noticing, he'd hidden in the barn to cry for the bear and its lost life of freedom, when it hadn't been doing anything more offensive than rooting under logs for bugs and grubs. For a long time, and with a child's sense of justice, he wished it were A. J.'s skin stretched out on his aunt's parlor floor rather than the bear's. He wasn't very close to his uncle after that.

This bear, alive and well, ignored him. Rocking from side to side, it pendulously swung its wedge-shaped head briefly in his direction as though considering whether or not there might be bugs or grubs hiding under *him*. Deciding on the negative, it proceeded on its way, wuffling quietly to itself.

After a second's hesitation, Sam followed. Though the bear's eyesight was poorer than his own, its other senses were not. This was its territory and it knew the lay of the land a whole lot better than he did. As long as he maintained a discrete distance, there shouldn't be any problem following his ursine guide. Though he still didn't know where he was going, Sam felt better for having even this small measure of company.

The mist continued to clear and show Sam more and more of his surroundings. The sky was at first a monochrome gray, matching the rest of the area, but tatters of fog shredded and suddenly there was blue sunlit sky overhead. The opportunity to see something familiar snatched his eyesight away from the murky surroundings. Smiling broadly for what felt like the first time in days, he turned in a slow circle with his arms outstretched and reveled in the pristine, sapphire blue of the sky. The sun warmed against his skin and sent tear-inducing daggers of light lancing up from the snow- and ice-covered land.

Around him, the landscape began to emerge and the lightening of the fog brought a lightening to his heart. Now there was nothing to stop him from finding Al! His pace lengthened and his face turned from the sun and forward, blue eyes purposefully studying the forested land around him.

The black bear had vanished, disappearing among the tall trees or behind a rock or gone to earth to sleep for a while. Sam didn't know which. He missed the animal's meager companionship, but not too seriously. He had more important things on his mind. His head swung from side to side as he walked, unconsciously imitating the bear's movements as he hunted the landscape for Al's familiar form.

What came instead was fear. What came was death armed with teeth and claws. What came was a rock beside the trail that was not a rock, but an enormous brown hunchbacked lump by the side of the unhewn path Sam followed, a ridge in the landscape that suddenly rose, taller than the elk, higher than the mountains, taking over the sky and the land and the entire world around it for no other reason than because it could.

Like the illusion in a Bev Doolittle painting, the grizzly bear rose unexpectedly out of the land around it. Grunting up onto its hind legs, it swung around at Sam with much more ponderous grace than the black bear possessed. Black-lipped mouth slightly agape with heavy ursine breathing, the bear gulped an enormous lungful of air and roared, swinging one front leg in an unerring arc toward the Leaper's head.

Sam turned and fled, running as never before in his entire life. The ground shuddered beneath his feet as the grizzly thudded onto all fours and charged after him in bawling rage.

Mind in a blind panic, Sam could not think of the "safety" precautions recommended when faced with a bear. All that mattered to him now was to flee the death thundering closely to his heels. He heard the bear breathing behind him, grunting in its lumbering rocking-horse-style run, and fought the desire to hazard a look over his shoulder to see just how close it was to catching him. That small and stupid move could mean the difference between survival and death.

A steep incline rose before him, blocking out part of the sky. Sam almost cried with terror and frustration. His lungs labored for breath they couldn't find. Chest and throat burned with the fire of his breathing, and a stitch burrowed painfully into his left side, cramping hard, making it difficult to breathe. As his boots hit the base of the incline and he began to climb, his eyes tracked to the summit arching high above his head. It was so far away!

Sam's feet and hands slipped in the loose gravel and shale, threatening to send him sprawling and sliding backward into the grizzly's clutches. His heart pounded agony inside his chest, thudding in his ears and drowning out the sound of the bear's pursuit. His hands clawed for purchase on the uneven terrain and came away torn and bloodied as he ascended. The pain meant nothing to him in light of what waited below if he should stop.

He glimpsed light above and knew he neared the crest of the slope. With a grunting cry, Sam flung himself forward, grabbing frenziedly at fistfuls of dry yellow grass to pull himself over the edge. He flipped onto the downslope, landing hard on his side, and struggled to his feet. His gaze flashed in every direction, seeking escape from pursuit, seeking anything that might afford shelter from the bear, and he saw the airplane. The image brought him up short in momentary confusion. The pause in flight was long enough for the bear to reach him.

Remembrance whirled Sam around to face his oncoming slaughter, but it never came. The bear was nowhere in sight. All that passed him was a fierce brush of unseasonably hot, gamey-smelling wind that flagged his clothing like sheets on a line and played havoc with his hair. Faintly, he thought he heard a roar, but he couldn't be certain.

He stared around in confusion. There was no way he could have continued to outrun the grizzly, or even given it a long enough chase to tire it and make it lose interest. Where it had gone was a mystery, but one he didn't ponder for long. He winged a thankful prayer skyward and turned back toward the valley and what it held.

At first his mind hadn't registered it was an airplane. It was just something odd in the landscape, something that could either help or hinder him in his flight from the bear. Now he started down the slope at a much slower pace, picking his way carefully in deference to the state of the ridge and the condition of his shaky, adrenaline-pumped legs. His eyes darted between the downed aircraft and the uneven footing continually threatening to trip him. The sun glanced piercingly bright off a hunk of metal lying to one side of the battered fuselage, bringing tears to his eyes, but he was halfway across the meadow before he realized what he was looking at.

A downed aircraft.

"*Al!*" Somewhere, despite having legs that no longer wanted to support him, he found the reserves for more speed and raced toward the airplane. He caught himself hard on the edge of the open hatchway and gasped for breath. "Al!" he croaked, his throat and mouth dry from prolonged heavy breathing. Sam swallowed hard and tried to get control over his laboring lungs as he grasped the edges of the hatch and started to clamber into the plane. "Al!"

"Sam."

The single word was spoken quietly and almost without inflection, but it was enough to spin Sam Beckett around like a top. His eyes popped and he steadied himself against the doorframe.

Al stood several feet away. His white suit had almost certainly once been immaculate and of the finest cut. Now it was covered with dirt and spattered with blood, but none of the blood seemed to be his. As a matter of fact, Al looked pretty good for someone who had survived an airplane crash.

"Al!" The strength left his body in a single rush and he sagged to his knees. Tears of relief filled his eyes and he let them flow unhindered. "My God, Al, I've been looking everywh—"

"You failed."

Sam blinked in confusion. "What? What did you say?"

"You failed. You didn't make it in time." Al paused to light a cigar and blow a large cloud of extremely black smoke toward the sky. "Do you need it spelled out for you? You blew it, putz. I'm dead."

Sam shook his head, brow wrinkled with confusion. "But . . . but you're *here*. You're okay."

Al snorted derisively. "You call this okay?" The fingers of one hand popped open the button on his jacket and spread the clothing wide to show just how un-okay he was.

Sam caught a glimpse of rendered flesh, gouts of blood, and bright particles of bone protruding through torn meat, and began to scream.

CHAPTER

EIGHT

Sam shuddered awake with an earsplitting scream of panicked terror and struck hard at the hand on his arm before he realized where he was or what he was doing.

Eric reeled back against the driver's door to get out of reach of the Leaper's flailing arms, and hugged his offended limb to his chest. "Dammit, Philip! Wake up!"

Still protesting inarticulately, Sam trembled all over and waved his hands in a warding off gesture, his eyes staring ahead unseeingly. "Get away from me! It's not my fault! I tried!"

"Philip!" The geologist raised his voice and dared to reach out and shake his shoulder hard. "Wake *up!*"

Eric's strident order finally pierced the fog of sleep and nightmare enveloping Sam's brain. He jerked and blinked hard, fully awake, but didn't know where he was. Disoriented, he blinked a few more times and his knees came into sharp focused familiarity a few inches from his face.

He was scrunched down in the seat in a near-fetal position, laying with his back curved uncomfortably, his neck bent forward painfully, his feet cocked up hard against the metal glove compartment and his knees in his face. One arm was entangled with the restraining straps of the seat belt and his feet had gone to sleep.

"Oh, my God," he gasped with relief. He straightened slowly, unkinking his knees carefully, and winced as circulation flooded back into his feet. He worked his captive arm free, but his hands trembled so violently that he had difficulty unbuckling the seat belt. When he finally fumbled it free, it snicked back to one side and he leaned forward shakily. Elbows on knees, he ran quivering fingers through his hair and over his face, feeling the stubble of nighttime beard against his palms. He ended the motion with his hands pressed so tightly over his eyes that colorful pinpricks emerged from the darkness behind his lids. Under the winter clothing, his body was slick with a chilly sweat despite the truck's warm interior. He felt clammy and dirty and in need of a hot shower.

"Are you all right?" Eric asked cautiously.

Sam didn't reply, unwilling to trust himself with words just yet. Instead, he stayed hidden within the barrier of his hands with the dream's already-hazy images playing over and over against the dark backdrop of his closed eyes. After several moments with no response, he felt the geologist's gentle, tentative touch on his shoulder. "Philip? Are you okay?"

Sam raised his head. Focusing on the dark blue dashboard, he slowly sat back, his hands laying flaccid in his lap with the fingers slightly curled. He took a deep breath and held it for a minute, then released it in a rush and finally nodded his head. "Yeah." He glanced at his companion and tried to work up a smile. It felt more like a death's head rictus, but he supposed it was better than nothing. "I'm fine, Eric. Thanks." His eyes tracked to Freeman's hands, one rubbing the other with a rhythmic motion. "Oh, gosh, I hit you, didn't I?" he asked shamefully. "Did I hurt you?"

Eric shook his head. "It stings, but I . . ." A corner of his thin mouth lifted sardonically. "I'll live."

Sam frowned with new knowledge. "That's not very funny."

Freeman snorted and the humor fled his eyes, replaced by something chitinous and cynical. "Tough shit."

"At least let me look at it." Quelling any residual shaking, he reached out.

The geologist drew back against the door, his hand held out of reach. "Mind your own business, Dr. Payne," he said nastily. "Save it for someone you can really help."

Maybe the real Philip Payne would be hurt by the cruel remark. Maybe the real Philip Payne could argue with that look and that tone of voice, but Sam Beckett *wasn't* Philip Payne except in form. Still too new in this body and too unfamiliar with the terms of his relationship with Eric Freeman, he didn't know how far he could push the ill man without having it be terribly detrimental.

Rather than test that theory right now, Sam let it drop. He took another deep breath to further clear his overwrought senses and turned away to look at their surroundings.

They were parked on a rise and it was just after dawn. The eastern horizon was a mountain silhouette sporting a ruddy line as testimony to the sun's recent emergence. Blood red color bleached rapidly into white-yellow and pearl gray as the sun rose above the skyline to lose itself behind a heavy canopy of dark gray clouds. Enough illumination escaped through the tiny crack in the cloud cover at the skyline to backlight a stand of trees to their left. The tall pines showed stark and black against the slender horizontal shaft of eye-watering brilliance, like strokes of charcoal against a palette of gold, and sent shadows racing obliquely along the snowy ground and across the road in front of them.

Sam didn't like the look of those clouds. They were too heady a predictor of more snow, not a smart thing to point out to Eric at the moment, considering the geologist's current state of mind.

The additional light made it easier to see details in the truck cab—the blue upholstery, the rigid folds of a roadmap shoved between the seats, and a detritus of Styrofoam cups, soda bottles, and candy bar and fast-food wrappers beneath both their feet. He picked a french fry pouch off his seat, sorry when it proved empty. He wanted something to eat.

The headlights burned a steady beam onto the road. Despite the overcast, they weren't much use in the rising light. A few miles ahead and below their present vantage point, Sam saw a collection of buildings that suggested the beginning of a town. Their sturdy presence in the bleak and beautiful land-scape gave him something normal to focus on, something to help banish the unsettlingly wild freakiness of the dream that lingered around his brain, and something he could ask Freeman about without inciting him to riot. At least so he hoped.

"What's that?" He nodded toward the group of buildings, then rubbed his eyes tiredly and sighed. Any good the sleep might have done him had been effectively shot to hell by the nightmare. His eyeballs felt as if they'd been rubbed with sandpaper, rolled in oatmeal, and deep-fried.

"Valemount. We made it." Freeman heaved a sigh of his own that sounded like relief and stared through the windshield at the small town. His blue eyes were hooded and pensive, his thoughts hidden. Even so, Sam suspected he had a pretty good idea of what was going on in the other man's mind. The way Freeman worried his lower lip with his teeth said it all.

Sam gave the man's wrist a squeeze. "We'll find her, Eric." He said it with more faith than he had any right to express, but a boost of confidence couldn't hurt either of them.

It was immediately obvious that Freeman didn't want to hear it, no matter how well intended. The shutters slammed down over his eyes so fast and hard that Sam was surprised his ears didn't ring from the noise. He took back his hand, but the other man didn't even look his way. Strike two.

Eyes gone glacier cold, Eric shoved the truck into gear without giving Sam a chance to put on his seat belt. "Lyndell's more trouble than she's worth," he said, his tone thick and bitingly bitter.

"You don't really mean that," Sam challenged gently, hoping it was true and that Ziggy wasn't off the mark in her information about the relationship between father and daughter and her speculated reason for this leap.

"You're overstepping your bounds, Philip," the other man snapped warningly. "Stick to what you know."

Freeze out. The silence coming from Eric was not some-thing easily breached and Sam was understandably hesitant to pursue this line of conversation and risk further upsetting the critically ill man. The best course of action was to lay low until he had a better idea of how best to proceed, if such a thing was possible with such an irascible individual. How did Ziggy expect him to get through the heavy armor Freeman wore? Even the best of friends found the going tough when it came to breaking through that kind of wall. This wasn't going to be easy, particularly since Sam felt stuff like this was never his forte. Wheedling, cajoling, and worming a way through a person's emotional defenses were more in Al's line of expertise. Why hadn't *he* been Leaped here and Sam to the injured passengers in the downed aircraft where he could be of more use? It just didn't make sense.

How much had in the last few years?

They drove on in silence, drawing closer to the town, then Eric cleared his throat. Out of the corner of his eyes, Sam saw the geologist flick a quick look at him. "That was some dream you had," Eric commented lightly, testing the waters.

It was probably the closest he was willing to come to an apology and Sam decided to accept it with silent grace. Playing up hurt feelings would only further alienate Freeman, so Sam just looked across and smiled slightly. Things still felt uncomfortable between them, but at least Freeman had made the overture. Sam didn't want him thinking that Sam was the sort to hold a grudge. He just hoped letting it slide wasn't completely out of character for Philip Payne. "Some *nightmare,* you mean." He nodded and drummed his fingers against one knee. "Yeah, it was pretty bad."

"What was it about?" Eric asked curiously.

"Oh, just . . ." Sam stopped and shut his mouth with a nearly audible snap. He'd had every intention of telling him . . . except he didn't have a clue as to what the dream was about. Not a single detail came to mind. He shrugged, his face screwed up in confusion. "I can't remember."

Freeman chuckled. "It couldn't have been as bad as you think, then."

"It sure seemed like it at the time," Sam muttered, scratching the side of his head and looking out the window to mask his confusion. It had been so real and so frightening at the time. Why couldn't he remember? *Why should you be able to remember?* he asked himself. Most dreams seem real when they're happening. That doesn't mean a thing.

"Well, all I know is you were certainly kicking up a fuss, whatever it was about." Eric sent him a quizzical look, one eye on the road ahead of them, and switched off the headlights. "Who's Al?"

"Al?" Sam squeaked in surprise, his voice thrown into its highest register by the question. He cleared his throat and coughed. "Al who?" he asked more normally.

Freeman shrugged. "Beats me. You were yelling to somebody named Al just before I shook you awake."

Sam scratched his cheek, appearing to ponder, and shrugged one shoulder. "I don't know anybody named Al," he lied. "I guess it must have been just a dream character."

"I guess." Another searching glance from those ice blue eyes. "Are you feeling any better?"

"Yeah. Sure. Lots better."

They spent the rest of the short drive in silence. At the outskirts of town they passed a sign that read Valemount. Underneath, someone had graffiti'ed Pop. 3000 . . . More or Less. The side streets were residential and mostly devoid of traffic in these early-morning hours. A few people were out and about, bundled to their chins against the Canadian cold as they cleaned snow off their cars or hurried along the sidewalks, and they barely gave the rental truck a glance.

Near the center of town, Sam noted the usual basic amenities—a single grocery store with a yawning clerk at the cash register; a couple of motels; and a few family-style restaurants, all open with the regulars bellied up to the counter and tables for coffee, hearty breakfasts, and the local gossip. A little further ahead on the left sat a broad, squat, two-storied building.

Seemingly every vehicle in the province was parked in front of it or just pulling up. A steady stream of people crossed the street and entered the building as the searchers assembled. There were truckers and loggers, men who knew the mountains and the lonely stretch of the Yellowhead Highway. There were locals with sturdy RVs, snowmobiles, ATVs, and cross-country skis, as well as a smattering of "winter people"—well-to-do sportsmen from elsewhere who staked vacation claims in the remote scenic mountains.

Eric angled for a parking space and beat out a bearded gent in a beaten-to-death pickup truck who just smiled tightly and waved them in. Sam read the sign hanging over the front door: Royal Canadian Mounted Police. *Sergeant Preston of the Yukon, here we come,* he thought, and didn't feel a bit like laughing.

"This is the place," Eric said calmly, his voice oddly atonal and without inflection. He parked the truck, turned off the ignition, and pocketed the key. For a moment he just sat there as though gathering himself for what lay ahead, then he opened his door and stuck out a foot. "You coming?" he asked over his shoulder.

"Sure," Sam said because he couldn't think of a good reason not to. Reaching into the backseat, he snagged the down coat he assumed was his, got out of the truck, and slammed the door. He slid his arms into the coat as he rounded the hood of the truck and came up beside Freeman. "You hanging in there okay?" he asked quietly.

"For the billionth time in the last twenty-four hours, I'm *fine,* Philip." He sounded tired of answering that question. He paused and rubbed a hand across his eyes and down the white stubble of his cheeks. "I'm just shagged out from the long drive, that's all. Don't worry about me."

"I *do* worry about you, though," Sam countered, striving to keep his tone light. "Lyndell will have my head in a bushel basket if anything bad happens to you."

"Everything bad has already happened to me," Freeman said resignedly. "And there's nothing you can do about it, so stop pretending there is." Halfway to the front steps, he paused and frowned.

"What is it?" Sam asked from behind.

The geologist didn't reply. Instead, he lifted his face slowly toward the wealth of heavy clouds overhead. In a moment he began swearing creatively in a low, intense voice.

Sam didn't need to ask the reason as his gaze followed Freeman's and several snowflakes melted across his lenses. He wiped them away with a finger, smearing water across the glass and blurring his vision, and continued staring upward at the thick white-on-gray falling dance of flakes. The cloud cover had lowered and darkened. It glowered threateningly as the snow fell in a whirling cloud. In another place and time he would have thought the sight beautiful. Now it was only ominous.

He looked at the geologist. Freeman's face was pale and angry within the ivory frame of his wind-touched, shaggily cut hair. He glared at the sky as though expecting the clouds to part and the sun to shine by his will alone. Just when Sam thought he might decide to stand there all day, Eric lowered his head. "Come on," he growled, and led the way up the steps and into the building.

Inside was pandemonium. The main hallway was tight with knots of men and women breaking and re-forming as they discussed urgent business. Some were dressed in uniforms of the Royal Canadian Mounted Police. On the jackets of others were insignias Sam couldn't read in the bustle and jostling movement. The rest wore generic winter clothing, open or off against the building's heat.

They stopped just inside the doorway, both of them momentarily confused by the disorder. Someone touched Sam's arm and he turned. "You here about the downed plane?" a pleasant-faced, dark-haired man asked in the rough burr of a Scots accent. A patch on the left breast of his heavy-duty parka read Yellowhead Helicopters and, beneath that, Dennis Bailey.

Eric answered for them, the skin around his eyes drawn tight with worry. "Yes. My daughter's on that plane."

Bailey swore unoffensively and shook his head. "My condolences. They're formulating a search plan in that room over there." He pointed across the corridor and down two doors. "Talk to Kris Gunn or Rich Selikoff. They're spearheading the effort." He smiled encouragingly. "Don't worry. A lot of fine people have gathered for this search. We'll find them."

"You don't know that," Eric said bluntly. He stared the man down for a few moments, silently challenging him to argue the point, then turned and began pushing his way through the crowd toward the designated room.

Sam was astounded by Freeman's rudeness. "I'm sorry." He felt compelled to apologize for Eric's bad manners. "He shouldn't have said that."

Bailey shrugged. "Water off a duck," he assured him, but his confident look wavered. "Ah, why shouldn't he be a little rude, then? He's frightened and he's right to be. There aren't any assurances, but we'll all try our best."

"Thank you," Sam said, grateful for the man's compassion. "I'd better go after him." He started following in Eric's wake, then half turned as he continued excusing his way through the throng. "Hey, thanks, again!"

A beefy hand raised in reply, then Bailey turned away. Flipping up his hood against the inclement weather, he stepped outside into the storm.

The Leaper caught up with Freeman as he entered the meeting room. It was less crowded here than in the hallway, with the majority of assembled searchers steering clear from the plan makers. A raised dais at the front of the room had a long table and a pedestal blackboard on it. Disordered rows of the uncomfortable desk-and-seat units like those used in schools filled the rest of the room. Several people gathered around the table looking down at its surface while they sipped coffee from Styrofoam cups. The smell set Sam's stomach to growling. He'd *love* a cup right about now, but there wasn't a coffee maker in sight.

They entered just in time to hear a lean man in a blue snowmobile suit say, "The two-twelve 'copters can take this area here." He gestured at the tabletop and the probable map hidden by the press of bodies. "Yellowhead's two-oh-sixes will cover this section, and the two-oh-fours out of William's Lake will take—"

Eric cut him off, voice raised to cut through the babble. "They won't take much of anything for a while. It's begun snowing."

His pronouncement brought a series of groans from those assembled. One man threw his wool hat against the wall and slumped into one of the uncomfortable plastic seats. "Now what?" he muttered. Another dropped his head between his shoulders and swore quietly.

A short, round, honey-haired woman, dressed in the heavy winter uniform of a high-ranking officer in the RCMP and standing at the center of the table beside the man in the blue snowmobile suit, raised an inquisitive eyebrow at the newcomers. "Killing the messenger on account of the message went out of fashion a long time ago, gentlemen, but I could be persuaded to reinstate it. I thought I knew everyone around here, but I don't recognize your faces. Who are you?"

Eric moved up the side aisle. "I'm Eric Freeman from Monterey, California. This is Dr. Philip Payne. My daughter Lyndell is a passenger on the aircraft that went down. I spoke to someone on the phone . . ."

"*Mon dieu* . . . shit! Yes!" The woman jumped off the dais and strode down the aisle to meet them halfway with her hand extended. "I'm Kris Gunn, Mr. Freeman," she said with a smile. "I head this outpost. I'm the one you talked to." She shook Sam's hand as well, but her eyes never left Eric. "I expected you to arrive last night."

Freeman made a face. "We would have if the airport at McBride hadn't sent my Cessna packing all the way back to Prince George to land."

"It's well they did," said the slender, brown-haired man who'd been giving directions as he joined their party without preamble or invitation. "We had one bastard of a storm last night. Everything iced up and visibility was nil. You never could have landed."

Eric looked as if he wanted to argue the point, but didn't, though he was obviously spoiling for an argument with someone if only to relieve the stress. Sam's concern was that there weren't enough arguments available in a day to calm down the tense geologist.

"Who are you?" Freeman asked bluntly, sizing up this new individual with his steely eyes.

Another set of handshakes as Kris made the introductions. "This is Rich Selikoff. He heads the Provincial Emergency Program in this area."

"Pleased to meet you," Selikoff said, evidently planning to excuse or ignore Freeman's ugly mood. "Come take a look at what we have." He shepherded them back toward the table. The others shifted aside to make room, and Selikoff handled the quick introductions. "These are our team leaders: Royal White, Wolfgang Kurth, Jim McMahon, Kate MacKrell,

Barbara Tandarich, and Chris Meyer." The men and women around the table nodded pleasantly and voiced quiet hellos, but it was up to Sam to return the salutations, because Eric ignored them all. He was engrossed on the map spread out before them.

"Do you know where they went down?" he asked, his voice strained as his eyes hunted the lines and whorls of the map.

"We don't have a solid fix on that yet," Kris replied. Her gray eyes imperturbably met the flash of his blue ones as he glared at her for a moment before returning to his study of the map. She traced an area with one finger. "The last airport to note them in its airspace was Williams Lake. That's approximately two hundred twenty-five kilometers from here as the crow flies and due south of Prince George." She shifted her hand. "Marge Robles up here in Barkerville reported hearing something on her scanner that might have been them. Times seem pretty concurrent, but the transmission was garbled by the storm."

"That old woman's nuts," Kate MacKrell protested. She rolled her eyes. "She says she bought that scanner special order to search for UFO's." Several of those present chuckled and nodded. Evidently, Ms. Robles was a legend in that area.

"That's as may be," Kris said flatly, her tone cutting off their jocularity. "What she does with it is her business, so long as she doesn't cause trouble. In all the years she's owned that scanner, she's never bothered me with reports about anything she's heard until now. Which is one of the reasons I'm of a mind to give it some weight." She smiled at Eric and Sam, evidently fond of the other woman. "Hey, I'm the first to admit old Marge is a little eccentric. Barkerville's an old gold rush town gone tourist. I guess she's been there forever and beyond, but she's not one to cause trouble or draw attention to herself for no good reason. And she's *not* nuts." A glare in MacKrell's direction accompanied that statement and the younger woman looked abashed. "If she says she heard something, then I'm likely to believe her until something comes along to make me change my mind." She straightened and rubbed the small of her back. "Anyway, the minute she heard about the downed plane she called me to say she might have heard it the other night on her equipment. The channel was awfully staticky so it was hard to tell much of anything, but she swears it wasn't any of the stuff she's used to picking up. I don't see any reason not to take that as a valid point until we're proven otherwise."

"I agree," Selikoff chimed in. He leaned over the map, drawing Eric's avid attention with the movement of one hand. "Taking that into account, we're concentrating our search efforts in this area." His palm covered the space below Prince George and between Highways 97 and 16, encompassing Bowron Lake Provincial Park and the upper portion of Wells Grey Provincial Park. He lifted his head to meet Eric's eyes. "You said it's begun snowing again?"

"Hard," the geologist replied with a sharp nod. "I'm no expert on snowfall, but this looks like it's planning on staying around for awhile."

"Shit."

Kris folded her arms and leaned a hip against the edge of the table. "It appears the weather reports are accurate for a change, boys and girls,'" she sighed. "Unfortunately."

Selikoff nodded. "Why can't it ever happen when it's to our advantage?" he asked of no one. His eyes tracked to the faces of those gathered around the table. It was easy for Sam to see these were hardworking people, familiar with the local terrain and comfortable within that familiarity, ready for what lay ahead. "Anyone hear the most recent report?"

"Lisa's been calling me with updates every half-hour," said lean, dark-haired Royal White. His arms were folded loosely over the front of his flight suit and he looked a whole lot more relaxed than the incessant jiggling of one foot said he was. He shook his head unhappily. "They're predicting one hellacious storm in the next couple of days if the front doesn't clear. Until then, it'll be sporadic storms and squalls."

"And probably right where we don't want them to be," remarked Jim McMahon. The blue-billed cap on his head read 'McMahon's RV Sales' on the front.

"Just as bad," Royal continued, "are the reports that there isn't supposed to be a break in the cloud cover until the end of the week or later. The air pressure's holding it low, creating fog in the melting boggy areas. Between all that *and* this last-hurrah snowfall, we just can't fly in this stuff. Not and risk putting ourselves down as well." He tipped his head in Eric's direction. "Begging your pardon, Mr. Freeman, but it's true. You know that from trying to get into McBride last night."

"I know it," Eric agreed unhappily. "I don't like saying it, but I do. Much as I want to find them, I don't want you risking your own lives to do it."

"That's good," Kris added. "Because I can't and won't risk the lives of all our air crews for seven people."

"So where does that leave us?" Sam asked to forestall the belligerent look clouding Eric's face. "We have to do something. If we can't do air recognizance, what are our other choices?"

Kris leaned beside him on the table, her arms rigid and every eye on her. Sam suddenly realized not only was she in charge of this RCMP outpost, but she was most assuredly in charge of everything else as well, at least as far as these people were concerned. Her gray eyes were stormy as they tracked the reaches of the map laid out in front of them. When she next spoke, it was obvious she wasn't happy with what she had to say.

"Okay. We can't leave them out there, so we'll use snowmobiles or we do it on foot. We've got skies, snowshoes, and dogsleds. We—"

"That's a damned big area to do on foot," Barbara Tandarich pointed out.

"We don't have any choice, Barbie." There was no arguing with that tone, had anyone even been so inclined. She looked at Eric. "Mr. Freeman—"

"Eric."

She nodded. "Does your daughter or the other passengers have any wilderness-survival training?"

"Lyndell's done some camping. I don't personally know any of the other passengers except the pilot, Dan Dodds, and Gordon Huckstep. He's a student of mine and he's an outdoorsman from way back." He paused and took a deep breath. Beside him, Sam felt his entire frame shake slightly like a tree teased by wind. "If they . . . if Gordon survived,

88

they might have a chance of hanging on for a while."

"Then let's make the odds even better, people." Kris straightened and her eyes were demanding. "You have your search grid landmarks, the names of your team members, the make and call number of the downed aircraft, and a list of the passengers and pilot. If you need anything else, now's the time to get it. I'm sorry as hell we can't do this from the air, but it just isn't possible right now. Just notify your standby pilots to be ready to hit the sky when and if those clouds break up. Mark your checkout time with Theresa or Sharri in the front office or I'll nail you to the wall. Radio in at the appointed intervals or I'll guarantee to have your ass in a sling the next time I see you. I already have enough to worry about without losing sleep over whether or not my search teams are intact. Capishe?" She wasn't joking, that much was certain, and her people knew it. Each one nodded seriously as they began shuffling papers together. Singly and in groups, they filed out of the room. From the corridor came shouts as they called their crews together for instructions.

Kris slowly released a pent-up breath and sat on the edge of the table. "I hate this crap."

"But you handle it so well," Rich Selikoff teased gently. He knocked his papers together into a tidy bundle, rolled them, and snugged them under his arm. "Time to get cracking. I'll be in touch."

"You bet your butt you will," she countered seriously. He gave her a winning, irreverent smile and was gone. After a moment, she glanced at the two men remaining. "When was the last time either of you ate or slept?"

"We had some fast-food on the way," Sam supplied, remembering the litter in the cab of the truck. "And we each slept a little while the other was driving."

"We don't have time for that!" Freeman erupted. "We're supposed to be searching—"

"And we're going to, Eric," she soothed with the patience of Job. "My promise. You're going to be on my team, in fact. But if looks are any indication, you're both going to drop in your tracks if you try searching on an empty stomach and without proper rest."

"You have no authority—"

She straightened and both feet firmly hit the floor. "I have all the authority of the Canadian government behind me, sir, and I'll exercise as much of it as I deem necessary. Now, if you want to join me on the search, you're more than welcome, but you'll do as I say. Otherwise, you'll stay here in town."

"We don't need your permission to search for my daughter!" Eric snapped angrily. "And we don't—"

Unafraid, she went right up into his face. "Let me explain something to you, Mr. Freeman," she said with a quiet authority that stilled his tongue. "I hold the reins here. There's an aircraft down and a lot of people going out to look for it. One or two more searchers might make the difference, but I will not have a handicap if I can prevent it. Neither you nor Dr. Payne—"

"Philip," Sam interjected.

She gave him a fleeting smile. "Are familiar with this territory, therefore you are a liability I can't afford to let free on its own. You either do as I say, or as another team leader says, or you remain behind." She lifted a finger, cutting off whatever Eric was about to retort. "If you give me a hard time, I'm within my rights as an officer of the RCMP to have you arrested and confined until this search is over. That's the bottom line. It's your choice."

"You wouldn't dare have me arrested," Eric said frigidly.

She folded her arms. "Try me."

Their eyes locked in a silent battle that was won almost before it had begun. Snarling with suppressed rage, Freeman spun on his heel and stalked out of the room without waiting to see if Sam would follow.

"I'm sorry," Sam began, wondering if he was going to spend this entire Leap apologizing for the other man's rudeness.

Kris waved it away, obviously annoyed by the confrontation but not made angry by it. "What's wrong with him?" she asked curiously. "I mean besides the worry and the fact that he's dead on his feet."

Sam chewed his bottom lip and decided it would be better not to throw patient-doctor confidentiality to the four winds.

She had a right to know, of course, being that she was going to be their guide on this search. But he didn't think she'd let Eric out of town if she knew about the leukemia. For now, what she didn't know wouldn't hurt them, so he settled for shrugging. "He hates waiting," he said lamely.

She snorted. "Him and everyone else." She hip-shoved away from the table. "Listen, I have a few loose ends to tie up here before I'll be ready to go. Take him across the street to the diner and get fed. Go big on carbohydrates and cram down as much as you can without making yourselves sick. The gent behind the counter is Kevin, Kate's dad. Tell him to put it on the RCMP ticket. If you can get Eric to take a nap, so much the better."

"I'd need a mallet," Sam said with a lopsided grin as he accompanied her out of the room. "What do I look like, a miracle worker?"

She patted her shoulder. "Philip, I'll take them where I can get them." With a final smile, she moved away down the less crowded corridor.

Sam watched her go, then zipped up his coat and went outside. The day was nothing but gray, watery gloom. Eric leaned against the hood of the truck, arms folded, collar pulled up, his head and shoulders covered with snow. "What took you so long?"

"I was apologizing for your rudeness," Sam replied honestly.

"Aren't we noble."

"You didn't have to get all bent out of shape back there. Kris was only doing her job. You know she's right."

"You're not my mother, Philip, so back off." Freeman looked up and down the street. "Most of the others have already left. How long are we going to have to wait for Her Majesty before we get started?"

Sam wanted to slap Eric for behaving like a spoiled brat. "I don't know. She didn't clear her itinerary with me." He gestured across the street at a brightly lit diner called Jollys. "She wants us to go over there and have some breakfast."

"You go," Freeman said obstinately, and his crossed arms tightened. "I'm not hungry. I'll wait for her in the truck."

"Eric, you have to eat something. You must be hungry by now. We haven't eaten since—"

"I said I'm not hungry!" the other man snapped with such unwarranted ferocity that Sam took an involuntary step backward. Eric's eyes fairly blazed within the frame of snow-flecked hair.

Suddenly Sam was angrier than he could remember being in a long while. He'd put up with Eric's bad humor almost since the moment he'd Leaped into Philip Payne. He thought he could ignore it and brush it off, but he couldn't. Their relationship and the man's health be damned. He wasn't putting up with any more nonsense.

Aping Kris Gunn, he went nose to nose with Eric, surprising the hell out of the geologist if the widening of his eyes was any indication. "For once you just shut up and listen to me! Be a bastard if it pleases you, Eric, but I came along as more than moral support and you know it." *Here's Sam Beckett,* he thought, *flying by the seat of his britches.* "I'm your doctor as well as your friend, and you wanted me here or you wouldn't have let me come. Now, I am not going to stand by and watch you do yourself more harm. You're not going to be any good to yourself, the search, or Lyndell if you don't take care of yourself. That means eating and getting some rest. If you won't do it willingly, I'll . . ." Sam lost momentum and floundered. What *would* Philip Payne do? "I'll sit on you and force-feed you."

Eric stared up at him . . . and then something extraordinary happened. A slight smile curled the edge of his lips. "You know, I think you would, Dr. Payne."

Sam's spirits rose, liking this glimpse of a different Eric. "Damned straight I would, Mr. Freeman. Just try me."

"I think I'll pass." Abruptly, all the energy went out of him. Eric's shoulders slumped and his face went a little gray. "Okay, Doctor. Lead the way."

The ready acquiescence startled Sam, but he decided not to look a gift horse in the mouth. "Alert the media. Eric Freeman agreed with me." He smiled good-naturedly. "Come on."

They crossed the street and entered the little diner. Sam forgot all about their argument the minute the smell of food hit him. He wanted to eat, he wanted it to be mountains of food, and he wanted it *now*. Evidently, Freeman felt the same way, despite his earlier protestations to the contrary. They found themselves a comfortable booth and within moments the man behind the bar (who was, indeed, Kevin MacKrell, father of Kate) served them thick white mugs of steaming coffee and took their order. Doubling as grill cook, he soon delivered plates piled high with scrambled eggs, hash browns, Canadian bacon, bangers, and toast.

Kevin grinned as he set down the plates. "You gents think you can get through all this without any help?" he asked in a thick Irish lilt.

"We'll do our best," Sam replied, fork at the ready. Eric nodded, already deep into his.

They ate in silence for a long time, both of them concentrating solely on the food and the bottomless cups of coffee Kevin provided. Finally, sated, Sam pushed back his plate. "I haven't eaten like that since I was a kid," he sighed.

When he got no reply, he looked up. Eric snored quietly, slumped sideways on the bench seat with his head pillowed against the window. For a moment Sam considered waking him and getting him into a better position, then decided against it. Freeman needed his rest, wherever and whenever he could get it. Instead, the Leaper poured himself another cup of coffee from the ever-present carafe, and settled back to watch the snow falling outside the diner.

What the hell am I going to do? he wondered, and sipped gratefully at the hot, fragrant brew.

CHAPTER
NINE

Lost deep within the wilderness of eastern British Columbia, Al Calavicci wondered precisely the same thing.

He lay curled on his side beneath a tarpaulin atop a makeshift mattress of cushions cannibalized from the aircraft's seats, hunched within the protection of his clothing, with his coat hood pulled up over his head and tied securely under his chin. His arms were folded across his chest with his gloved hands crammed into his armpits to conserve body heat. The air was frigid against the bare strip of skin around his eyes, and tepidly moist where the breath hissed in and out of his nostrils beneath the protective scarf. He pulled down the scarf to his chin and gently chafed his face against the wool glove, tingling the skin and stimulating circulation. A night's growth of beard tugged gently at the tightly knitted material. Shifting his head slightly, Al stared at a ceiling he couldn't see and waited impatiently for daylight to arrive.

He had survived the night. From the quiet sound of breathing in the darkness around him, he deduced that evidently the other passengers had as well. He couldn't tell for certain if they had actually slept or just lay awake thinking as he was, and it didn't really matter. Both constituted rest and neither changed a thing. Even so, he hoped they all found the temporary relief and oblivion of sleep at some point during the long night. It was the best thing they could do for themselves right now. And passing out from exhaustion and stress sure beat lying awake and staring at nothing as he had done for several hours.

Having the "hindsight" Ziggy's report provided gave him a feeling of near certainty that this Leap wasn't going to be easy. Unfortunately, he couldn't tell that to the other survivors without looking like an idiot or a fatalistic doomsayer (a position that Gideon seemed to have handily and almost enthusiastically appropriated for himself).

Someone whimpered off to his right and back toward the tail section. There was a rustling sound as someone rolled over, and Al thought it might be Faye, caught deep in her dreaming or trying not to awaken the others with her crying. A sense of duty pricked sharply at him to go ease her fears, but before he could get up and inch his way blindly to her, he heard someone else move. A moment later, his ears picked up the quiet sound of Hugh Bassey's distinctive voice as the Australian began a comforting, monotonous murmuring. Al smiled slightly in the darkness where no one could see, grateful for the man's presence and his gentle, never impatient way with the distressed woman. He suspected Hugh could charm sharks out of the Great Barrier Reef given the right incentive. Al knew with certainty that if he hadn't had Bassey to keep an eye on Faye, he didn't know what he would have done with her.

He sighed, thinking about it. Every group had a weak link and he was afraid Faye Marlowe was going to be theirs. The woman hadn't been much help at all in gathering wood and making the slap-dash campsite secure for the night. She seemed unable to keep her attention focused on the task at hand, no matter how simple they made it for her. Hugh kept finding her with a piece of wood held limp and forgotten in her hand as she blankly stared off into space, seemingly unaware of the snow that pelted her face and soaked through her expensive clothing. Al wasn't altogether confident she understood the severity of their situation. She seemed so out of touch. He hoped a night's rest would break her out of the shock or whatever it was that had circumvented her soul and, at the same time, prayed the reality of their situation wouldn't send the pendulum soaring in the other direction and plunge her into hysteria. They already had enough handicaps without one of them going off the deep end, and Faye seemed the most likely for that course. What they needed now was everyone doing their best to keep each other alive. In her present condition, about the best he felt he could hope for from Faye was to tie her to a tree to keep her from wandering into everyone else's way.

A warm flush of shame stained Al's cheeks at the uncharitable thought. He knew it wasn't Faye's fault she reacted as she did to the crash. It could just as easily have been any of them or, heaven forbid, all of them. Instead of finding fault with the woman and laying some sort of erroneous blame at her feet, he should be thankful she was the only one so affected.

There were other positives to their situation, now that he bothered to make himself think about it. Though he mourned the loss of Bob Bachellor's life, he was also grateful no one else had died. He appreciated the woodland experience of Dan Dodds, which might make the difference between life and death for them all in the time to come. He appreciated the levelheadedness and support of people like the pilot and Hugh Bassey. He was glad Lyndell's and Gideon's injuries weren't more severe. He was . . .

He paused and sighed. *I should be doing everything I can to think of a way to get us out of here alive,* he thought sourly. *According to Ziggy, that's part of my job. Time for an attitude adjustment, Calavicci, and right now.*

Unfortunately, that was easier said than done. All the forced good thoughts in the world weren't going to change the fact that Al thought they were up to their eyebrows in deep doo-doo.

His eyes felt grainy and coarse in their sockets when he rubbed them, as though someone had sprinkled them with sand while he slept. He'd been exhausted when they went to bed and had dropped off almost immediately, but he hadn't slept well. His rest was disturbed by dreams of Tina, and of Sam and the Project. He dreamed of the crash, reliving it in the echoes of his mind in lurid flashes of fear playing against the black backdrop of his brain with more detail than he actually remembered. He wondered if these visions were Gordon Huckstep's memories rather than his own. Some of it seemed so real, but he couldn't remember any of it from the brief, disorienting glimpse he'd experienced just prior to the crash.

He'd also dreamed of his years in the Navy and of Beth, oddly enough. It had been a long while since he'd allowed himself to think about her in more than a passing manner. Even that hurt after all these years. It was one of those Beth dreams that drove him to wakefulness inside the dark hull of the plane, coming to consciousness with the weight of Lyndell's head against his upper arm and a wisp of her dark hair escaping her hood and tickling his nose. For an instant his heart leaped with hopefulness, for it was Beth again, together with him in their bed. For a heartbreaking moment the years rolled back and they never parted in war, she never lost faith in the belief of his return from Vietnam, and they never divorced. All that past horror was nothing but a bad dream.

"Stop it," Al muttered sternly, trying to ignore the sting of tears behind his eyelids and the thick, clogging feeling that hurt his throat. "Just drop it right now."

Lyndell shifted at the sound of his voice, but did not awaken. Despite the unwieldiness of her splinted leg, she inched closer to Al and buried her face against his bicep. The sharp edge of her nose pressed against the arm through the thick down of his coat.

After a second's hesitation, he carefully lifted that arm free and snugged it around her shoulders, pulling her close against him. Might as well conserve all the body heat they could, right? Sure. Besides, it felt good to be close to someone right now, and if Al Calavicci had ever needed to feel close to someone it was at this moment. He only hoped if Lyndell awoke this wouldn't be too far out of keeping with their relationship to make her question him. He hadn't a clue to what he would say if she did.

Lying there staring into the darkness with his arm around a woman he barely knew (nothing unusual there), Al let his mind wander over the last several hours since the onset of the storm and before their escaping flight into sleep.

In their relatively short time abroad before the storm hit, the scavengers collected enough wood to get them through the night providing they didn't build too large a fire and waste their fuel. That could prove disastrous, for not only must they keep themselves warm enough to stay alive, but if the snowstorm held on for longer than they hoped, it would be difficult collecting more wood without the risk of becoming lost in the poor visibility. Thought of the storm had Al straining his ears to listen beneath the fury of the wind for the pinging whish of snow against the fuselage. He heard something out there, but couldn't tell if it was storm-driven snow or the wind just moving things around.

Returned from their foraging, Al and Hugh helped Dan clear an area near the front of the plane in which to build the fire. Conceding to experience and his obvious ability to outdo them in this area, they stood aside and pitched in only when called upon to do so (though Al admitted to the singular certainty that *Gordon* knew what this was all about).

Using one of his many tarps ("What'd you do, man? Corner the market on them?" Hugh asked, impressed by the quantity of carefully folded and packed colorful plastic the pilot produced), Dan rigged a lean-to angled to catch the fire's heat and not the teeth of the wind, and banked it back toward the aircraft. Another strategically placed tarp served as protection for the fire from the storm's onslaught. Using delicate pine branches and a few flakes of magnesium from the fire-starting kit in his pack, Dan soon had a little bundle of tinder glowing. Slowly feeding twigs and tiny strips of wood into it produced a small blaze. Though it threw meager heat as yet, just the sight of it made Al feel warmer and he wondered briefly at the mystical properties of fire that brought *Homo sapiens* through the ages. Evolution, schmevolution. Manipulation of fire made humankind what it was. That and nothing more.

"What's next, boss?" Bassey asked, his shoulder lightly

touching Al's as he leaned beside him against the airplane while they watched Dan's expert fingers coax a larger flame despite the damp wood and rising wind that occasionally blew gusts of snow around the protection of the billowing tarpaulins and into their faces.

Dan answered for him, glancing up as he worked, his fingers moving seemingly by rote. "One of the things foremost in our minds at all times should be fuel," he said, sitting back on his heels and tipping his head at their hastily gathered stockpile. "That there will last us until morning if we're very careful, but we need to do better if we intend to survive." He snugged his cap further down his forehead. "Storm or no storm, we must maintain a large supply of wood. I'd like to gradually get the flame to bonfire proportions and keep it going as a signal until help arrives."

"*If* help arrives," Gideon remarked sardonically from his perch just inside the passenger hatch. He had Lyndell's injured leg in his lap as he gently set and splinted it with wood supplied by Dan and strips torn from someone's sweatshirt. The younger woman was still out, snoring gently with her head lolling to one side. Al noted that she'd drooled on herself again.

Bassey's jaw tightened at Daignault's words. He shot him a nasty look, but it was lost on the zoologist, who was concentrating on his work (or pretending to, at any rate) and not looking at them.

Dan carried on speaking as though he'd never been interrupted, which was probably a far more effective rebuttal than any remonstrance from Al or Hugh would have been. "That means gathering wood on an almost continuous basis. Hypothermia is our greatest danger right now, even more than hunger or thirst, because not all of us are dressed for this kind of weather." His eyes flicked briefly toward Faye, who stood a few feet away. Al's gaze followed his.

She stared unblinkingly at Lyndell's somnolent form and shivered slightly, shuddering back and forth like a sapling in the wind. The shoulders of her wool coat were wet from the falling snow and her expensive slacks were damp to the knees. She wore no hat and her well-coiffed hair had come undone in damp tendrils around her face. Her gloves were thin and stylish, made for protection from the house to the car and not for the frigid temperatures of British Columbia in March. The older woman's lack of adequate clothing wasn't her fault, of course. She expected to find herself attending an environmental conference in an expensive, heated hotel in Prince George, not surviving an airplane crash in the remote mountains of British Columbia.

"A lot of trees got blasted in the crash," Dan continued. "We'll use them first. The smaller bits can be easily gathered and we have the ax to take care of the larger ones. The wood is wet, but I think we can make do with the addition of the magnesium. At least the trees are close by so we don't have to do any distance foraging just yet." He fed more wood into the fire, watching with a critical eye as the flames licked almost disinterestedly at the damp offering. "Unfortunately, most of these trees are coniferous."

"Pardon me for a dolt, but why is that a problem?" Bassey asked curiously.

"They're soft woods," Al explained, glad that he finally knew the answer to something. "And they're filled with pitch, which makes them burn hot and fast. Dry pine is great for starting a fire, but we should try to find some hard wood to keep the blaze going and give it longevity. Otherwise we'll be running our legs off trying to keep this burning." He sighed and looked around at the gathering darkness. The light had faded fast. Soon they would have to get inside out of the storm and Bob was still inside.

"What about the fuel in the airplane?" Hugh asked, squinting against a particularly vicious blast of wind. "Couldn't we use some of that on the fire to get it started and keep it going? And speaking of that, how safe is it to have a fire this close to the plane?"

"I'm way ahead of you on that," Dan answered, feeding more kindling into the fire. The tiny blaze smoked more than it actually burned, but even that was a comfort. "I've already siphoned the remaining fuel out of her." He steadied himself against the aircraft's battered side as he shifted his feet. "That makes the fuselage safer for us to use as protection against the elements. As for using the gas on the fire, Hugh, that's definitely an option we'll consider. I'll use it if I can't convince the fire to burn on its own, but I'd prefer to wait and see for a little while. There might be some other use for the fuel we haven't anticipated. I don't want to cut short our opportunities by using it where we don't need to."

"Makes sense to me, Dan. You're the expert."

Dodds chuckled quietly. "I don't know if I'd call it that, but thanks." He spoke to Bassey, but his eyes were on Al. The look he gave him was overlong and terribly expressive, but it took the Navy man a minute to understand what the pilot was silently trying to express, that while the gasoline could be used on the fire, it could also be a defensive advantage against predatory animals.

Al wondered fleetingly just how big a grizzly bear or a mountain lion really was close up and personal, and whether or not all those stories were true about wolves never attacking human beings. He swallowed hard and gave Dodds a slight nod, scratching his nose to cover the movement lest the others pick up on the silent communiqué. There was no big secret, but he didn't want to start a panic, either. They'd already survived a crash. That was enough stress for one day.

A momentary tightening of the lips was all the indication Dan gave that anything had passed between them, but he looked confident that he'd gotten his exact message across.

Where does that leave us, though? Al wondered. He had no great desire to go up against some hungry animal with a burning torch blazing in his hand like a peasant yelling "Burn the beast!" in a bad horror flick or some hero out of a T & A medieval fantasy. *Calavicci the Barbarian.* Terrific.

"Okay, so fuel," Hugh said, drawing Al's attention back to the conversation. "We're agreed we can't do much more about that until morning, yes? What else, then?"

"Assessing our food supplies and the other stuff in the cargo hold would be a good idea," Al suggested. "And forming some sort of game plan."

"Good idea," Dan agreed. "Since I brought most of the stuff in cargo, I've got a pretty good idea what's back there. But the rest of you should know, too." The last part of that sentence, *in case something happens to me,* didn't have to be said. Dodds's tone implied it all, and Al was just as glad that the pilot hadn't felt the need to voice it outright. The thought of Dan gone gave him the willies. "The food situation is going to be tight, since I brought enough for myself for a little more than a week. It's mostly freeze-dried stuff, so we don't have to worry about spoilage. We're going to have to ration it carefully, though." He hesitated, then continued. "I've got a gun and fishing line in there, too. I don't mind taking an occasional salmon to supplement things, but I'd like to avoid killing anything larger unless we absolutely have to." Again, his sentence was left hanging.

"It would be a good idea to make a list of everything available and keep it updated as things get depleted, so we don't come to rely on something that isn't there anymore," Al recommended.

"I'm onto that one, mate," Hugh offered, obviously eager for something constructive to do. He pulled himself into the aircraft though the pilot's hatch, then paused and swiveled on his heels in the doorway. He had an unreadable, weird look on his handsome features and it was a moment before he spoke. "If it's all the same with you lot, I think I'll put Bob in the cargo hold once I've brought the stuff into the cabin to take my tally. It might make it a little more comfortable for everyone not having . . ." The corner of his mouth twitched. ". . . his body around," he finished.

Al was heartfeltly grateful to Bassey for taking on such a task. Maybe it wasn't Lyndell whom Faye had been staring at all this time, or maybe she thought Lyndell was dead, too. That thought chilled Al to the marrow. If she died, then Eric died, too, and Al and Sam might be trapped in the past forever. No matter what happened to him or any of the others, he had to find a way to make certain Lyndell Freeman survived.

Anxiety made him want to check on the younger woman, just to make certain she was still breathing normally. He bit back the inclination and stayed where he was. Gideon was beside her. If anything was wrong, he would have said something. Wouldn't he?

"That's a good idea, Hugh," Dan said gently. "You want some help?"

"Nix to that, mate." The lanky Australian shook his head, and a ghost of sadness that hadn't been there before crossed his eyes. "Me and old Batch, well, we knew each other from way back. We've slugged down a few brews together and done the old pub crawl once or twice. I'll take care of him." He shrugged. "If it's all right with you, I'll just roll him in a tarp or a blanket or something and put him aside for later."

Al cursed silently. Gordon might have known that the two men were friends and acted accordingly, but there was no way *he* could have known and made Bob's passing any easier for Bassey. The lack of knowledge wasn't his fault, but that didn't keep Al from wishing he could know everything Gordon Huckstep knew. Whoever was engineering these Leaps sure wasn't doing a very good job in not letting him access his host's brain!

This was a hell of a thing for one friend to have to do for another.

"Put him aside for *what* later?" Gideon asked, sitting up straighter beside Lyndell with his legs dangling outside the open passenger hatch. If Bassey's expression had been weird, Daignault's was downright odd. "You planning on carving him up for filet mignon if the food supplies run low? I can see it now," he continued in the wake of their shocked silence. He held up his hands, squared to make a marquee or a camera lens. "Welcome to the Donner Party Cafe."

Hugh stared at the injured man, eyes wide with hurt and pain. His fists clenched whitely in anger. He dropped smoothly from the hatch to the ground and took a dangerous step forward.

"You listen to me, you carky son of a bitch—"

Al caught his arm and held it firmly before the Australian could reach Daignault and throttle him by the throat, though he had a sudden mind to let him do just that. "Stop it, Hugh," he said firmly, keeping his voice from stridency only by sheer force of will. "Get back inside the plane and go do what you

103

need to. Don't listen to him." He stared Bassey down until the man vented a shuddering sigh and nodded. Only then did Al feel safe in releasing his arm. Without looking at any of them, Hugh turned, climbed back into the plane, and vanished from sight.

CHAPTER

TEN

Al listened to Bassey's steps pace the length of the aircraft and enter the cargo hold before shooting Gideon a look that should have made the zoologist burst into flames had the weather conditions been right. "You're a callous S.O.B., aren't you? Would it have cost you so much to keep your mouth shut? Comments like that aren't going to help our situation any."

Gideon shrugged and declined to answer Al's patently rhetorical questions in favor of making another remark. "Just make sure he takes Bob's clothes off before rolling the body in a tarp," he added brusquely. "We could use them."

Dan's eyes were stark with shock. Al sympathized with him. He couldn't understand Daignault's crude, hurtful behavior. Certainly there were other ways, kinder ways, to get your message across.

Despite his choice of delivery, though, Gideon was right. Al hated admitting it, but he was saying the words, agreeing with the rat bastard son of a bitch, almost before he realized they were going to be uttered. He raised his chin and called out, "You hear him, Hugh?"

A moment's silence greeted the question, then the Australian responded, his voice made hollow sounding by the fuselage around him. "I heard him, Gordon. So what?"

"So he's right." Inside his coat pockets, Al's hands curled into fists which he'd have liked to use on Daignault. He stepped closer to the hatch and ducked his head inside so he wouldn't have to speak so loudly and risk waking Lyndell. "Clothing won't make a bit of difference to Bob now, but Faye could really use his stuff," he urged gently, wishing he could see the man's face and better gauge his reaction to all this. "She's freezing. She needs something warmer than what she has on."

Hugh stepped into sight in the cargo bay entryway and stared silently at Al with his arms wrapped around the rolled bundle of Dan's sleeping bag. All the momentary fire had sagged out of the photographer's expression and he was as gray as dishwater. "Right, right," he muttered sickly. "Batch would want her to have them. He never liked to see anyone suffering."

"I'll help you," Al offered, ready to pull himself inside the aircraft. "There's no reason why you should have to do this alone."

Hugh shook his head. "I want to do it alone, Gordon." His sad eyes searched Al's face. "I'll be okay, mate. Really. Batch and I have a few things we want to say to each other." He turned away without another word. Al stared for a moment at the place where he'd been, pondering on the truthfulness of Bassey's words, then turned back to the others.

Dan had rounded on Daignault like a pissed-off bulldog. "Well, that was tactful," he said sarcastically.

Gideon almost appeared surprised by the pilot's tone. He shrugged lightly, as though nothing he'd said had mattered (and maybe it hadn't to him), and stared at his mittened hands, turning them over and over, palms to backs to palms again for no apparent reason. "What's the point of tact, Dan? Dead is dead and reality is reality. Bob Bachellor won't be hurt by anything I say and maybe my so-called rudeness will keep the heat burning in Bassey's bones long enough to get him out of here alive." His hands went still in his lap as he looked up at them both. "I was only trying to help, you know," he added defensively. "You agreed with me about the clothing."

Al was dumbfounded. He couldn't believe the higgledy-piggledy defensive run of Daignault's logic. What a convoluted way to justify being mean to another person. He stared at Gideon, convinced the zoologist was hurling a load of bull at them, but he knew by the look on Gideon's face that he felt perfectly and honestly justified in his behavior. As far as Gideon was concerned, he *had* been only trying to help.

Al nodded tightly. "So you were right about the clothing. Let's alert the media. One good idea doesn't give you the right to be nasty to Hugh or anyone else and excuse it under the heading of 'helping' them. It wouldn't have put you out to be considerate of Hugh's feelings. He and Bob were friends, for pete's sake! And that stupid crack about steak was too far over the line no matter what it was you intended." He felt an unexpected twinge of guilt. There but for the grace of God went he, had Sam Leaped into this situation, cracking Donner party jokes without thinking before putting his mouth in gear. Maybe he felt justified in stepping down on Daignault because of his own propensity for tasteless remarks.

He leveled a finger, a little surprised by how *very* angry he felt. "I'm warning you, Gideon, and this *isn't* as leader of the party. This is just me talking. *Don't* make remarks like that again. All it does is hurt people unnecessarily. We have to keep our spirits up, not drive one another down."

Gideon's eyes flashed fire and he slowly levered himself onto his feet, one leg cocked gingerly to ease the pulled groin muscle. "You're *warning* me, Huckstep?" he asked, as though he couldn't believe what he'd just heard. "And what dire consequence will you heap upon my head if I don't comply with your command?" He snorted when Al remained silent, trying to stare him down. "Keep your bogus threats to yourself, Gordon. I'm just as stuck here as you are and I'm entitled to my opinion the same as anyone else." His lip curled. "Just be glad I didn't suggest we toss the body into the snow for the bears to find."

"What held you back?" Al fumed, unmindful now of waking Lyndell or having Hugh hear their argument. The Australian could hardly have failed to, being only on the other side of the aircraft's walls. "It sounds like your style."

"Does it?" Daignault said dryly. "Good. At least my style is a lot more practical than the rose-colored glasses you all seem to be wearing." He jabbed a finger at them. "Let me clue you in on something, folks. We're stuck here! Glinda the Good Witch is not going to come floating over the mountain and tell us how to get home to Kansas, no matter how many campfire songs we sing!" He shook his head sadly. "Wake up and smell the coffee, Gordon."

Dan's hand curled around Al's arm, stilling his response. "Let it go, Gordon," he said, and his quiet voice suddenly sounded tired. "We're all strung out and stupid from the crash. If we keep on like this, we're all going to say things we'll later regret. Blow it off. There's no point in having a stupid argument. He—"

"Bears?" Faye asked, interrupting them as though the conversation going on around her had suddenly pierced through her lethargy. She looked at them, her eyes speculative in the taut paleness of her face. She was shivering even harder now and Al knew she had to get warm soon or risk the consequences. "There are bears?" The question tipped up at the end, rising on a note of fear that might spill over into panic at any time.

Annoyance soured the inside of Al's throat. His hot eyes sought Gideon before the zoologist could fashion a suitably sarcastic reply to what essentially was a rather ignorant, as opposed to stupid, question. "You're so good at the explanations, Daignault, *you* set the lady's mind to rest." Without another word, he turned away and climbed into the cockpit, glad to see as he left that Gideon looked a little ashamed and was already squirming under Faye's steady, unwavering gaze as she waited for him to tell her there was nothing to worry about.

Good, Al thought as he moved back in the aircraft to help Hugh whether he wanted it or not. *Let him deal with some of the responsibility for a change.* He didn't feel the least bit guilty to hear Gideon fum-fuh'ing a lame explanation.

That incident had undoubtedly been the capper of the day. The rest of their short evening was spent noting their assets (a reasonable amount, thanks to Dan's foresight and knowledge of winter camping) and preparing the aircraft for habitation. At Dan's recommendation, they stripped the cushions off the seats and made one giant mattress for everyone to share under a protective layer of tarpaulins. The seats' skeletal metal frameworks were tossed into the snow, discarded until someone thought of a use for them.

Everyone layered on from their suitcases as much extra clothing as they could comfortably wear without cutting off circulation. Rather than wake Lyndell to dress herself (a feat that seemed prodigious and unlikely given her injury and the depth of her drug-induced snooze), Al wrestled her into another sweater and two more pairs of socks while Hugh gently convinced Faye into going behind a temporarily strung blanket to change out of her wet clothes and into those bequeathed by the deceased environmental activist. Bob Bachellor's jeans and shirt were huge on her small frame, but also enabled her to layer on even more clothing underneath them. When she was done, she looked like something out of Santa Claus's North Pole workshop (as designed by Tim Burton), but no one dared laugh at the resemblance. Three pairs of socks adequately filled the dead man's boots so she could walk without tripping all over herself. An extra set of mittens made her hands look more like paws, but at least now she was adequately dressed.

Looking at her face framed in the faux fur trim of Bob's parka hood, Al was struck by an odd dichotomy. On one hand, bundled up as she was, Faye looked even more handicapped than before. Yet, on the other hand, she looked almost normal decked out like that, and not nearly so automatonic as she had earlier. He couldn't decide which was the reality of the woman and finally figured there was probably a little truth to both viewpoints. Faye Marlowe was, like the rest of them, undoubtedly more and less than she appeared.

Despite the exertion and the stress (or perhaps because of it), none of them felt particularly hungry. Even so, Dan brought out his propane stove and made a pot of coffee, then passed around a large bag of a trail food charmingly labeled gorp (*g*ood *o*ld *r*aisins and *p*eanuts . . . plus chocolate chips, coconut, and peanut butter) for them to munch on while it brewed. Dubious at first, Al found himself full after consuming surprisingly little.

There was no argument when Al suggested they bed down for the night in a tight huddle, like puppies. No one particularly wanted to sleep close to Gideon and he seemed to realize it, finally choosing to make his resting place on the other side of Faye, bracketing her between himself and Hugh ostensibly to keep her warm through the night. The men drew straws for the watch, with Al earning the first and Dan the last.

Now hours had passed. He'd been relieved by Hugh and sought his bed sleepily, but rest was light and infrequent. Still wide awake now despite the ruminations he hoped might ease him back into sleep, Al slid his arm from around Lyndell and raised his wrist just enough to be able to squint at the luminescent dial of his digital watch. According to the clock, Dan was outside now or curled within his sleeping bag just inside the front hatchway, keeping an ever-watchful eye over their fire and the possible presence of curious predators.

They'd had a devil of a time over that damned sleeping bag. Dan and Hugh thought Lyndell should have it, being that she was the worst injured of the party, chiefly immobile and needing to be kept warm. The brunette had been too wigged out on painkillers to give them any argument, but Gideon supplied one just the same, stating that he felt everyone should get a chance to use the heavy-duty down protection. That led to more arguing and sniping until Al, surprising everyone, sided with Gideon again out of desperation to end the pointless go-around. His only stipulation was that the person using the sleeping bag was also the one currently keeping watch. When the zoologist pointed out that solution didn't include Faye and Lyndell and was, consequently, unfair, Al countered that keeping awake on watch was more important than a comfortable night's sleep. Lyndell was exempt from watch because of her injury. As for Faye, well . . . He didn't come out and say it in so many words, but he let them (and her) know that if she wanted to use the sleeping bag, she'd damned well better get her shit together. It was tough and maybe it was unfair, but he knew from experience that if they continued coddling her, the woman would never function appropriately because she wouldn't need to. Sometimes the best in a person only comes out when others expect it of them, even if the only one doing that is oneself.

No further argument was posed. If Faye heard him, she gave no indication that his words had anything to do with her. Gideon subsided into grumbles, which everyone ignored, and Al decided that his favorite passenger was poor dead Bob Bachellor. At least Bob wasn't arguing semantics every time a suggestion came up and he certainly didn't insist every course of action be put through committee. He hadn't even complained about being rolled in a tarp and tucked safely into the cargo bay.

At this rate, Al thought, still wanting to box a few ears, *I won't need to worry about saving them. The way things are going, I'll probably kill them all out of sheer frustration.*

An eerie ululation sounded faintly in the distance, tugging at his hearing enticingly and making him sit up fast. It was enough to send him scrambling from under the tarp and toward the hatch. Lyndell querulously protested his abrupt movement, half sitting up and groping in the dark with one hand for her glasses, but he didn't respond to her sleepy, half-voiced question.

Wading clear of their bedding, Al slipped down the short aisle to the cockpit. As he'd thought, Dan sat in the hatchway with the door half-closed, his round body swathed in the puffy red contours of the down sleeping bag and his Remington M760 Gamemaster cradled across his lap. He raised his head at Al's approach. His eyes were red-rimmed and shadowed with tiredness and his face bore a scratchy night's worth of beard to rival Al's own, but somewhere he managed to work up a smile. "Good morning, Gordie. Welcome to a new day."

"That makes it a very good morning," Al replied, bracing himself with a hand on either side of the hatch frame and eminently glad it was Dodds's face he had to see first thing in the morning instead of Daignault's. He leaned through the

111

doorway's narrow opening to get a look at the day and let the chill of the freshening wind slap any remaining vestiges of sleep from his brain.

It was much lighter outside than the interior of the plane had indicated. Al was confused by that until he remembered they'd pulled down the shades over the windows before going to sleep. No wonder the airplane was as dark as the proverbial cave. He felt monumentally stupid for forgetting.

The sky to the east was pale with watery light. Clouds crowded the tops of the surrounding mountains like herded sheep brought in from forage. The heavy overcast was streaked briefly with crimson and gold at the eastern end of their valley, highlighting the tips of trees and making them look like streaks of black felt-tip against the gray sky. The snow had stopped during the night, though the moisture-laden smell of it hung heavily in the air. There was a quality to the air here high in the mountains that made Al feel as though he were looking through old glass, the kind with waves and bubbles in it before the process had gotten all the kinks and charm ironed out of it. It smelled like an old sponge.

He looked at the snow, which lay drifted against the side of the aircraft and decorated the rocks and the branches of the trees like sugar frosting on gingerbread. It lay in smooth lines against the rigged tarpaulins, holding them solidly at least until the wind picked up. For now, it had blown itself out and gusted gently against his face rather than howling as it had during the night. Speaking of howling . . .

"Did I just hear wolves?"

Dan grinned. "I'm surprised they didn't wake you earlier. They've been pretty vocal for the past few hours. All things considered, it was kind of nice to sit here and listen to them."

Al nodded because he didn't want to argue. It wasn't that he had something against wolves, because he didn't. In fact, he was a little disturbed by the media-produced paranoia he felt gnawing at him toward the animals. "How much snow did we get?" he asked, changing the topic.

"Hard to say," Dodds replied, groaning as he stretched his legs. Gun caught in the crook of one arm, he massaged a knee with his free hand. "It blew around a lot. I'd make a poor guess

112

at about a foot or so, but I'm really not sure."

"I'll take your poor guess to anybody's educated one, Dan."
Al nodded toward the east and the brightening underlayer
of clouds. "It looks like it might be a nice day," he said
encouragingly, not quite ending the sentence with the lilt in
his voice that would denote a question. He wasn't certain he
wanted to be told otherwise.

Dan canted his head to cast a jaundiced eye through the
windshield and toward the heavens. "Maybe, Gordon, but I
wouldn't put the family jewels up as collateral. I've seen skies
like this before and I'm willing to bet you dollars to doughnuts
those clouds are going to get lower than before and give us
some more of something—rain, snow, whatever." He glanced
at Al. "I don't want to be the bearer of bad news, but I don't
think there are going to be any planes out searching today,
amigo. At least not around here."

The corner of Al's mouth twitched unhappily. "I don't
suppose it ever occurred to you to lie to me just this once?"

Dodds chuckled. It was a warm, friendly sound despite
the cold, the man's tiredness, and everything else that had
occurred, and it lit his face like a beacon. It made Al think of
Santa Claus again for the second time in as many days. Decked
out in a red suit, Dan Dodds would have made one hell of a
good Saint Nick. "Sorry, pal. It's not in my nature."

"That's a damned shame."

"What's a damned shame?" someone asked around a yawn
and Al turned to see Hugh Bassey behind him. The Aussie
stretched like a lean cat, careful not to bang his head or his
arms against the low ceiling, and blinked sleepily at them.
"What'd I miss?"

"Nothing," Al replied, shifting sideways to give the taller
man more room in the cramped confines of the cockpit. "We're
just catching up on old news." He glanced back toward the
sleeping compartment, watching to see if anyone else was
stirring. "Dan says it looks like more snow, maybe," he said,
pitching his voice a few notches lower than normal.

Bassey genially gave vent to an expression Al had never
heard before, but which had something to do with sheep drov-
ers, kangaroos, and the gross manipulation of a didgeridoo. In

the surprised silence that followed, he blinked placidly at the two startled men as though he'd merely asked them the time of day.

Dan grinned with delight. "Well, if I wasn't awake before, *that* sure did the trick. I'm going to spend all day trying to figure out how someone could actually *do* that."

Bassey winked. "It can be done, mate, let me assure you."

"I'm almost afraid to ask how you know that," Al countered archly. A connoisseur of the barbed comment, he silently repeated the phrase over and over again to cement it firmly in his mind. If he went home from this Leap with nothing else, he was going home with that expression. Gooshie would pop a rivet when he heard it!

"I never kiss and tell," Hugh sniffed haughtily, one hand splayed across his chest like a prima donna's feather fan.

"*I* think I need some air," Dan commented dryly, and pushed the door open the rest of the way with his foot as the other men laughed. "And maybe a pair of hip waders," he added. "It's getting a little cramped in here." He slid out of the cockpit on his rump and stamped his feet to pack down the drifted snow. "I'd forgotten what circulation felt like," he grunted, massaging both thighs with his hands. He indicated the remainder of their wood pile with a sweep of his hand. To Al's eyes it was a woeful little heap. "We did pretty well keeping last night's consumption to a minimum, but we've got our work cut out for us today, particularly if it starts snowing again."

"Don't remind me," Hugh pleaded. "At least not on an empty stomach. Is there any coffee left?" he asked hopefully.

Al bent and lifted the pot, swirling the contents to gauge the amount. "Probably enough for the three of us, then we'll make a fresh pot for the others."

"Suits me," Dan agreed. "Use the propane stove while I stoke this up a bit." He began tossing selected limbs onto the fire. It licked hungrily at the wood and slowly began to grow.

"It was dead silent for me last night," Hugh remarked, his eyes tracking the flight of a small bird. "You blokes have any action?"

Al shook his head as he pumped the stove's propane canister requisite to lighting a burner. "I didn't see or hear a thing, but the storm was in full swing, so that's not surprising. How about you, Dan?"

"Once the wind cut down I heard some geese go over, probably headed for their spring breeding grounds." He tossed another log on the fire, then used a long branch to further prod the coals to wakefulness. "And I was telling Gordon I heard—"

"Wolves?" Lyndell's voice piped up from the doorway. The men turned. She was sitting on her butt in the open hatchway, blinking owlishly at them from behind the round lenses of her glasses. Her eyes looked overly bright and her cheeks were flushed with color. Al wondered if she might be running a low-grade fever and wanted to check as soon as possible. It wasn't unlikely. She held her injured leg stiffly out in front of her, the ankle still securely bound in its brace.

"Odd position, that," Hugh commented, straightening and reaching to help her inch her way into a comfortable position.

"Number seven hundred ninety-six in the *Kama Sutra*," she returned brightly. "I thought I heard something in the night, but it seemed awfully far away."

"It's the weird mountain acoustics," Dan agreed, wiping his hands on the seat of his jeans. "But the wolves were definitely out there somewhere and in full voice."

"Did they come close?" she asked concernedly. "Do you think they'll be any problem for us?"

"There's no documented evidence of wolves attacking a human being, Lyn," Dan said soothingly but firmly, so as to get his point across. "I think we're safe in that regard." Al couldn't help but notice the pilot didn't say anything about bears. "I didn't see anything out there, but my night vision was ruined by the firelight and it didn't cast very far, anyway. Besides, wolves are pretty good at ghosting around when they want to. I think they were just out sending word of us along the wilderness telegraph."

She smiled sadly. "Too bad humans don't listen in on it."

Dan returned the smile with understanding. "Yes, it is."

Listening, Al remembered the haunting cry he'd heard just before getting out of bed. Wolves. Real wolves, not something out of *Little Red Riding Hood* or *The Three Little Pigs*, and nothing like the sad specimens he'd seen at the zoo. Out there somewhere were wild flesh-and-blood *Canis lupus*. He shivered and tried hard not to recall all the werewolf movies his traitor mind suddenly made him remember. *Loup-garou*, the French called it . . .

He frowned to cover his discomfort. "What are you doing out of bed?" he asked Lyndell, his voice sharper than he'd intended.

The look she gave him told him to mind his own business, but she answered him anyway. "I can't stay in bed all day, Gordon. I'll turn into a mushroom. Besides, I didn't walk on my leg. I shuffled out on my ass."

"Just as long as you don't jar it around," Dan cautioned, obliquely siding with Al. "It needs to be immobile and elevated. Did you sleep well?"

"Not bad," she shrugged. She seemed pleasantly surprised by the admission. "Actually, I was kind of surprised to find myself *in* bed and in all these clothes." She shot Al a wicked grin and he knew he'd been caught red-handed. "But I guess drugs will do that to you."

"Are you still in a lot of pain? You look kind of flushed." Without asking permission, Dan lay the palm of one hand flat against her forehead and frowned consideringly.

"Uh . . ." Her face screwed up and Al practically heard the gears grinding. "Well . . . yeah, I am in pain, sort of."

Dan arched an eyebrow as he took away his hand. "Sort of? Being 'sort of' in pain from a broken ankle is like being 'sort of' pregnant, Lyn. You either are or you aren't, and I think you are. You're also running a fever. I want you to take something to bring it down. Do you want something for the pain, too?"

"Well, I do but I don't." She sighed in frustration. "I know I'll need something later, Dan, but I'd rather dope myself with drugs only when I really need to. I hate feeling like I'm not in control of myself and I really hate that I'm not contributing."

"I understand. I'd feel the same way." He nodded and squeezed her shoulder. "Okay, it's your call regarding the pain medication. When you want it, you just tell me or Gordon, okay? Until then, you *are* taking something for the fever." He beetled his brows at her. "And no arguments."

"It's a deal," she agreed. "Anyplace out there for a person to sit down?"

It took them a few minutes to rig a serviceable resting place by the fire and out of the wind. While she waited, Lyndell drank a cup of tepid coffee and downed the two aspirin Dan gave her. No sooner was she settled on her makeshift couch of gathered pine branches and an old blanket than they were joined by Faye and Gideon. The older woman looked a little better this morning, though her eyes were red and looked sore. She brightened slightly when Hugh smiled her way and gave her a cheery "'Morning, ducks." Gideon looked as sour as he had when he went to bed, and barely grunted when the others wished him good morning. Hunkering down near the propane stove, he reached for the pot and appropriated the remaining cup of coffee without even asking if it was already taken. Cupping it between his gloved hands, he moved away to settle on the opposite side of the fire from Lyndell and the rest.

"Is there anything for breakfast?" Faye inquired.

Al was heartened to hear the question. It was the first real interest she'd shown in their situation. Dan must have felt the same way, for he gave her a grin that would have melted a glacier. "Another pot of coffee will be ready in a few minutes, Ms. Marlowe. I don't promise haute cuisine, but I'll whip up something to fill the empty spot a little."

"How little?" Gideon asked sourly and blew across the top of his mug.

Al felt like performing Hugh's curse on the other man. "Enough to keep us going," he answered curtly. "It's probably not what you're used to, but if you don't want your share I'm sure the rest of us would be glad to divvy it up."

They glowered daggers at each other across the fire. Faye hunched her shoulders unhappily and withdrew back into herself. Lips pursed, Hugh shook his head over the propane stove as he checked the coffee's progress. Dan threw another log on the fire, sending a shower of sparks climbing into the drab, gray dawn.

117

It was Lyndell who broke the silence. "Well, aren't we just one big happy family," she remarked sourly to no one in particular. "Reminds me of home." She drummed her fingers on her knee and glanced at Al. "What's on the agenda for today, kimosabe?"

It took him a minute to pull his eyes away from Daignault. He sighed and started to speak, then stopped to accept the cup of coffee Hugh silently handed him. Al smiled gratefully and took a sip. Ah! Black and strong enough to tar roads. Just the way every Navy man he knew liked their java. "We were just going to get into that. Any ideas from the rest of you?"

Dan nudged him. "It's your road show, boss," he said quietly. "What are *your* ideas?"

God, but Al hated being put in this position. "Okay." He hunkered down by Lyndell's injured leg and she rested a hand on his shoulder blade. "As Dan said yesterday, wood has to be our first priority. Hugh and I can take care of cutting and hauling. Even if it starts snowing again, we should be able to get in a sizable load before nightfall."

"What about the rest of us?" Lyndell asked. "I mean, I know I'm practically useless, but . . ." She let the sentence dangle, but her eyes flicked toward Gideon and away before the other man noticed.

Al bit back a smile at her subtle show of support. "Your job, as long as you can handle it, Lyn, is to maintain the fire. We'll make sure the supply is close enough so you don't have to get up to reach it and Dan can give you an idea of the size blaze we want."

Dan nodded. "Something large enough to keep us warm *and* attract the attention of anyone who's looking for us."

Al continued. "We can melt snow for our drinking water, but I'd like someone to take a look around and see if they spot a close waterway of any kind. It'll make for better drinking, possibly supply a few fresh fish, and give us a focal point to follow."

"I can do that," Dan volunteered, and Al nodded.

"To follow?" Faye looked up questioningly. "Follow where?"

Al sipped again at the coffee and regarded her steadily over the rim of his mug. "If we're not found in a few days, Faye, we may want to consider packing our way out of here if we can."

"But . . ." The woman wrung her hands. "But what about Lyndell and Gideon?"

"There are ways to get them out. Trust me on that," Dan put in. "We'll worry about it when and if we reach that point."

From where Al stood, she was going to worry about it anyway, but she subsided with a weak sigh and nodded, staring at the ground. "All right. It's just that I thought it wouldn't be a good idea to leave the airplane."

"That's true," Al agreed. "Normally it's not, but we have to consider all of our options."

"What sort of options?" She raised her eyes again.

Al saw Gideon's head slowly come up, saw the look in his eyes, and knew the zoologist was within breaths of saying something cruel. "We'll talk about that later," he said firmly, cutting into the conversation before Faye got crazy, Dan lost his patience, or Gideon stuck in his two cents' worth.

Hugh spoke quickly to cover the possible flare-up. "What about an S.O.S. signal stamped into the snow?"

"That's another good idea," Al nodded. "An S.O.S. can be filled with pine boughs or even those seat frames. Anything to make it stand out and be seen from the air."

"We can also stamp out ground-air codes," Dan suggested. "I have a listing of them in the cockpit."

"Good. We'll use them." Al felt a warm glow begin in the pit of his stomach that had nothing to do with the coffee. It was coming together. *They* were coming together. If they could continue to work like this, sharing ideas and the work load, everything should be okay until help arrived.

"The bigger and deeper the letters, the more effective the signal," Dan explained. He stuck his head back into the cockpit long enough to retrieve a sheet, which he handed across to Al. Printed on it were sixteen straight-line codes, denoting everything from "require doctor" to "will attempt takeoff."

"They recommend making the letters thirty-three feet long and three feet wide for maximum visibility," the pilot continued. "The message should face north or south and snow should be piled highest on the south of the letters for maximum shadow. Who wants to take that on?"

There was silence. Just about the time Al was going to make a few rude remarks of his own, Faye raised a tentative hand. "I'll do it, Mr. Dodds."

Al wanted to hug her. Dan did, reaching across and surprising the hell out of her. "Good for you, Ms. Marlowe! We'll pick you a nice flat spot to work. Just take your time and go slowly to conserve energy. As soon as I'm finished trying to find some local water, I'll come back and help you, okay?"

She nodded and there was an expression on her face Al hadn't seen there before. "Okay."

"I suppose you have something planned for me?" Gideon asked, curling his mouth into a forced smile.

"As a matter of fact, there *is* something you can do that won't require too much exertion on your pulled muscle," Dan said, refusing to rise to the bait the man's tone implied. "Snow acts as a natural insulator. Pack as much of it as you can, as high as you can, around the fuselage. Don't let it be any thinner than twelve inches, and more if you can manage it."

Gideon nodded and Al thought that for once he might just accept something as given and let it go. No such luck. "Does anyone happen to care what *my* opinion is?"

Al's voice was tightly controlled when he replied. "We're interested in everyone's input, Gideon. What's on your mind?"

"I think we should just pack it out of here. Get on the move as soon as we can." He jabbed a hand skyward. "Those clouds are too damned low for a plane to search for us. We're doing nothing but wasting time by just sitting here."

"We're making provisions to stay alive," Lyndell broke in hotly.

Al rested a hand on her shoulder, quieting her. "The first rule of survival is to stay put, Gideon, at least initially. People know our itinerary. They know by now that we've gone missing. A search party will have more luck locating us if we're not on the move. We've got water and heat and shelter. There's enough food to keep us going for a while and maybe we'll be able to supplement it with some fish if Dan's search pans out." He lifted a hand as the other man started to protest. "You make a valid point, Gideon. I'm not saying you don't. But if we leave and it *does* start snowing again, we'll be without shelter altogether in the middle of nowhere."

"I still think we should risk it."

Al waved a hand in a circle, encompassing all they could see. "Then be my guest. Which direction do you intend to start out in? Any clue where we might be or where the nearest town is? Where will you find shelter on the way?"

The zoologist stared at him. The muscles in his jaw worked furiously as he ground his teeth together, but there was little he could say that wouldn't make him look monumentally stupid. Al was right and Gideon knew it. He sighed in exasperation and rose, tossing the dregs of his coffee into the snow. "I'll get started as soon as I take a piss," he said brusquely, and stalked around to the other side of the airplane.

"Don't you want some breakfast?" Dan called, trying to keep a straight face. When there was no reply, he shrugged. "Guess not."

Some freeze-dried something-or-other better left unidentified with gorp stirred into it made for a nourishing if unimaginative repast that even Gideon returned to partake of. Dan cautioned them to burn all food scraps, and Lyndell took it upon herself to become the clean up detail so the others could get started on their tasks. Within a few moments, they were coordinated and on their way.

Al worked for a long time hauling wood to the campsite. Larger logs were brought in by him and Bassey working in tandem like a couple of farmer's drays, but most of the time they worked apart, dragging in tarpfuls of scavenged timber.

Now and then Al cast a curious eye around to check on everyone. Dan was out of sight, disappeared into a stand of trees in search of water, mucking about atop the snow on his single pair of snowshoes. If it weren't for the crash, the pilot would have been as happy as a pig in mud. For certain, he was in his element. Faye was off a short distance into the meadow, a lonesome figure against the surrounding white as she shuffled her feet in the snow like a child playing choo-choo and slowly carved out the letters and signals of their S.O.S. Now and then, he caught a glimpse of Daignault when the zoologist came around the side of the airplane to warm himself by the fire for a few moments before returning to his work. Al wasn't close enough to judge the progress but, if activity was any indication, the quarrelsome man seemed to be pulling his own weight. Every so often, Lyndell raised her hand in greeting if she caught him looking her way, and he always waved back. It was hell for her to be left sitting immobile by the fire. She asked for her cameras before the others split off, intending to make a photo-journal diary of their crash. Enthused by the idea, she and Bassey agreed to collaborate as soon as he had a free moment to take some distance shots for her.

Al's fingers and toes were growing numb, so he decided to take a break and warm up beside the fire. He tramped in with a final load of wood dragging along behind him and further packing down the trail he and Hugh had worn in the pristine snow. The fire had thrived under Lyndell's tender loving care and blazed away merrily, the pine logs popping and sizzling in the flames. She was inched back several feet from where they'd left her, still within reach of the growing woodpile and an arm's throw of the fire, but back far enough that she wouldn't be roasted. Her cameras were on the blanket beside her and her head was bent over something. Gideon was nowhere to be seen.

"Hi," Al called as he approached. "What are you reading?"

She looked up and gave him a smile. Lines of strain showed around her mouth and he wondered how well the pain medication was working. She'd asked for some a few hours earlier and it might be time for another dosage. "It's some magazine Gideon dug up in the back and tossed my way." Finger in her place, she held it up, cover foremost, for him to see. It was a familiar magazine, no longer in print in Al's time, but one that he remembered with fondness for its radical approach to science. "You've *got* to read this one article if you get a chance." She flipped open the magazine to the place she marked and folded back the page. "It's about time travel, for God's sake! What tripe." She made to toss the magazine aside.

"Wait! Let me see that!" Al dropped the end of his tarp and reached to take the periodical with hands he hoped didn't shake too much. He smoothed the page and took a close look at the article. Sure enough, it was all about the quantum leap theory of moving through time. Accompanying the article was a faded color picture of Sam Beckett somewhere in his early twenties, wearing his usual earnest expression, a white lab coat, and horn-rimmed glasses that made him look like the quintessential computer geek.

It was the facial expression over which Al lingered the longest, especially the emotion caught in the depths of the eyes. That was Sam, all right, charged up and enthusiastic. He hadn't changed much in the past fifteen years or so. Al was surprised the way his heart gave a painful clench.

"Gordon? Are you okay?"

Al looked up, embarrassed to be caught with his real self showing. Lyndell was watching him steadily, her head tilted fractionally to one side. He cleared his throat gruffly and handed her back the magazine. "Just having trouble believing anybody would buy into this kind of stuff. It must take a pretty remarkable person to convince people that something like this could actually be viable." He smiled slightly.

She mistook the reason for the smile, of course, as he'd intended. "You've got that one right, bucko. What a dumb article. I'll bet this guy pandered himself as a rainmaker in a past life." She looked up quickly when Al dissolved into a fierce bout of coughing. "Geez, Gordon, that sounds like hell," she said concernedly. "You're overdoing it, aren't you?" She nodded, answering her own question. "You always do." She scooted over and patted a spot beside her on the blanket. "Come sit down for a minute. No one's going to fault you for taking a break to rest and warm up. In fact, it probably wouldn't be a bad idea if everyone did."

He did as he was told, crossing his legs and settling down Indian fashion beside her. His protesting muscles gave an appreciative sigh as he edged a little closer to the fire. "Is Dan

123

back yet?" he asked, needing to retreat from the time-travel conversation before he broke into laughter.

"A while ago. He found a river. The ice is out and he thinks he'll have no trouble fishing. We might actually have something edible for dinner tonight." She jabbed a thumb over her shoulder. Following her direction, Al saw the pilot out in the field with Faye. "He promised her he'd help finish the letters, then I think he's planning on trying to catch some fish." She glanced at him. "Do you think she'll be all right?"

"Faye?" He shifted to warm his back and shrugged. "Sure. Yeah, I guess so. She just needs to be kept busy so she doesn't have time to worry about where she is and what's happening."

"That's pretty good logic, Huckstep."

"Thanks, Freeman." Al grinned and was startled by the sudden welling of friendship he felt for this slight, albeit hard-as-nails woman. Since he didn't really know her, this had to be Gordon coming through. At least he thought so.

He took up the slender branch she'd been using as a poker and gave the fire several prods. This seemed as good a time as any to get to the real work at hand. "Your dad must be half out of his mind with worry, Lyn."

Silence as old and cold as the grave greeted the remark. This wasn't just someone being quiet. This was a freeze-out. This cold made the day and the surrounding snow feel like a visit to the Bahamas by comparison. Slowly, he raised his head and looked at her.

She wasn't staring at him, as he'd thought, but at the blanket past her knee, staring at the rough worn nap of the olive drab wool, but not really seeing it. Her eyes glistened with what might have been tears if they hadn't looked so cold and hard. "I don't think my dad feels much of anything anymore, Gordon," she said quietly.

"I don't know about that," he said cautiously, gingerly testing the waters and seeing which way to navigate. "I think you're probably wrong about that. I mean, I know you guys have had your differences and all, but—"

"Put a lid on it, Huckstep." Her eyes met his and there was pain and anger and hurt and betrayal printed there for all the world to see. Her voice was flat and emotionless, and warned that no argument would be tolerated. "I know you and Dad are friends, but you're stepping out of line. You don't know what you're talking about." Her voice began to shake. "You're not in my shoes and you don't know what it's like to *be* in my shoes. You and dad still talk. He still communicates with you. Try living with someone who's cut himself off from the entire world, from *you*, just because he thinks he got a bum rap called cancer. Just try it." She suddenly shrieked, a short, sharp bark of pain-filled sound and flung a piece of wood into the fire as hard as she could. Sparks exploded upward in a volcano-like shower of color. "Christ! You don't know what it's like dealing with that! Dealing with him refusing to speak, pulling away a little more every day until there's nothing left when there's still so much more we could do! He won't let me be close and it's the one time in life when we *should* be!" She started crying, her chest heaving with huge, in-rushing sobs of pain.

Beyond her, Dan and the others headed in at a run, drawn by her scream of frustration, and Gideon came around the end of the aircraft. Al reached out to put his arms around her and she struck out, hitting him hard enough to hurt.

"No! Save it for someone who wants it, Huckstep! I don't need your sympathy or your concern." She brushed a hand frenziedly over her face, smearing tears and snot, and sniffed loudly. "I need my father." Struggling, slapping his hands aside when he tried to help, she lurched to her feet and hopped toward the plane on one foot. She caught herself against the hatch and leaned there a moment, panting with effort. When she turned around, her face was pale from exertion and pain, but her eyes blazed hotly through her tears. "Don't bring it up again, Gordon," she grated through clenched teeth. "I mean it. Just don't do it." Grunting with effort, she pulled herself into the plane with her arms and slid out of sight. Al heard the rustle of tarpaulins, followed by the sounds of ragged crying muffled by blankets.

Sighing in frustration, he turned and stared into the fire, ignoring the others as they came questioning into the camp. Talking to Lyndell about the rift between her and her father—

and seeing what he could do to help mend it—was going to be a lot harder than he had first thought. How do you help people when they don't want your help?

Wind riffling the pages of Lyndell's discarded magazine caught his attention and he stared at the old photograph of Sam Beckett as it wavered back and forth in the breeze. If the Freeman father-and-daughter tag team was anything at all alike, Sam had his work cut out for him.

CHAPTER
ELEVEN

Sam's ass was numb.

He'd long ago lost track of how many hours they had been out on the trail searching the wilderness for the downed aircraft. It helped knowing others were out here hunting as well, but all he really knew for certain was a deep-boned dog-tiredness. Hours of uncomfortable riding on the noisy, jostling snowmobile had fused together his rump and spine into a single solid line of throbbing white ache that threatened to push the crown of his skull through the top of his head.

He'd stopped glancing at his watch early in the search. The futile gesture only made the passing hours seem longer than they were, restraining their progression to a sloth's pace agonizing enough to put his teeth on edge. He felt tense and agitated, frustrated and tired. He had no reason to assume this Leap would be any easier than the others had been. He had no reason to suppose that merely setting out on the search would immediately bring them to the crash site. He was aware of his task—how he must find a way to locate the crash site and reunite the Freemans. But, more than that, he was poignantly aware that Al was one of the crash survivors. Sam didn't know if Al would die in real time if his host body died here in the past, but prior experience had taught him to lean on the pessimistic side of things. If he didn't make it in time, that might just be the last the world knew of Al Calavicci and there was no way he was going to lose Al without a long, hard fight.

He glanced around as he throttled down the machine to a whirring crawl to get over a particularly convoluted piece of corrugated terrain without upending the snowmobile and spilling himself into a drift. The snow under the caterpillar treads was fresh in some areas. In others it appeared to have softened and refrozen several times, leaving it with the yellowed, brittle appearance of old cottage cheese. The tree verge along their route had darkened with the gathering gloom. Shadows huddled against the stately trunks and beneath the sweeping needled boughs as though seeking sanctuary or secrecy from prying eyes. As daylight began to fail, the conifers turned from dark green to black. Hollows in the rolling expanse of snow shaded to blue and faded purple, like an old bruise. The sky was gray and heavy with low-hanging clouds pregnant with moisture and the threat of more snow (or, worse, rain), which he hoped would not be fulfilled. The going was tough enough without adding weather to it.

Zipped warmly inside the snowmobile suit he'd borrowed from the RCMP station in Valemount, Sam felt padded and trussed up like some cross between a sumo wrestler and Tutankhamen's mummy. Even so, he couldn't deny the difference it made in keeping him from freezing to death. Jeans alone wouldn't hack it out here at this time of year. The air against what little showed of his face between the scarf and ski mask was cold as evening closed in, but not bitingly so. Spring thaw was definitely under way. It meant a return of life for this barren landscape. It meant the reemergence of bear and the threat of flash flooding as the mountain snows melted.

Couldn't you just once think of something uplifting instead of depressing? Sam asked himself, and sighed. Soon it would be dark, with full night catching them out in this unfamiliar, mountainous, somewhat frightening territory. He wondered if

Kris Gunn would stop before then to set up some kind of camp, or if she intended to hunt all night. That just didn't seem feasible, but he was out of his element to know otherwise.

His eyes tracked ahead to her, riding the lead snowmobile with all the familiar ease and assurance of a cowpoke aboard a recalcitrant horse. With a confidence almost awe-inspiring, she took her machine up and over or around or under obstacles that would have daunted almost any other person of Sam's acquaintance. She knew where she wanted to go and seemed unable or unwilling to consider the possibility that something might actually impede her determined progress to get there. Quietly and confidently, she demanded nothing but full effort from the people and resources at her disposal, and appeared used to getting it and accepting of nothing less. Able to swiftly, but calmly, think through a plan before implementing it, she was the best sort of person to have leading an expedition of this kind, and Sam was glad to be part of her team.

Trails led off in every direction, each with its assigned search crew, and Kris Gunn knew them all, trails and people alike. Some of the passages where she led her team of three were wide, well maintained, and well marked, like miniature highways used to a lot of traffic. Others were narrow footpaths winding through hilly areas where speed was an impossibility, and they slug-crawled the machines around hillocks and over tussocks. Still other passages were the faint trails left by animals, deer mostly, though Sam saw a few larger prints he thought might be moose, and there was the broad, hand-sized print he was certain was a wolf's. Here the snowmobiles must be halted and left behind while Kris and the men paced ahead on foot to the nearest ridge or outcrop to get a look through binoculars at the lay of the land and periodically converse with the other team leaders via radio. Never had Sam met anyone who knew their home area as well as she did. Her calm assurance did not carry false security. She knew how serious the situation was, yet Sam somehow found it difficult, despite his sour thoughts, to believe they would not succeed in their endeavor. Kris inspired that kind of confidence.

The pace she set since leaving Valemount in the early morning was swift, but not grueling. Joining them was a clean-limbed and stoic, seasoned camper named Tom Greycloak, with waist-length brown hair and piercing dark eyes. His snowmobile growled along behind Sam's, just as Sam followed Eric, and the geologist followed Kris's lead.

Sam wondered how Eric was doing. He couldn't see his face, so he had to make a judgment by the set of Freeman's shoulders and the droop of his head as he rode. The geologist had seemed a trifle winded at their last stop. That was hardly unexpected, given his physical condition, but it hadn't seemed bad enough for Sam to be overly concerned or to think about suggesting a halt to the day's search. Besides, trying to stop the search while it was still daylight would only serve to throw Freeman into a tirade. He was as driven in his own way as Kris was in hers. If the present sag to his back was any indication, he was pretty tired by now. Sam was glad the day's search had to be winding to a close.

The bumpy snowmobile ride wasn't the only pain in the ass Sam had to contend with that day. Freeman contributed a hefty share as well.

The geologist was still asleep in the diner booth when Kris came slowly across the busy main street to join them. There was a newspaper rolled under one arm and someone with her, leaning heavily on her other arm. It wasn't until they stepped inside the warm diner and threw back their hoods that Sam saw the newcomer was a stoop-shouldered Inuit elder with steel gray hair and a face as whorled as the lines on a topographic map.

Kris flashed a quick grin and started toward their booth as Kevin hailed her from behind the counter. " 'Morning, Kev. Two coffees, please, and some breakfast for Grandfather."

"Right-o, Kris." He set to rapid work over the grill table.

She slid into the booth beside Freeman and Sam shifted over to make room for the old man. Closer now, the Leaper clearly saw the milky film covering both of the Inuit's formerly dark eyes. The man was completely blind.

Kris slapped the newspaper onto the table between them. The sound roused Freeman. He jerked awake with a startled grunt, blinking rapidly and trying hard to focus his red, weary eyes. "Are we ready to go?" The question caught in the middle of a huge, jaw-gaping yawn.

"In a few minutes," she assured him, and reached for the carafe, swirling it experimentally to gauge how much coffee was left inside. She tipped the dregs into Freeman's cup and signaled to Kevin for more all around. "Have another cup of coffee while you wake up."

Eric's blue eyes clouded over immediately and Sam saw the response forming on the geologist's lips. Before he could utter it, Sam kicked him sharply under the table, masking the movement and Freeman's surprised yelp by reaching across the table to turn the newspaper right-side-up to him. "What's this?" he asked curiously.

Kris's expression was almost puckish. She knew precisely what had just happened. "The newspaper out of Vancouver," she replied, and stretched with her arms straight over her head. She didn't look up at Kevin's sneakered approach until he put a huge plateful of food in front of her. She stared at it, then across at the enormous breakfast the Inuit elder was tearing into with peaceful, methodical vigor, and wrinkled her nose up at the cook. "What's this?"

Kevin gave her a pitying look. "It's called food. You might be more familiar with it if you ate some now and then. Stop worrying about seeing everyone else stoked up and take care of yourself for a change. You gotta eat, too, if you're going on a search." Bantering though his tone might be, it left no room for argument. She wasn't getting out of the diner without tucking that gargantuan breakfast behind her belt buckle. Bestowing a final shit-eating grin intended chiefly to annoy her, Kevin set down two more carafes of coffee and departed for the sanctuary of his realm behind the counter.

She shook her head, but Sam couldn't tell if it was at the cook's behavior or at the newspaper article she flipped to with one hand as she began eating. She tapped the page with an index finger to get the Leaper's attention. "You're from the States, so maybe you can explain this to me. With all the problems going on in the world, and with all of its *own* problems, can't the United States government find better

131

things to spend their money on than *this*? I mean, let's face it. *Time travel?* Who does this guy think he's fooling? Would anybody really take this seriously?"

"What?" Tiny jolts of anticipation clipped through him as Sam picked up the newspaper and peered at the tiny article shoved into the bottom left-hand corner on the thirteenth page. Laughter perked within him, tickling the inside of his nose like carbonation when soda is drunk too fast. His eyes scanned the scant two inches of newsprint he'd never seen before, noticing the reporter or typesetter had spelled his last name wrong. The vague, almost tabloidlike report on the early efforts of Dr. Samuel "Becklett" to gain monetary support for the project called Quantum Leap made a grin slowly spread across his face.

Kris nodded, misinterpreting his expression. "That's what *I* thought, too. Pretty weird, huh?"

"Oh, that's for sure," he agreed, and couldn't stop grinning. He lay the paper flat, wishing he dared cut out the article, all the while knowing he couldn't take it with him anyway. He hoped he'd remember the newspaper name and date so Al could have Ziggy do a search for it later to add to their files. "But who knows what the future will bring?"

"Yeah, and pigs will fly out our butts," she replied, cheerfully derogatory. She glanced almost guiltily across at the Inuit, who had yet to break away from his plate except to hold out his blocky mug for more coffee. As though sensing her scrutiny, he met her eyes with his sightless ones and his lined face creased into a beatific smile, which Kris returned.

She dropped her eyes to her food. "I was raised to believe in things like that," she said quietly, forking up more eggs. "Time travel, I mean. Our shamen sometimes travel in time, using meditations and herbs, things like that." She paused in chewing for a sip of coffee, grimaced, and added more sugar before finally looking at Sam. "It's one of the ways we learn about our ancestors and what they have to teach us. I've seen it happen, so I know it's true. It's very real and very natural. It's part of the world around us. But building a machine that will let you travel in time?" She shook her head. "I don't know if I can make myself believe in *that*. I think this guy's bitten off

132

more than he can chew. Either that or he's a consummate con artist trying to bilk the government." She chuckled. "They'll probably go for it. It's funny what people will lay their hopes and dreams on."

Sam's smile broadened, the secret warm inside him like a second heart. Attempting to bilk the government was precisely what he had been accused of by one senator. "Tell me about it."

She nodded and stuck her thumb against her chest. "Well, this is one woman who is going to stick to reality for at least a while longer."

Eric put down his coffee mug with more force than was warranted, drawing their attention. "What's any of this got to do with finding the plane?" he demanded bluntly. "And who's this?" He jerked his chin toward the silent native who smacked his lips with obvious relish as he devoured the last of his breakfast.

Kris's smile tightened at the edges, narrowing her lips into thin lines. Sam could tell she didn't much like Freeman's attitude and he could hardly blame her. She was trying above and beyond the call of duty to be patient and civil with the ill-tempered, strung-out man, and the effort earned her high points in Sam's book. "I'm sorry," she said without one whit of apology lighting her eyes or coloring the tone of her voice. "I let the conversation take over." She gestured toward the old man. "This is my paternal great-grandfather, He Who Sees. Grandfather, this is Dr. Philip Payne and Eric Freeman. They've come to help search for the missing aircraft and Mr. Freeman's daughter."

The old Inuit turned unerringly toward them, holding out his hand first to Sam and then to Eric. "Dr. Payne. Mr. Freeman. It's a pleasure to meet you." His voice was soft and scratchy, warm and soothing on the ear. It was a wool-and-whiskey voice that would have smelled of strong tea and fragrant woodsmoke if voices had scents.

Sam was amazed to be greeted accurately when the man obviously couldn't see which was who or where. The urge to ask how it was done itched him like a healing scratch, but he didn't know how to ask the question without it sounding like he wanted the old man to divulge a particularly cunning parlor trick. "It's nice to meet you," he replied politely, and left it at that.

All Freeman managed was a brief handshake. "He's not coming with us, is he?" he asked as though He Who Sees wasn't even there or was somehow incapacitated and couldn't respond to a direct question.

Kris's gray eyes flashed balefully and Sam was glad he couldn't read her mind. Her thoughts were undoubtedly caustic. "Grandfather asked to meet you," she said tightly. "I don't know how he knew you were in town, or even that you existed at all, but he came to me and asked to meet you." She shifted, turning a shoulder to Eric, and picked up her coffee cup too fast. Hot liquid splashed onto her fingers and she hissed in pain, swearing under her breath. She set the cup down too hard, spilling more coffee, and sucked the burned spot. "God knows why," she muttered sotto voce.

He Who Sees chuckled and pushed his plate aside, reaching for one of the carafes and pouring himself another cup of coffee before anyone could offer to help him and doing it all with an effortless grace that went beyond mere sight. "My granddaughter is angered by your rudeness, Mr. Freeman. She hasn't yet learned rudeness almost always masks a bleeding soul."

For the first time, Sam saw the vitriolic geologist struck dumb. Eric blinked stupidly at He Who Sees and for an instant Sam caught a glimpse of the man inside the shell and the burden of pain and torment he carried. It reminded him suddenly of a quote from Gerald Kersh: "There are men whom one hates until a certain moment when one sees, through a chink in their armor, the writhing of something nailed down and in torment." In that instant, he felt he finally understood Eric Freeman, if only just a little.

He Who Sees nodded and blew across the top of his mug. "Your child and the others will be found if you follow the right path. It will all work out as it should."

Eric's moment of poised silence passed in a flash. The shutters slammed down over his eyes and the corner of his

134

lip curled into a sneer. "Really? I guess it's like something being in the very last place you look, right?" He leaned forward belligerently. "You know, everyone's been throwing that kind of optimistic drivel at me without having anything to base it on, so I'm calling your bluff. Just what the hell do you think you know about it?"

He Who Sees's eyes locked onto Eric with an intensity that shook Sam and evidently rocked Freeman by his expression and the way he suddenly sat back in his seat. In that moment, Sam knew the old Inuit might be physically blind, but there was nothing at all wrong with his sight.

When He Who Sees spoke, his quiet voice held the charged power implicit in the gathering of thunderheads. "The path I speak of is no trail through the forest, Mr. Freeman, but a path of the spirit. You can't touch it except with your soul. Somehow, you wandered off it and can't or won't find your way back. Your heart and mind are sick with the disease of it." He held wide his large and callused hands. "I make you no promises you'll find your daughter. That possibility is in the hands of the Great Spirit. But I know you'll never find her in time if you don't strive to return to the path of your true nature. Your heart has made you bitter toward the world. You must learn to trust in it again." He shook his head sadly, his gray hair moving gently with the motion. "I do not speak of the world of men. The world of men is nothing at all compared to the real world, the natural world. Learn to trust it, to believe in it again, and you'll find what you most seek."

The Inuit elder reached into his coat pocket and pulled forth a jumbled handful of leather, beads, and wood, which he placed carefully in the center of the table. It took Sam a moment to recognize the conglomeration as a collection of necklaces.

He Who Sees's fingers sorted through the pile, separating the individual strands, but his eyes never left Eric's intent face. "Trust the world. Trust the animals. They will show you the way. There is a different civilization out here than you are used to. It has its own rules. Learn that and you will be okay." A particular strand of beads worked free and he lifted it toward Eric. "The elk—"

"I've had enough of this shit!" A sweep of Eric's hand sent the necklace winging through the air. It hit the mirror behind the counter and dropped to the floor, skittering crablike across the waxed linoleum to stop at Kevin's feet. The short-order cook looked down, then back up again to stare at Eric malevolently.

The other patrons all stared at him in shock, but Sam thought the most shocked by his actions might just be Eric himself. He was half standing, caught awkwardly between the bench seat and the table. His face had a waxy pallor to it that made the pale blond spikes of his overnight beard stand out in stark comparison. His eyes were enormous and stunned, and his breath came in sharp, thin bursts that whined through his nose.

"Eric . . . ," Sam began.

"Let me out of here!" he demanded. He shoved against Kris's legs with a panicked urgency. "Let me out!" He practically climbed over her in his desire to be free. She slid out of the booth and he blundered past her, nearly tripped, and grabbed blindly for his parka on the coat rack beside the booth. Shoving his arms into the sleeves, he hurried into the cold gray morning. Sam tracked him across the road, where he stopped by the rear bumper of their truck and looked around as though seeking a panicked avenue of escape. Abruptly, Eric's head slumped and he dropped his forehead against the side of the truck. Chest heaving, his breath puffed bursts of steam into the frigid air as though he'd just run the four-minute mile.

Sam started to rise, wanting to go see if he was all right, but Kris's hand on his wrist stayed him. "Why don't you leave him alone for a few minutes?" she asked, showing a compassion she hardly owed the temperamental geologist.

Sam nodded, his eyes once again tracking beyond the windows to Eric's dejected form. After a moment, the white-haired geologist straightened. He glanced once, quickly, toward the diner, then climbed slowly into the cab of the truck and closed the door. The engine roared to life and white exhaust plumed out of the rear pipe. For a moment, Sam worried that Eric might drive away and leave him stranded in Valemount, but the truck remained where it was, idling gently.

The Leaper glanced at the others and smiled faintly. "That didn't go so well, did it?" he asked rhetorically. "I'm sorry. He's worried about his daughter."

"The apology isn't yours to make, Dr. Payne," He Who Sees said quietly, though he didn't look the least bit offended by Eric's violent outburst. He smiled up at Kevin as the cook silently returned the necklace, dropping it onto the table as he passed to serve some customers at another booth. His hands, never still, sorted through the other two necklaces, untangling their strands. He handed one to Kris. "May the wolf guide you, Granddaughter."

She accepted the medallion with a smile and hung it around her neck without hesitation, tucking it inside her shirt before Sam could see what it looked like. "Thank you, Grandfather."

The other two necklaces he gave to Sam. One in each hand, the Leaper studied the jewelry. The thongs were of beaded leather while the medallions themselves were quarter-sized pieces of wood, sanded smooth and varnished, with a design etched into each and stained black. It took him a moment to realize he was looking at the stylized images of two distinct animals.

He Who Sees touched Sam's right hand, his thumb brushing lightly across the face of the medallion. "This one is for you to wear. It's a bear. He will guard you and lend you his gifts." His fingers strayed across Sam's wrists in a feather touch to reach the second necklace. "This one is for your friend. It is an elk." His sightless eyes sought Sam's. "Rockreader must trust in the animals," he stressed. "They will guide him."

The Inuit's impromptu use of another name for Eric caught Sam off guard, particularly as it was so appropriate. Puzzling that over in his mind, one corner of the Leaper's mouth quirked up. "I don't think I'm going to have much luck convincing him of that," he sighed, putting Eric's necklace into his pocket and fitting the other around his neck.

The lines around He Who Sees's mouth firmed and tight-ened into something close to a frown. His eyes, unable to see, studied Sam's face with an intensity that made the younger man want to fidget. "Believe it yourself first," the old man retorted, not at all angrily, but more like a teacher patiently pointing out something stunningly obvious to a dunderheaded student. "It's easier to convince someone if your own beliefs are solid." He smiled then, his face cracking into such a wealth of wrinkles that Sam couldn't help but smile back. He patted the Leaper's hands, whispered a word in a language Sam didn't recognize, and stood. Leaning across the table, he kissed the top of Kris's head, chucked her under the chin as though she were still a little child, and left the booth.

"Shouldn't we help him?" Sam asked, watching him zip his parka and pull up the hood as he headed for the door.

"That's the last man in the world who needs helping," Kris remarked with fondness as He Who Sees opened the door and stepped outside, then made his way down the sidewalk.

Sam glanced her way, intrigued. "He called Eric 'Rock-reader.' Did you tell him that he's a geologist?"

She shook her head. "He never heard it from me. Maybe from someone else, but don't be surprised if it's just something he knew. Grandfather is like that." She slid out of the booth and reached for her coat. "Come on, we'd better get this show on the road."

"What about that word?" the Leaper asked, shrugging into his coat as he followed her toward the door. "Your grandfather said something when he touched my hands. I didn't understand it. What did he say?"

Kris chuckled, pulling on her gloves and flexing them for a perfect fit. "Oh, that. Don't let it floor you. I think he was making one of his little jokes, poking fun at what we talked about earlier."

"What do you mean?"

She grinned at him over her shoulder as she opened the door and stepped into the cold morning. "He called you a time traveler."

CHAPTER

TWELVE

His mind distracted by thoughts of the near past instead of in the present, where it belonged, Sam didn't notice that Kris had called a halt. He collided with the rear of Eric's snowmobile, giving the geologist's vehicle a hard bump that could have been worse if he hadn't broken from his reverie just at that moment and engaged the brake. He stopped hard, so the collision was slight, but it was still enough to lurch the other man up against the controls with a grunt.

Back hunched, Eric looked around at him. All the Leaper could see of his face was his startlingly blue eyes above the protective covering of a red scarf, but one look at those orbs was enough to convince him that Eric was patently too tired to do more than deliver a halfhearted glare.

Sam smiled apologetically, realizing too late that it couldn't be seen beneath his own multicolored scarf. "Sorry," he said, his voice muffled by the intervening wool. "I guess I wasn't paying attention."

Standing spread-legged astride her machine, Kris tugged her ski mask up over her head and grinned back at him. Loose strands of hair moved gently in the evening's breeze. Roses bloomed in her cheeks and at the end of her nose, and her breath puffed in the air. "It looks like I'm not the only one starting to fall asleep at the wheel. This seems like a good place to call it a night." For a moment, she looked as though she expected a fight with Eric over that decision, and who could blame her, given the geologist's track record? And for an instant, Sam thought that might actually be the case. A stubborn demeanor settled briefly over the other man's features, but then he nodded and slowly dismounted his machine. Silently, he waited for the others to decide what to do next.

Sam frowned, watching him. Freeman had been unusually quiet since leaving Valemount. There were one or two minor flare-ups, mostly involving Eric challenging Kris's authority, but certainly nothing like what Sam had come to expect. The scene in the diner with He Who Sees seemed to have taken something out of Freeman. Whether or not it actually gave him something to think about, Sam didn't know. All he knew for certain was that all day Freeman seemed to be a little less than himself.

A sense of depression settled over Sam. He was a doctor back in his own time. He was a doctor in the present Leap. Still, there was nothing he could do for a man dying of leukemia and driving himself to the point of exhaustion in the search for a daughter he wasn't even friends with anymore.

Kris's eyes met his over Freeman's bent head as the geologist stared at the small stepping motions of his feet packing down wet snow. A tiny line creasing between her fine brows was the only indication she was concerned about something. "Tom?" she called to the man behind Sam.

The Leaper turned. Greycloak was stretching in all directions, slowly easing the painful stiffness of cramped muscles with gentle manipulation so as not to risk a pull.

"Yeah?" he grunted, bent over backward with his long fall of hair reaching nearly to the ground. He cocked his head around to peer upside down at her over his shoulder. Where her cheeks bloomed pink, his were bronze from the cold, hinting at the dual heritage he shared with Gunn, though his blood ties to the native locals seemed closer than hers.

"When you finish contorting," she said with a grin, "why don't you and Eric start setting up the tents and getting an area ready for a fire so we can fix some dinner and hit the sack? Philip, let's you and me gather some firewood."

"Okay," Sam replied readily, but concern niggled at him. Some sixth sense told him there was more to this pairing up than immediately met the eye. He swung his right leg up and over the snowmobile seat, and bit back a yelp of pain as he stood and straightened with his full weight on his feet for the first time in hours. Tom had been right to move slowly, easing the muscles back into their familiar positions. Sam hadn't felt this sore for more than a decade, ever since the last time he let himself get talked into going horseback riding. He'd walked oddly for three or fours days afterward, during which he barely endured Al's seemingly ceaseless repertoire of "Mr. Dillon" jokes and songs about bowlegged women.

The unexpected memory tugged a grin to the corners of his mouth and he fought back the desire to chuckle. God willing, he would be the brunt of those awful jokes once again some time soon.

"That sound all right with you, Eric?" he asked, slowly extending his arms over his head in parody of Greycloak and grimacing with the pull of tight muscles the entire length of his back.

The geologist's bony shoulders lifted in a shrug, his eyes still riveted on the nothing-to-see between the monotonous motion of his slowly stamping feet. "Sure. Fine. Whatever you guys want to do." Freeman finally looked up when he sensed Sam still staring at him. He'd loosened the scarf around his throat and pulled it down to expose his face. His eyes were red rimmed and sore looking, bloodshot with weariness. His cheeks were sunken cadaverlike against the bony framework of his face, hollowed and shadowed beneath a jut of cheekbone that hadn't seemed quite so prominent earlier in the day. His skin was gray with fatigue. The patches of cold-bloomed skin that blazed with high good health in Kris's and Tom's faces looked feverish and sickly on Eric Freeman. This close look at the geologist after so many hours sent a chill jab of fear through Sam's gut. In her transmission, Ziggy had said that his and Al's jobs were to ensure the survival of the crash survivors and reunite Eric and Lyndell, patching the differences between them. That would be kind of difficult to do if Freeman turned heels up somewhere on the trail.

Knowing his hands had been tied from the start (and hating every moment of it), Sam was still sorry he'd agreed to let Freeman participate in the search. It had probably condemned the man to an earlier death than that which he already anticipated, and there wasn't a damn thing Sam could do about it.

If Eric saw Sam's concern, for once he didn't react to it. He blinked slowly and tiredly, and his head bobbed in what might have been a nod or just a nervous jerk. "That sounds great," he added, and managed to dredge up from somewhere the ghost of a smile that looked ghastly on his drawn features. "We could all use a fire and some rest. You two go on and we'll get started here."

Sam wanted to pry at him further, to ask if Eric was sure and if he felt okay, but he couldn't do that without raising suspicion in Gunn and Greycloak (which, to his mind, suddenly sounded like a medieval detective team. The thought almost made him laugh out loud and he suddenly realized just how tired *he* really was, never mind how the others felt). "Okay," he agreed, because he didn't have any other choice. "We'll see you two in a bit."

"Make it a quick bit," Tom cautioned, stepping up to stand beside Eric, nearly touching his left elbow. "Night's coming on fast."

"We've got our flashlights," Kris assured him, patting her hip with one hand while she waved her other arm for Sam to join her as she started toward a stand of trees.

"A flashlight'll do you a shitload of good if that storm I've been smelling all day hits," he replied. His tone was conversationally cheerful, but his dark eyes were deadly serious.

142

Sam expected Eric to make a rude remark to the observation and was surprised when the geologist merely glanced at Tom with a sad, world-weary expression in his eyes. His gaze dropped back to his gently stamping feet, which hadn't paused in their unconscious repetition since he'd gotten off the snowmobile. His shoulders rose and fell in a restrained sigh. Sam sensed it wasn't an expression of his annoyance but, instead, an expression of his concern and worry. Another snowstorm would only hold up the search even more and further threaten their chances of successfully rescuing the stranded crash survivors.

Freeman's reaction wasn't lost on Kris. The line between her eyes deepened and she shot Tom a glance of annoyance which he parried with one of placid, unruffled aplomb that probably annoyed her all to hell. "Noted," she replied flatly, a somewhat sardonic tone to her voice. "We'll be back in a few minutes. Come on, Philip."

Sam started after her, wincing with each step as his stiff muscles and sore behind protested the movement and whined imploringly at him for a long hot bath and a masseuse. Maybe those would be waiting for him at the next Leap. He hoped so . . . and then instantly rescinded the prayer. Through his years of Leaping he'd learned to be careful about what he wished for. All too often, he got it.

Skirting a series of steep cliffs, he followed Kris toward the nearest stand of trees, his eyes on the gaudy magenta coloring of her coat and suit leggings. She could be found in a blizzard in those lurid clothes. He glanced back once at their soon-to-be campsite. Tom still stood near Eric, his eyes on Freeman's back. He seemed to be studying him with a quiet intensity that was almost disconcerting, and Sam thought he heard the soft murmur of words carried on the breeze. Eric stood where he'd been, his head up and following their progress with his eyes as though waiting for them to disappear from sight before he tried using muscles too tired to support his wasted frame.

That, in fact, may have been precisely the case, for as he and Kris passed behind the first line of overhanging tree limbs and lost sight of the camp, Sam thought he heard a noise that sounded, to his imagination at least, an awful lot like the exclamation of one man catching another as he fell. There was no chance to turn around and step back for a better view, no opportunity to divine whether or not Freeman was okay, for at that exact moment Kris suddenly turned, grabbed him by the front of his snowmobile suit in a grip that was surprisingly firm and almost impossible to get out of, and slammed him up hard against the nearest pine tree.

Well padded as he was, it still hurt. His shoulder blades ground painfully against the tree's rough, resin-scented bark, but she was up in his face, her nose inches from his, and Sam didn't have the leisure time to stop and smell the trees.

She barely came to his chin, but she may as well have been eight feet tall for the anger coming off her. For the first time in his life, Sam really understood why an animal strives to make itself seem larger than it really is in order to daunt and intimidate an enemy, only Kris Gunn wasn't playing pretend. Right now, she really *was* eight feet tall . . . and every inch was spitting mad.

"Okay, Philip," she grated, warm gray eyes gone icy cold. "Out with it. All of it. *Now*."

He blinked at her, afraid to raise his hands and test the tensile strength of her forearms and wrists. "Out with what?" he squeaked, and swallowed hard. He sounded like he was going through puberty again. Her anger was certainly enough to make a person do so.

He thought she might let him go then, but she didn't. Her fingers tightened in the puffy material of his collar and she pressed him even harder against the tree. "I should knock you on your damn ass right here and now. I could do it," she threatened. It wasn't the blown-up intimidation of someone trying to be cock of the walk. She meant every word.

"I believe you," he agreed, wide-eyed and nodding rapidly. "What have I done?"

"It's what I think you *haven't* done. What you haven't done is be completely up front with me." Her clouded breath blew across his vision. "And you're going to rectify that situation right here and now. Just what's going on?"

"Going on?" Her fingers tightened again, working deeper into the down suit, in all probability headed for his jugular.

144

He coughed for effect. It wasn't far from the truth, and he risked having her bite him by raising his hands and curling his fingers gently around her wrists without threat. "Kris, you're going to choke me into passing out."

"The thought crossed my mind."

He leveled his gaze at her, trying with everything he possessed to put all of Philip Payne's supposed honesty and integrity into that single look. "Just tell me what you want to know, and I'll do what I can to answer you." She continued glaring at him and he sighed. "I can talk a whole lot better with my air passage unblocked," he prompted, and wheezed for effect.

She didn't laugh. He hadn't really expected her to, though he'd kind of hoped she might. Sam felt her take a step back in spirit, though for a moment her physical presence never altered. Then she released him, slowly lowering her arms to her sides, but never changing her rigid stance or stepping back an inch to give him more room. Her eyes held him against the tree trunk as surely as had her hands, pinned like a butterfly to a board.

"What's wrong with *him*?" she asked. One arm raised and she rigidly pointed a gloved finger back the way they'd come. "Freeman, I mean, before you decide to pretend I'm talking about Tom. I've seen exhaustion before, Philip. I've suffered from it myself, so I know there's a lot more going on here than just being tired from a day on the trail." She shook her head, her eyes holding him immobile. "I've seen grief and concern before, too, and there's more wrong with Eric Freeman than a father being worried about his missing daughter. So you tell me exactly what's wrong with him and you tell me now." She went up on her toes in the snow, nose to nose with him so closely Sam had to practically cross his eyes to see her clearly. "And if you dare try to tell me 'nothing,' I promise I *will* knock you on your ass and have both of you back in Valemount so fast it'll make you think you'd never left at all. Count on it. I don't make empty threats. I make promises."

He swallowed hard. "I don't doubt you." He wished he could step back a bit and get out of such close proximity. As she'd no doubt intended, it was making him nervous.

She knew that and for a minute she let him twitch. Then she stepped back to a more comfortable distance. Stance wide in the snow, she crossed her arms over her chest and waited silently, her hard eyes never leaving his face.

Sam breathed deeply and let it all out in a rush. Dammit. He hadn't wanted to do this, but he wasn't about to lie to Kris Gunn. Not only would she kill him for doing it, but she was helping them, after all. She was his and Eric's lifeline out here to not only rescuing Al and the others, but to getting their own carcasses back to Valemount in one piece. Without her help, he and Eric were sunk. Without her help, his Leap (and Al's, consequently) would fail. And where would that leave them both?

There was no easy way to prelude this so he just took the plunge. *Mom always used to say the water is only cold for a second.* "Eric has leukemia," he informed her bluntly. Cringing inside (and giving serious thought to cringing on the outside in the hope she might take pity on him), he waited for her reaction, half expecting her to kill him outright and leave his bones for the scavenging animals awakened by the spring thaw.

She didn't, of course, though he wasn't stupid enough to assume the thought didn't at least cross her mind. For a moment there was no reaction at all, just the continued, steady, unwavering regard of those pale, ice-chip eyes. Sam was rapidly coming to an understanding of how she rose to her position of authority in the RCMP and how she came to obviously command the attention and respect of the local citizenry. Only some idiot with a death wish would do otherwise, particularly when confronted by those eyes.

She stared at him almost long enough to make him squirm, which wasn't very long at all. He felt as if he were back in the second grade and Mrs. DeAcetis had once again caught him scribbling science fiction stories in the back of his notebook. "I beg your pardon?" Kris finally asked quietly. "I think I heard you correctly." Her tone implied she hoped she hadn't. "But I want to make certain there hasn't been some mistake. What did you just say?"

"Eric has leukemia," Sam repeated quietly. "He's dying."

Kris rolled her eyes heavenward, exposing the whites all around like a crazed horse or an animal with rabies. "I was really hoping I heard you wrong. I was *really* hoping you didn't say that." Her arms dropped and her hands curled into fists. "I don't believe this," she said softly. Actually, that was what Sam thought was the gist of what she said, because what she really said actually involved several languages (most of which he couldn't identify), the gross manipulation of body parts, and more than a few words beginning with the letter *F* (all of them definitely in capitals).

The entire diatribe was delivered in a voice held low and in check by a woman obviously wanting to run amok and murder the entire population for several hundred miles around, starting with Sam. When she finally wound down, her face was flushed and she was breathing hard. She inhaled deeply, visibly taking control, and looked up at him. "Why didn't you tell me before we left?" she queried.

He hoped no one looked at him like this ever again in his life. "If I had, would you have let us come along?"

Her expression told him it was a stupid question, though he already knew that. "Of course not."

He nodded. "That's why."

She swore under her breath. "I'd love to hit something," she muttered. "Believe it or not, Philip, I *do* understand your reasoning. But there's something you've failed to understand. I'm responsible for finding that downed plane. I'm responsible for the well-being and safety of the people out here, possibly risking their lives to find that plane. Sure as shit, I'm responsible for the safety and well-being of my own team. You've allowed, and by purposeful omission of information made *me* allow, a man to put his life at risk."

"To him there's no risk," Sam divulged. "He's terminal. He's going to die, regardless."

"That's not the point!" Her voice rose. She stopped and took a moment to almost physically put herself in check. "I don't want him dying on me, do you understand that? I don't want him dying while he's part of *my* team. Eric Freeman has no right being out here."

"The way he sees it, he has every right." Sam shifted away from the bole of the pine that he'd allowed to hold him up for much of this conversation. "His daughter's out here

147

somewhere, Kris." He waved a hand to take in the surrounding wilderness. "He's scared to death of the leukemia, but he's even more frightened of losing Lyndell." The rightness of that observation suddenly warmed him, urging him on. "If you hadn't brought him out here, guiding him, he'd have found someone else to do it, maybe someone less qualified. Or, knowing Eric, he would do it himself, relying on topographic maps and a compass and with not a clue to the surrounding terrain. And he probably would die out here without ever learning whether or not his daughter is safe."

"And you'd have let him do that?"

He couldn't tell for certain if there was condemnation in her voice or just curiosity . . . or a mixture of both. "I wouldn't have any choice. Just like I don't have any choice now."

She drew breath to argue with him, then paused, thinking better of it. She studied his face for a moment, weighing what he'd said. "And you'd have gone with him. Just like now." It wasn't a question.

Sam answered it, anyway. "Yes, just like now." He returned her look unblinking and wondered what was going on behind her eyes.

After a moment, Kris turned to study the trees and glanced up at the indigo sky with its sprinkling of early stars. "That's quite a friendship you have, Philip Payne. I don't pretend to understand it, because it's way out of my experience. Still . . ." She let drop whatever she'd been going to say. "I'm not happy about this."

He smiled with understanding. "I wouldn't expect you to be, Kris. I'm sorry I didn't tell you sooner, but I didn't feel I could without putting our participation in the rescue in jeopardy. And I couldn't do that."

She snorted through her nose, laughter that had nothing whatsoever to do with humor. "Well, you got that one right for sure." Her face sobered. "I can still send you both back. I should, just to teach you a lesson. Not that I think it would work," she added wryly.

"But you won't," he countered, a large dollop of hope coloring his words.

"Oh? And what makes you so sure of that?"

148

"I'm *not* sure," he replied with utter honesty. "If I were in your shoes I'd probably do just that, except you know Eric won't back down. He won't take no for an answer any more readily than do you. He'll find a way to search for Lyndell even if it kills him in the process."

"He's going to die anyway," she replied, bluntly paraphrasing his earlier words. She cocked her head sideways and gave him a look from beneath peaked brows. "What the hell did I do wrong in my life to deserve you two?" She waved away a reply before he could even think about voicing one. "Forget I asked. I don't think I want to know. I don't think there's enough good karma in the world to make up for it." She sighed. Reaching for the flashlight clamped at her waist, she flicked the switch with her thumb. A beam of circular light stained the snow at their feet, bringing each tiny crystal to radiant life. She bent and picked up a piece of wood in her free hand, and handed it to him without meeting his eyes. "We'd better gather some wood and get back before Tom comes looking for us." She gathered another limb, playing her flashlight beam across the ground in front of them in search of likely deadwood.

It was then they heard the wolf. The initial sound started low, thrumming Sam's eardrums before he was consciously aware he was hearing anything. The low moan rose eerily, then cut off. A moment later, it started again, taking the song further and joined this time by several more voices. Sam stood transfixed, mesmerized by the feral beauty of the sound, until Kris jabbed him in the kidney with a length of wood, reminding him not only of her presence, but also of the great need he had to make a bathroom stop somewhere soon.

Bottom-lit by the flashlight, her face looked like something scary out of an Inuit legend. "Come on, Philip. Let's hurry up and get back to camp." She looked around, worried, and bent for another piece of wood.

"What's wrong?" Sam shifted his load to one arm so he could gather with the other as they turned back toward the campsite. "I thought wolves didn't attack people."

"They don't, so far as I know," she replied. "At least that's what David Mech and his people say, and I don't have any reason to disbelieve them."

149

"Then what's the problem?" It was hard keeping up with her as she hurried through the soft lumps and drifts of snow and narrowly skirted the edge of the cliff.

"It could be funky acoustics, but those howls sound awfully close," she replied cryptically.

"So?" Sam stumbled. He nearly went down on his knees and almost spilled his entire load. Fear of the cliff edge hammered his heart in his chest. Struggling, he lengthened his stride to keep up with Kris's ground-eating dog trot.

She sighed. "Sorry. I forget you're not inside my head." She watched the beam of light as it bobbed before them. Up ahead, Tom and Eric had turned on their lights and trained them on the ground so as not to blind the others on their return. "The only territory in this area that I know for certain is patrolled by a wolf pack is directly east of us in the Mount Robeson area. Those cries came from the west, toward Mount Watt."

"So?" Sam asked, still not getting it. "Maybe another pack came into the area."

"Maybe," she agreed dubiously, though she didn't make it sound likely. "Or maybe the old pack has moved its territory." She flicked a glance at him. "If they have, I want to know why."

For a moment, he couldn't read her expression, though he felt he ought to be able to. Then, suddenly, Sam remembered He Who Sees's big gentle hands untangling the strands of two necklaces and handing to his granddaughter the one with the face of a wolf.

"So do I," he panted, and hurried to keep up.

CHAPTER
THIRTEEN

By the time they reached camp again both Sam and Kris were winded, neither having realized how far they'd walked.

Tom and Eric had been busy in their absence. The snowmobiles were drawn up to make four of the sides of a pentagon around an area of packed-down snow. The center area was scraped to the bedrock to form a safe fire pit. The two two-man tents supplied by the RCMP made up the final side of the geometric figure, side by side and facing in toward the fire pit. Night gear was unpacked and stowed, and a four-burner propane stove was lit with a pot of coffee brewing gustily and sending its enthralling odor into the air, making Sam's mouth water.

Back slumped, Eric sat near the stove with his legs drawn up under him on the seat of one of the snowmobiles. A metal mug of coffee was cupped loosely between his hands. He did not acknowledge the others' arrival or the distant howling, but continued staring at a small but steady flame in the center of the firepit. His hooded eyes flicked sideways in tiny, jerky motions like physical ticks, watching something in the movement of the fire that was unknowable to the others.

It was Sam's guess that Tom was the one who did all the work of setting up camp and kindling the flame that so held Eric's fascination. The woodsman had fed the fire with bits of wood chipped from the dry insides of nearby deadwood and shaves of magnesium off the block he still held, along with an expensive knife, in his left hand. Tom stood at the edge of the encampment, facing the woods with his back to the fire, both his and Eric's flashlights held in one long-fingered hand, which he swung, pendulumlike, back and forth and around in front of him as a beacon to guide them safely home.

He smiled now as they came into view, his teeth a stark contrast against the darkness of his face, but the emotion didn't quite reach all the way to his worried eyes. "It's not everyone who has their very own human lighthouse to get them home. I thought maybe you folks had gotten turned around out there."

"We were talking," Sam said immediately, then blushed, realizing how that might sound to someone who hadn't been there. Before he could try to say something else equally stupid to make up for it (and, in all probability, making it worse than it already was), Kris broke in, allowing him to keep silent and die a quiet, unremarked death.

"Give me *some* credit, will you, Tom?" she asked, dropping the wood she carried and helping Sam to off-load his. "I had my compass with me."

He nodded. "Good. If we could teach you to read it, you'd be all set." His smile widened, taking the sting away from his teasing.

From the way she wrinkled her nose at him, it was evidently an old joke between them. "Funny man. Just remember I grew up out here and know my way around pretty well, white man."

Tom snorted. " 'White man,' huh? Now who's the pot calling the kettle black? I've got more native blood in me than you do, daughter of pirates."

Kris ignored him, letting the placid argument lie where it was and refusing to rise to any further bait the woodsman might dangle. She dusted bits of wet bark from her gloves

152

and nodded at the heap of wood they'd delivered. "It's not much and it's wet to boot, but it'll have to do."

"We'll make it do," Tom agreed with a sharp nod. A brief gesture of his hand drew her attention to another modest pile of wood stacked between the two tents. "Eric and I gathered some, too, before we lost the light. We should be fine until morning. At least we don't need to waste it on cooking." He knelt before the portable cookstove. "Beef Stroganoff sound good to everyone?"

Kris stepped up behind him and took a deep, appreciative breath through her nose. "Is that my favorite blend of coffee brewing?"

He grunted and rolled his eyes up at her as he began unpacking cups, plates, utensils, and several freeze-dried food packets from a large rucksack. "You packed it, so you should know." His smile was lazy and genuine. "I thought it would be a good, quick warm-up for us while I fix dinner. I've got some—" His voice cut off as, from the distance, the otherworldly cry of the wolves sounded again.

It was a nighttime chorus of energy so primal that, for a moment, they were all transported back to a simpler, more basic way of life. Even Eric looked up, fine white hair falling back from his alabaster features as he turned toward the sound, a flower following the path of the sun, and listened.

Sam glanced overhead at the unimaginable wealth of cloud-cut stars blazing this far from civilization's encroaching, invading lights, and imagined how all this looked from the sky. It would be a tableau often seen throughout mankind's short history—a tiny gathering of human beings huddled for companionship and safety around the meager assurance and protection of their fire while all about them the true essence of the earth roared and swam and wallowed in a cacophonous miasma of emotion and silent sound. It brought to mind the words of He Who Sees back at the diner, seemingly a million years ago: "There is a different civilization out here than you are used to. It has its own rules." That had to be the understatement of the century.

Of them all, it was Greycloak who seemed most wolflike and less an intruder in this other world. He turned toward the sound, tracking it with every pore and rising to his feet with the silently fluid grace of someone totally comfortable with their surroundings. The brightness of his eyes caught the flicker of the campfire, mirroring it in their dark depths like a spark held against the encroaching night. He raised his chin, turning his sculpted, beardless face into the night and the cool wind. His nostrils flared and Sam half expected him to howl in return. With his face lit from the bottom by the stove's steady flame, he reminded Sam for all the world of a hunting animal testing the air for prey.

"They're certainly vocal tonight," the woodsman quietly remarked to no one in particular, his voice hushed as they listened to the convoluted song wend its nearly visual spiral dance of notes toward the clouding heavens.

"I wondered if you heard them," Kris breathed from beside him, her voice hardly above a whisper and almost too faint to hear. She rested a hand lightly on his shoulder and he shifted slightly in her direction, his eyes never moving from the distance where the wolves sang, but patently aware of her presence.

Seeing them together like this suddenly made Sam smile gently. Here was a pair mated for life if he'd ever seen one, though he didn't think they'd figured it out yet.

"Hard not to hear them," Tom responded with a smile and finally looked down at her. "Only problem is, those calls are coming from the wrong direction."

Kris's palm slapped her leg, her attention riveted on his face. Any emotions the eerie calling may have produced were forgotten as her mind tracked back onto the situation at hand with a single-minded relentlessness. "Exactly! That's what I told Philip!"

Greycloak nodded, turning to include Sam and Eric in their conversation, though the geologist didn't seem the least bit inclined to join in. His attention had wandered from the wolves' ululations and returned to the dancing fire. His eyes were expressionless, his features slack and blank. "We could expect howls from Mount Robeson, sure," Tom agreed, pointing easterly. "Or from down south in Glacier National Park, absolutely. But west of here on Watt?" He shook his head.

154

"I haven't heard of any wolf sign, though that's not to say they couldn't have traveled in from another area and just been particularly cagey up until now. But it seems strange no one else has even heard them."

"It *is* the tail end of winter," Sam offered helpfully. "Maybe there's been no one around to hear them."

"Maybe, but it's not very likely." Tom turned his back toward the night and faced the fire once again. "There's always *someone* out here. Skiers, ice climbers, mountain climbers, trappers, loggers. *Somebody.* Not to mention the few who choose to live out here the year 'round." His tone implied his great admiration for those hardy souls. "There are enough people out here, hell there are enough people throughout all of Canada, with a healthy dislike for wolves that we would have learned about it if any had been sighted or heard in the area. A lot of the locals would have been screaming themselves blue in the face for the government to trap or poison any wolves." He shook his head, obviously disgusted, but perplexed as well by their discovery. "I don't understand it. There's something going on and whatever it is, is damned peculiar. It's like the wolves came out of nowhere to set up shop."

"Maybe they did," Kris said cryptically, gray eyes narrowed contemplatively as she stared for a moment at the fire. That remark earned her an odd look from Greycloak that she didn't see, but Sam did. She was busy fingering the beaded thong holding her grandfather's wolf pendant around her throat, stroking it with a motion Sam guessed was totally unconscious, given the look that crossed her face the moment she realized she was doing it. She tucked the necklace back inside her collar and looked up at Greycloak. "I want to throw a couple of ideas past you, Tom. And I need to talk to you about some other things, too. Privately." The brief look she cast Sam's way told him that, like it or not, Greycloak was about to learn about Eric's failing health. It only made sense, given their circumstances, but Sam couldn't help but wish he'd just been forthright with the information from the outset and not tried to keep it a secret, even though his reasoning had been sound. *Oh, what a tangled web we weave,* he thought with a sigh.

155

"Sure, Kris." Tom nodded and stepped away from the fire.

To make their desire for privacy a little more comfortable, Sam moved around to hunker down in front of the stove. He picked up one of the foil food packets lying in the snow. Turning it over in his hands, he scanned the words on the back. "Will everything turn out all right if I just follow the directions?"

Greycloak grinned. "That's all I ever did, Philip, until I learned the routine by heart and started experimenting with technique. Following along step by step will still make a decent meal and I can throw together some one-pot spoon bread when we get back. This shouldn't take long." A glance at Kris earned him a confirming nod.

"Take your time," Sam urged, already involved in the task he'd set himself. Stripping off his gloves for fear of setting himself alight, he rummaged in the rucksack with one hand for an appropriate container in which to put the freeze-dried concoction. When he looked up again, Kris and Tom had vanished into the darkness.

He experienced a sudden thrill of fear up his spine. For an instant, he was completely and utterly alone in what was essentially hardly more than primordial forest, returned to being man the prey, not man the usurper of power, not man the ruler. It was a singularly humbling realization.

Then Eric coughed, breaking the moment.

Sam glanced at him, but the geologist hadn't so much as stirred from his spot atop the snowmobile. Both legs of the insulated suit he wore were wet, further evidence that Sam was right in thinking the ill man had collapsed after getting off his machine. Whatever the geologist watched, be it the fire or the Leaper's hands as Sam worked at making dinner, he evidently wasn't really *seeing*. Fine white hair blew about in the wind, framing his hawk-visaged face in long strands as delicate as gossamer. He looked haggard and as utterly beaten as a man can get.

In retrospect, Sam realized later that probably he should have kept his mouth shut, but he didn't like Eric's silence. He wanted to draw the other man out of his deep blue funk and back into an active participation in the world around him.

He didn't bother thinking at the time that maybe Freeman had momentarily withdrawn into the only safety he could find.

"That's quite a sound, isn't it?" Sam asked as the wolves gave vent to another chorusing cry. Even after hearing it a half dozen times or more, it still raised the hair on the back of his neck.

Eric shifted slightly, turning his body to catch more of the fire's mediocre heat, but didn't say anything.

Sam fought back a sigh. He finished preparing the beef Stroganoff and put it over the stove flame to heat, then raised himself onto his knees to peek into the other man's cup. It was empty. He picked up the coffeepot and, without asking, refilled Freeman's mug with the fragrant beverage. After a second's thought, he reached for another cup and poured one for himself.

The first sip was bliss. The second was nirvana, and the third took him straight to heaven as the brew warmed the lining of his stomach and sent tendrils of heat into the chilled remainder of his body. "How's your coffee?" he asked pleasantly, settling onto one of the other machines and turning toward Eric.

He didn't get much of a reply, but at least it was something. Freeman's head dipped fractionally in what would have to pass as a nod, but he didn't look away from the fire. "Good, thanks."

"Great." Sam pursed his lips, wondering what to say next. Freeman's words hadn't exactly been the best conversational opening of all time, but they would have to do. He glanced around, wondering where Kris and Tom had gone and if they were okay. That last thought made him snort gently into his coffee. If anyone was okay out here, it was those two. Besides, their not being okay didn't bear thinking about, since that would leave him and Eric up the proverbial shit's creek without a paddle. He didn't know if he could find his way back to civilization from this east end of nowhere.

He pursed his lips. What to talk about with the silent geologist? The weather? Looking up and noticing the steady influx of clouds obscuring the night sky, he thought that might not be *quite* the topic to broach with Freeman. Should they talk about their upcoming dinner? How far could a conversation be expected to go on the topic of freeze-dried beef? (He imagined Al could make a night's work out of it, but the Italian, unlike homegrown Sam Beckett, had a genuine gift for the gab.) He was just about to say "How about them Mets?" when the wolves howled again and inspiration, good or otherwise, struck.

"That's great to hear, isn't it?" he asked, swirling his coffee around and around in his cup.

Eric grunted noncommittally, raised his mug, and sipped at the steaming brew.

"You don't hear that sort of thing where I come from," Sam added, remembering the small bits of information Ziggy managed to pass on at the inception of this Leap, as well as some of his own esoteric knowledge garnered along the way. "There aren't any wolves in England anymore. They were hunted to extinction years ago. It's a real treat to hear this." He paused as a lone howl echoed across the mountainside, stark in its singularity after hearing the chorus of voices for so long. It hung in the air with the crystal clarity of an icicle.

Eric shot him a dismissive glance before resuming his study of the fire. "I'm so happy for you," he replied brusquely.

Sam counted to a quick and silent ten, then reached to stir the bubbling pot on the stove. "This should be done soon," he said, attempting a different approach. "I sure am hungry. How about you?" Silence greeted the question, but he pressed onward with what he felt was the unfailing optimism of the totally clueless. "I hope the others hurry up and get back or there might not be anything left for them." He forced a chuckle. Eric didn't respond and Sam's laughter watered away to a weak dribble.

"Funny thing about those wolves," he said, going back to the former topic. "When I first heard them, I didn't know what they were, you know? Just for a second. And then I started thinking about He Who Sees and what he said at the diner in Valemount."

Eric's head came up slowly. Eyes still on the fire, he didn't look at Sam, but it was obvious he was now listening. Heartened, the Leaper kept right on talking.

"Remember when he was talking about the animals? He mentioned wolves. Wouldn't it be strange if—"

"Christ, Philip!" Freeman's explosion was so unexpected and so sudden that Sam shut up as though someone had shoved a sock down his throat. The geologist lurched to his feet, dropping his cup and spraying dregs of coffee across the stove and into the fire. Both hissed and sizzled, burning away the drink and leaving a nasty smell in the air.

Eric rounded on Sam, face tight with emotion. "If you're going to buy into stupid native mumbo-jumbo that's your business, but don't make it mine!" He stamped one foot, for all the world like an ill-behaved child. "Dammit!" he railed in frustration. "If I'd known you were prone to that kind of crap, I would have left you behind! I don't need this shit on top of everything else, Payne. I just don't!" He turned and stalked away, and the night closed around him like crow's wings.

Sam sat there a moment, humbled by Freeman's vehemence and his own stupidity at bringing up a topic already proven to be tinder to the acrimonious man's explosive nature. Then he suddenly realized that Eric, unfamiliar with the terrain, had gone off angrily into the darkness without a flashlight.

And the cliffs were out there.

"*Eric!*" He lurched to his feet, grabbing hastily for one of the lights left behind by Tom and Kris. Flicking on the halogen beam, he started after the geologist at a trot, calling for the others as he ran.

The strong light found Freeman almost immediately, spraying across his back in a splash of white that brought to life the dark color of his parka. He was walking fast, arms pumping hard, and already had quite a lead on Sam. Out of the dark, someone called out to Philip, but Sam barely acknowledged it. "Eric, wait!" He hastened his pace, the flashlight beam bobbing and wobbling in front of him as he ran, but Freeman didn't stop or turn around. "Be careful! There are cliffs—"

Suddenly, Eric stumbled, almost falling to his knees, and cried out in startled surprise as the ground vanished from beneath his feet. His hands flew up, clutching for purchase where there was none to be found. Before Sam's horrified

159

gaze, he toppled forward and fell over the cliff edge with a sharp cry.

"*Eric!!*" Later he would wonder where he found the energy to slog with such speed through the knee-high semi-thawed snow rapidly hardening under the cold night's not-so-tender embrace. He raced for the cliff edge, terrified by what he expected to find, what he knew he would find, and confident he had just destroyed every chance he and Al had of making things right here and returning home.

He came upon the cliff too fast. His feet slid on wet, congealing mud and shale and twisted out from under him. Fingers clenched hard around the flashlight, his arms flailed wildly, pinwheeling spastically in an effort to stop his forward momentum. A hand shot out of the darkness, grasping for him, but it was too late. The fingers closed on air as the ridge edge, loosened and softened by the thaw and the wear of geologic age, disintegrated under Sam's feet and he followed Eric over the drop.

He landed hard, eight feet below. The impact drove every ounce of air out of his body with a jolt of paralyzing agony. Every nerve and muscle screamed hot white and chilling black as Sam fought to retain consciousness. For long, agonizing moments, he hitched and coughed, struggling to bring breath back into lungs that didn't want to comply with this most basic of orders.

Suddenly he gasped, drawing air successfully with a loud whooping intake that made him cough hard, scraping the inside of his throat. Oxygen made the pain recede to a manageable level and he struggled to sit up. Rubbing his eyes to clear the last stars from his vision, he looked around.

The flashlight still shone, lying in a jumble of snow and mud a foot to the left. Trembling, he rolled onto his hands and knees to reach for it and played the beam around the immediate area. About five feet away, Eric lay sprawled flat on his back amid a scattering of dirt and brush, arms and legs splayed akimbo, blue eyes staring into the night. Sam just knew he was dead.

"Eric." His voice was an old man's despairing croak. He started forward and had almost reached Freeman when his knees abruptly went to water as the geologist slowly began struggling to sit up. "Eric!"

"Philip!" Kris's scared voice, coming from the top, echoed off the cliff face. "Are you all right?"

On his knees beside Eric with one supporting arm around the geologist's shoulders and bowed back, Sam shifted around and trained the flashlight beam up the steep incline. Kris's and Tom's faces, bleached by the white light, looked down worriedly from where they stood a safe distance from the disintegrating cliff edge.

"I'm sore as hell, but I'm okay," he called back. "I don't know about Eric, though." He turned concerned eyes on the geologist, fingers already probing with clinical detachment.

Freeman's slight weight was all on Sam's arm, but it was little enough to hardly trouble him. Already, the other man had rallied, shifting around, blinking hard to regain orientation, and taking stock of himself. Sam was amazed at his resiliency. "Eric? Are you all right?"

He rolled his eyes toward Sam's voice and slowly sat up a little straighter. Groaning quietly, he drew away from the support of the Leaper's arm. He shut his eyes a moment, wavering from side to side as though he might suddenly crumple, then opened them again. "I think so," he finally replied in a voice as close to normal as could be expected. "Just got the wind knocked out of me."

Sam's breath rushed out of him in a huge sigh of relief. "He's okay," he called. Up above, Kris vented a sharp yip of delight and Tom's face split into a huge grin.

Moving slowly with Sam's hand always at the ready just beneath his elbow, Eric moved his arms and legs experimentally and testingly prodded his rib cage. "There doesn't seem to be anything broken," he said quietly, but Sam knew how much the geologist was hurting from the fall. The pain was imprinted in the skin around his eyes in indelible lines. Philip Payne was in good physical condition and Sam knew how poorly *he* felt. In a body that was declining, it could only be worse.

"Don't move around," Tom called from the top. "Just rest and get your breath back. We'll get to you as soon as we can."

Sam angled his head up toward the cliff and shone the flashlight back up that way. Several tiny snowflakes danced in the beam and his heart fell with dread. Not that, too. "What do you mean?"

"We don't dare try bringing you up via a rope," Kris continued, sparing a look of disgust at the whirling flakes and then casting her eyes skyward with an expression that said it all. Sam's eyes followed hers. The sky was completely clouded over now, with not a single star showing. "This cliff edge is just too unstable," she continued. "We have to come around from the west where the terrain's a little more manageable. We're going to try coming part of the way on snowmobiles, so the trip back will be less hard on you." She glanced at Tom. They conversed for a moment in a low-voiced mutter, then she nodded. "It shouldn't take us much more than twenty minutes or so. Hang tight and stay warm. We'll be there as soon as we can." And they were gone. A moment later, Sam heard the sound of two of the machines gunning to life and starting away. Shortly thereafter, he couldn't hear even that.

Aware his knees were cold even within the snowmobile suit, Sam shifted onto his rump for a while and scooted a little closer to Eric whether the geologist liked it or not. It was getting colder and the snowfall was picking up at an uncomfortable rate. Conservation of body heat was of prime importance, particularly while they awaited the arrival of the others. Eric, staring stoically into the darkness and breathing deeply, seemed to hardly be aware of him.

Their single flashlight beam reminded Sam of the proverbial candle in the window, a beacon to guide the far traveler home. He wondered if anyone at home was burning a candle in the window for him.

The sound of a soft voice turned his attention toward Eric. Head tilted back, the geologist stared at the cloud-covered sky, blinking away each snowflake as it fluttered against his lids and lashes. "What the hell are you doing out here?" he asked himself quietly, unaware of Sam's scrutiny. "You're an old man dying of leukemia. You don't have any right to be out here traipsing across the face of British Columbia. You gave up that right. The others are competent enough to find

162

Lyndell without having to drag your failing carcass along." He shook his head and his hair waved gently around his face. His eyes clenched tightly shut for a moment, the lashes damp with unshed tears.

The water's only cold for a moment, Sam thought, thanking his mom again for that bit of good advice before he plunged in. "Lyndell would really give you a tongue-lashing if she heard you talking like that," he hazarded quietly, watching the other man closely.

"I know. I'd like nothing better right about now," Eric replied in a voice tight with emotion. He opened his eyes and looked at Sam despairingly. "Do you really think we'll find her, Philip? Do you really think they'll be okay?"

Here now was the opening of the century, the opening with the geologist for which Sam Beckett had prayed. But he couldn't take it. Rather, he *wouldn't* take it. He'd learned honesty, no matter how brutal, was the way to handle Eric Freeman, and he wasn't about to prattle platitudes in the face of the man's pained hopefulness. Instead, he shook his head and reached to squeeze the man's shoulder. "I don't know, Eric. I hope so. I really do, but I just don't know."

Freeman studied him closely, expression blank, then sighed quaveringly. "I hope so, too." He stared at his gloved hands curled cuplike in his lap. "I've done a really bad thing to her, Philip. A heinous thing." He shook his head before Sam could speak. "I don't mean the leukemia, though that's part of it. I mean backing away from her, pushing her out of my life. I don't want it to be like that, but I just don't know how to make it better between us again."

"Acknowledging the problem is a good start," Sam encouraged, heartened by this break in the man's veneer. "Maybe you both could—" He stopped, hearing something.

Or, rather, *not* hearing something. The world around them, quiet with night and the muffled chiming of stars hidden behind the cover of falling snow, had fallen suddenly *silent*. Sam had never heard such quiet in his entire life. Even the wolves ceased howling. The only sound in the tomblike hush of the woods was the crispy whisper of falling snow landing on the ground and dusting the surrounding trees with a coating like confectioner's sugar. Beside him, Eric was utterly still, also listening, his only movement the tracking back and forth of his eyes for what little could be seen.

Suddenly, with a certainty he could neither express nor explain, Sam Beckett knew they were being watched. Turning fluidly, rising up onto his knees as he moved to protectively block Eric's body with his own, he swung the flashlight in a broad arc and lifted the beam.

It stood at the edge of the tree line, veiled in light and falling snow, supremely alive, its sheer presence immense. It was his dream come true.

The elk, *wapiti* to some native tribes and *Cervus canadensis* to zoologists, was smaller than the animal of his dream. (Had that been only earlier today?) Something over five feet tall at the massively muscular shoulders, the impressive rack of palmate antlers atop the thick neck and elegant head added another five feet to its height. From nose to white-patched rump was easily eight feet. The impressive bulk was balanced delicately on thin, deerlike legs, and when the animal moved it was with balletic grace.

It moved now, stepping toward them slowly, mindful of where it placed its feet, and all the while never taking its dark eyes from them. Its expression, if it could be said to have one, was of grave consideration, a judge come to deliver verdict on people not of this place, people not welcome.

Except Sam felt no threat from the beast. There was no curiosity, either, as one might experience sometimes when meeting a wild animal. There was only silent, burrowing concentration and unblinking regard.

Dun, white, and black, it halted six feet from where they crouched unmoving in the snow. For another long moment it stared at them, then it lifted its head and blew a long plume of steam from moist, black nostrils. The black line of mouth parted, showing blocky, yellowed teeth, and the beast grunted softly several times, its sides heaving with each utterance.

Sam's foot had fallen asleep. Wincing, he shifted slightly to ease it and the elk's eyes found him. *No,* the Leaper abruptly realized. *Not on* him. *On Eric.* The animal watched Eric with a steadiness that bordered on fascination.

Sam glanced sideways. If aware of his regard, the geologist gave no clue. Transfixed, he stared back at the huge beast in awe.

Taking another few steps forward, the elk lowered its head with those dark eyes still steady on Freeman's face. A foreleg lifted and the animal pawed the ground three times, the leg rising and falling rhythmically, striking the earth with a precise movement and gouging a track in the mix of fresh and old snow beneath its hooves. That done, it stepped back away from the men, turned, and vanished silently into the night.

There was a moment of intense silence and then the world remembered to breathe again. Once more, Sam heard the fall of snow, the sough of wind in the pines, the in-and-out rush of his breathing, and the pumping of his own heart. Eric breathed shallowly and rapidly, the air wheezing through his nose. His eyes were still fixed on the spot where the *wapiti* had been.

"Eric . . ." Sam was cut off again by the crunch of rapidly approaching footsteps. *Now what?* he wondered, until he realized he never heard a single footfall preceding the elk's appearance. Flashlight beams broke the distance, bobbing at the trot as Kris and Tom arrived.

"We made it quicker than we thought," the woodsman said with a grin. "There's a decent wash back there with a good, solid floor," he said, cocking a thumb over his shoulder. "We brought the snowmobiles almost the entire way in."

Sam blinked. He hadn't even *heard* the snowmobiles approaching.

If Tom had been about to say more, he changed his mind, falling silent to stare at them, one side of his face screwed up quizzically. "What happened?" he asked. "You two look . . . odd."

Sam chuckled weakly. "You would, too." Ignoring his protesting body, he got to his feet and quickly told them what had just occurred. Throughout his narration, Kris kept pointedly shooting looks at Freeman and Sam, periodically including Tom in her scrutiny. Sam knew only too well what she was thinking, because his thoughts followed a similar track. Eric just kept staring off into the distance, his expression puzzled.

"And it went off that way?" Tom asked, pointing back the way they'd come. He shook his head. "I never heard or saw a thing, but that's not surprising. Elk can move with amazing silence, just like a moose." A sudden gust of wind made them all shiver within the swirling dance of flakes. "Come on," he urged. "Let's get back to camp. We have a dinner to salvage and some badly needed sleep to pursue." He started back toward the snowmobiles, trusting in them to follow. Eric and Sam fell in behind while Kris brought up the rear.

"Pretty eerie about the elk, wasn't it?" Sam asked.

Hands deep inside his pockets, Eric didn't look up from his feet as they followed Tom's tracks. "Unusual, maybe, but certainly not eerie," he said obliquely. "Animals do strange things sometimes. He was probably just curious."

"Oh, come on! Eric! When was the last time anything like that happened to you?" When the geologist didn't reply, Sam pressed on bravely, certain that now he could bring up the topic without inciting Freeman to rage. "Seems kind of weird to me that first we hear the wolves like on Kris's necklace, and then we see the elk like on the necklace He Who Sees wanted to give you."

Eric looked up. "What necklace?"

"Don't you remember?" Sam reached into his pocket to withdraw the beaded necklace and pass it to Freeman, who considered it for a long time, his thumb brushing lightly over the intricate carving of the elk.

"Did he give one of these to you, too?"

"Yeah." Sam snaked a finger inside his collar and teased out the bear necklace for Eric's inspection. Freeman gave it little more than a passing glance before returning the elk necklace.

Sam stared at him in surprise. "Don't you want to keep it? Don't you want to wear it?"

"Why should I?" Eric's voice was softly mocking, softly challenging, but Sam thought there was something going to bay in his eyes.

"Aren't you the least bit curious about what's happening here?" the Leaper challenged. "Don't you see it? First the wolves and now this?"

166

"Jesus, Philip." Freeman shook his head sadly. "I never pegged you for the type to get caught up in this sort of thing. It would be nice if it were true, but this is nothing more than coincidence." He reached over and tweaked Sam's necklace hard, setting it swinging back and forth. "Maybe I'll start believing in this stuff when we see your bear." He held up a finger. "*Maybe*," he stressed, and sped his pace a little so he wouldn't have to walk with Sam.

Only later would Sam think to tell him to be careful what he wished for.

CHAPTER
FOURTEEN

"Goddammit!"

Al dredged up from his memory every common as well as
obscure curse he recalled ever having heard in his long and
illustrious naval career. Jaw clenched, he turned in a tight
circle, hardly aware of the silent group of people gathered
nearby around the remains of the past evening's watch fire.

Angry and frustrated, he jammed his curled fingers back
through his hair with enough force to make it hurt, as though
the pain would somehow help assuage his looming sense of
hopelessness. The compulsion was strong to scream at the top
of his lungs and he only just barely bit it back. He couldn't
afford the luxury now, but later he intended to make the forest
chime. It should have been now, with his initial cry echoing off
the enclosing mountain range, making them ring and setting
any local avians to riot. Instead, his voice fell dead at his feet,
muffled and suffocated by the seemingly impenetrable wall
of unmoving fog enfolding them in its deceptively innocent
shroud of opaque white.

The temperature was noticeably warmer this morning, with
a chilling humidity that soaked into Al's clothing and straight
through to the marrow of his bones, making it impossible to
feel anything but cold. It was this warmer air that caused the

fog to form, vying with the cooler temperatures of the earth and the softening snow underfoot. This wasn't just mist like that often seen over a lake at dawn, semitransparent and tinged with the red welcome of the rising sun. Nor was it the eddying filaments that sometimes wreath the tops of distant hills with a faerie-like gauze. What Al stared at, with malevolent eyes, was good, old-fashioned, thick-as-cotton, dense-as-pea-soup, can't-see-your-hand-before-your-face, pick-the-cliché-of-your-choice *fog*.

Al wanted to kill something. No, make that some*body*. And he had just the person in mind. He turned to face those clustered around the meager warmth of the fire and his motion was so abrupt they all jumped just a little. Dan, squatting to poke the flames with a long stick and encourage them to wakefulness with the introduction of fresh kindling, flinched when Al's stony gaze swept over him, though Dodds, true to form, had done nothing to rouse Al's ire.

Lyndell perched on the sheared-off stump Al had vacated upon waking, her injured leg propped stiffly out in front of her atop another log and cushioned underneath by someone's soft-sided suitcase. Al's abandoned blanket lay balled damply in the snow beside her, where he'd dropped it just moments before. She held her elbows in tightly against her sides. Her hands were crammed rigidly into her coat pockets, pulling them awry to clearly show the tensely balled fists within against the sheer nylon of the shell. Her short, dark hair was sleep-skewed and spiking in all directions. She looked troubled and unhappy. The lines of her face had dropped into an uneven scowl and the rims of her eyes were still red from weeping. Al didn't think she had yet forgiven him for upsetting her yesterday by bringing up her father as an unwanted topic of discussion, though he couldn't for the life of him figure out another way to solve this Leap . . . not that she would know anything about *that*.

God, had that argument really happened only yesterday? Why, then, did it feel like a year of yesterdays ago? And why did he feel like Methuselah's great-grandfather?

Across the fire from Lyndell, Faye Marlowe sat on another log, bundled to the chin inside Bob Bachellor's discarded

169

clothing. Knees primly together with her elbows on her knees, she leaned forward slightly over her lap and extended her hands toward Dan's rapidly growing fire. Her fingers splayed wide inside their gloves, reaching for the flames and their life-giving warmth, but if she felt any pleasure from the fire it didn't show on her face. Her features were pale and waxen, pinched and tense with worry, and her eyes tracked Al as though afraid he might suddenly take a notion to vanish into the encompassing wall of water droplets and hide himself away in the forest forever. Al had to admit the idea held a certain appeal.

Standing behind Faye, almost close enough for his bony knees to touch her back, was Hugh Bassey. The Australian's lanky form was ramrod straight and stiff with tension. It was the first time since Al awoke in Gordon Huckstep's body that he could remember the lean man being anything but at ease, or at least giving the impression of such. Hands in his pockets, he stared at Al from eyes that showed the strain of what they all had endured so far, yet his expression was one of the utmost faith and confidence. No matter what else, Hugh Bassey was sure to his boot soles that Al (or Gordon, rather) would get them out of this latest conundrum with flying colors.

Al wished he had the guts and the gall to slap that look right off Bassey's face, but he possessed neither. It wasn't the Australian's fault any of this had happened, just as it wasn't Hugh's fault, per se (if fault it could be called), that he believed in Al.

That completed the morning's happy little roll call. Gideon Daignault was nowhere to be seen, having traipsed off on his own sometime before dawn. It was he, and not the fog, who had drawn forth from Al the spate of indignant, sarcastic, blue-tinged profanity.

"Did anyone see which way he went?" Al asked now, only barely keeping his tone civil when what he really wanted to do was spit nails. "Did any of you hear *anything*?"

They all shook their heads silently, every eye on him except Lyndell's. She was looking off toward the east, or what Al thought he remembered as being the east. It was impossible to discern direction in the foggy mire. Her eyes were hooded and pensive with hidden thoughts, and her teeth worried at her bottom lip, chewing it gently.

"We were all asleep," Dan offered apologetically, as though they shouldn't have been, as though they should all have stayed awake throughout the night, bright eyed and bushy tailed and never mind that they had spent an exhausting and grueling day making their camp secure and carving out a variety of SOS signals in the now mushy and useless snow. Even if a plane going overhead could have penetrated through this airbound mud, they would never have been able to make sense of the hopeless sprawl of packed snow and pine branches that just yesterday had been crisp, well-defined signs for help.

"You were the one on watch," Bassey added quietly, unable to stop himself from making that observation. He looked instantly contrite for having said anything at all and started to apologize, but was waved to silence.

"I know." Al sighed as another wave of frustration welled up inside. He turned away from their unwavering scrutiny to stare belligerently at the white wall of nothing boxing them in on all sides. He hated having to admit it, but Hugh was right. Too damned right. That was the worst of it. Al *had* been on watch, so there was no one to blame but himself.

Yesterday had been terrible, not just for him but for them all. The morning's useless argument with Gideon put everyone on edge and off stride, and had sent tiny fractures through the fragile unity they so desperately needed to maintain if they hoped to survive this ordeal. Emotions already fraying at the edges from stress, little sleep, and a poor diet had loosened a little more, leaving them all skittish and irritable, liable to snap at the least little perceived slight, real or imagined. Despite their peevish ill humor, they had still worked like dray horses throughout the day, coming and going from the campsite like a colony of industrious insects and stopping to rest only when forced to by hunger, exhaustion, or someone else's gentle persuasion. Even Gideon, despite his complaints and lack of any constructive comments or redeeming value (as far as Al was concerned), had fallen in with the closest he probably ever came to a willingness for hard labor and spent the morning hours and part of the afternoon packing snow in a high, thick wall against the aircraft's northern side to insulate it from the encroaching cold. A satisfactory supply of wood had been cut by Hugh and Al, enough so they wouldn't run out in the course of one night's passing provided the next day they replenished what was used. Thanks to the crash, they didn't have to go far to find usable fuel. Faye and Dan had worn themselves to the nubs stamping out letters and signals in the snow and lining them with anything available to make them stand out. Once she'd cried herself out, Lyndell had emerged from the aircraft and silently, though not resentfully, taken up her assigned spot beside the fire.

Light's failing found them crawling back to camp in ones and twos, exhausted and aching to the bone with the day's exertions. It was difficult to compensate such hard work with nothing more than a pot of weak coffee (they were carefully rationing Dan's small camping cache) and the cardboard refinement of reconstituted food which might have tasted good (or at least passable) on any other occasion, but which now lay on Al's tongue like sodden sawdust, even if the package *was* labeled Chicken Dijon. A tasty "dessert" of well-watered ketchup soup was enough to make everyone feel profoundly gross.

They had been silent during the meal, the only sounds being the clink of shared plates and silverware and the soft slurp from mugs. Even if there was the desire for conversation, the strength wasn't available to do more than ask the salt to be passed. Strained and exhausted nerves thrummed just beneath the surface of the silence, rippling it like the dorsal fin of a killer whale slicing the still waters of Puget Sound. Al felt like a tuning fork caught among them. The latent energy made the hair of his arms stand on end even inside the warm and slightly redolent confines of his down coat.

Bedtime came with the complete fall of night and the start of another snowfall. No one uttered a single sound as the first few flakes fluttered into sight and guttered to death within the fire's flames, but Al felt every soul there hit rock bottom and die a tiny death. More snow meant their signals must be redone come morning. More snow meant no helicopters or airplanes searching, and they all knew in the pit of their heart that an airborne search was their only real chance of rescue from the outside. Another day of the same and Al knew they would have to come to a decision about attempting to pack their way out of wherever the hell they were. It just wouldn't be prudent for them to sit tight any longer.

Because of the snow, or perhaps just using it as an easy excuse for avoidance, none of them felt the least bit inclined to gather, in true camper fashion, around the fire and share companionship. Leaving Hugh alone to take first watch, they crawled one by one into the wrecked fuselage and bedded down beneath the hodgepodge of tarpaulins and blankets. United in body, pressed together by the need for warmth, Al felt they had never been farther apart in spirit. The only thing holding them together now was the commonality of their pain. There was no one thing toward which he could point an accusatory finger. Everything that happened since the crash contributed to this moment of despair, and there wasn't a single damned thing he could do to make it better.

Maybe sleep will do it, he thought, fastening his hood close around his head and face, and noticing Lyndell had chosen to find a bed spot as far away from him as she could possibly get without forfeiting the warmth of the others. *It had damned well better, because I'm shit out of ideas.*

That was the last thing he remembered as sleep claimed him, and he didn't stir a whisker until Dan roused him to take his watch in the deep of the night. Grunts of acknowledgment were about all they managed as they passed the symbols of the watch office. Tilting the stump backward until he could lean against the side of the aircraft, Al tucked the blanket around his legs and lower back and settled the gun across his lap. Dan hadn't reported anything. There was nothing moving in the night or, if there was, its motions were hidden behind the curtain of snow. Even the wolves of last night had been silent in the hushing, crystalline fall, no doubt curled up in some warm den with their tails over their sensitive noses and their heads full of whatever it was that good little wolves dream of.

If their circumstances had been different, if their lives hadn't been in danger and the outlook becoming progressively dire,

173

Al thought he could probably have actually enjoyed some of this. He'd forgotten how nice it was to be in the woods and listen to the murmuring voice of the planet and her people. He'd forgotten the pleasure of watching snow fall or the enjoyment of sitting around an open fire at night with friends . . . though an enclosed fire in a penthouse somewhere with champagne chilling nearby and a blonde heating up close at hand was not to be knocked, either.

He'd gone to sleep. He hadn't meant to. Far from totally rested, he still felt coherent and lucid enough to stand watch without the threat of nodding off. He'd had to do it often enough in the Navy. But "nodding off" didn't come close to describing the depth-plunging plummet he had taken into sleep not more than twenty minutes after taking over the watch. While he slept, snoring gently with his chin tucked against his chest, the snow covered his head, shoulders, and lap in a contour-softening heap of white. While he slept, the temperature rose and turned the snow soft and melting, dampening his clothing and the blanket. While he slept, the fog had come in on Carl Sandburg's little cat feet the size of a puma's paws and settled in to patiently wait. And while he slept, Gideon Daignault had left the airplane with a pack full of food, gingerly stolen the gun from Al's lax-handed grip, and vanished into the night.

Al didn't know whom he was angrier at—himself for falling asleep or Daignault for being such a sneaky son of a bitch. Hands on hips, he stared at nothing, wishing he could pierce the veil with his eyes and spear Gideon through the heart with a look. "Did he say anything to anybody yesterday?" he asked quietly, uselessly. "Anything that might give a clue as to what it is he's up to or which way he's gone?"

"Ummm . . ." Dan's quiet little murmur brought all their eyes around to him. Al felt the sudden and profound relief of having their regard removed from his person, if only for a few moments, and heartily sympathized with the pilot's discomfort at the sudden close attention. Evidently Dodds wasn't much used to being at the center of things, but he was certainly there now.

174

"What is it, Danny?" Hugh prompted, twangy voice gentle and coaxing as he'd used it with Faye.

"Well, I don't know for certain that it's much of anything," he preluded with a self-deprecating shrug. "Maybe I should have said something to you sooner, Gordon, but I really didn't think it *meant* anything." His brow puckered worriedly.

"Didn't think *what* meant anything?" Lyndell asked tersely, her spectacled gaze intent and intimidating.

"Lyndell," Al said quietly. "Put a sock in it." He didn't bother acknowledging the startled look she shot his way, but kept his eyes on Dodds instead and nodded encouragingly, though his insides were cold with the expectation of what he would hear. "Go on, Dan. What happened?"

"Well . . ." The pilot settled his rump back onto his heels and rested his hands atop his thighs. "When I took a break yesterday and tried to catch some fish, Gideon came along to the lake."

The fishing expedition had been a hearteningly good idea that would have turned wonderful had it successfully panned out and given them something to eat other than the freeze-dried asbestos they were rationing at every meal. The thought of pan-fried brown trout or sock-eyed salmon made Al's mouth water. (Hell, the thought of pan-fried *dog* made his mouth water at this juncture.) Unfortunately, no fish were intrigued by any of Dan's lures, and he managed to accomplish little save make himself frustrated. Remembering all this, Al nodded for the other man to continue.

"He wasn't interested in fishing," Dan went on, eyes on his knees rather than any of their faces. "Said he just wanted to take a breather and work the kinks out of his pulled muscle. He asked if I minded if he came along and I said no, even though I don't much like him. Hell, I guess I really didn't care, so long as he stayed quiet and let me fish in peace."

"And did he?" Faye asked.

Dan shrugged one shoulder. "For the most part. As I recall, he walked quite a distance along the shoreline by himself, heaving sticks and some stones onto what's left of the ice cover. I don't remember how far he went exactly because I was minding my fishing rod. After a while, he came back and sat down beside me and started talking. He kept his voice low, so I didn't bother shushing him up."

"What did he have to say?" Al prompted.

Dan looked up. "I should have guessed what he was getting at." He rubbed between his eyes. "He asked me about lakes and runoff, inlet and outlet, in which direction the lake flows, that sort of thing. I'm used to studying bodies of water when I'm camping so I told him what I knew for certain about this lake and most of what I guessed. I never thought it was anything more than idle curiosity to pass the time." His expression was miserable. "It's my guess he's seeking the outlet along the western shore of the lake and intends to follow the stream down the mountain, hoping it'll eventually lead him to a road or hiking trail." He shook his head. "I feel so *stupid*."

"You should." Lyndell's flat-voiced pronouncement brought Dan's eyes hurtfully to her face. One side of her mouth lifted slightly in contempt. "After the way Gideon's behaved, you didn't have a *clue* what he was getting at by asking you those questions? Jesus, Dan."

"Lay off me," Dodds said quietly. "I didn't do it on purpose. I'm sorry. I screwed up. I wasn't thinking—"

"That's for sure."

Al jabbed a rigid index finger into Lyndell's face, silencing her with the force of his thrust. "Just shut up!" he shouted, glaring into the upturned surprise of her dark eyes. "When you're perfect, then you can start tearing down Dan. Until then, keep it shut! You don't have anything constructive to say, so just put a plug in it, Lyndell, or I'll do it for you!" He was breathing hard and his chest hurt. "Dan's not the guilty party, here, so stop trying to make him a scapegoat. I don't recall you being so bright that you've never made a judgment error, and until I do remember such a time or you point it out to me, you can just keep quiet! And that goes for the rest of you, too."

Faye's quiet voice startled him and made him realize how loud he had been. "Gordon's right, Lyn. Dan made a mistake, that's all, and it wasn't even that. We were all so exhausted yesterday, I don't think any of us knew what we were saying half the time. I know I spoke to Gideon a half dozen times yesterday and I can't recall a single word of it. It could have been any of us Gideon talked to and we'd still be where we are."

"You've got that right, ducks," Hugh added softly, lending his support to hers. He stepped around her to rest a long-fingered hand on Dan's bowed shoulder. "You did well, Danny. At least you remembered what he asked. Now we have an idea of where he's gone."

Al nodded. "And an idea of where to search for him."

"You're not serious." Lyndell's voice was incredulous. She waved an arm at the fog cutting them off from everything that was temporarily familiar. "You can't go out in that stuff, Gordon."

"Gideon's gone out in it."

"Well, bully for him!" She bounced on her seat, frustrated with her immobility. "If he wants to take his life into his hands by doing something so stupid as to leave the site in this fog, then that's his choice!" Her cheeks flamed red with emotion.

"He's *my* responsibility," Al added quietly, silencing her vehemence with his calm tones. He smiled gently. "Either verbally or by implication, you all elected me leader of this expedition. Even Gideon, whether or not he likes to admit it. So it's my job to try and haul his silly, sorry ass back to the campsite, even if it means I have to do it with him kicking and screaming the entire way."

"He probably will," Hugh said.

"That might provide an unanticipated opportunity to land a good right cross," Dan offered with a slight smile, and the others laughed.

Al returned the smile, grateful for the slight, albeit serious, joke. "If the opportunity affords itself, Dan, I just might take it," he agreed. "God knows I want to."

"I'm next in line," Hugh said darkly. Faye glanced up at his ominous tone and he smiled briefly to ease her concern. "He needs a good walloping."

"After me," Lyndell put in, brows drawn down together over her nose. "He's got it coming to him in spades, and that's exactly what I'd like to hit him with." She held out one hand not quite imploringly as Al straightened, stretched, and zipped up his coat. "Gordon, please don't do this until there's better visibility. You don't know what's out there. . . ."

"I know Gideon's out there and he's just as handicapped by this stuff as I am."

"And that's supposed to make me feel better?"

"There's no telling how much of a lead he has on us, mate," Hugh pointed out.

"I'll have to take my chances," Al shrugged. "I don't have any other alternative." His eyes silenced Lyndell when it seemed she would protest again. "Or, rather, there's no other alternative I'll consider. I need to get him back here as soon as possible. Remember, he's hampered by that pulled groin muscle. I'm willing to bet he didn't get far before having to pull up and rest for a while. I'll catch up with him. Don't worry." He smiled to reassure them all. "Chances are the sun will burn this off before too long."

He was surprised when it was Faye who snorted. "Mr. Huckstep, we haven't seen the sun in days. What makes you so sure it will shine today?"

"Luck of the Irish?" he asked winningly.

Lyndell's laughter was a bark. "If you're Irish, I'm Paddy's pig," she retorted. She looked across at Dan. "I don't suppose you have another gun with you?"

He shook his head unhappily. "I only figured I'd need the one." He stood and slapped the snow from the knees of his jeans. "But you're not going out there alone, Gordon."

"Dan—"

"No!" The pilot's voice was low, but so vehement as to still Al's tongue in his mouth. "Don't argue with me on this, Gordon. I've done more camping than you have and I know my stuff. It's bad enough Gideon's out there stumbling around alone, even if he did bring it on himself. That isn't going to happen to you. One lost person is enough." He folded his arms stubbornly. "I'll stay behind if you push the point . . ."

"Thank you."

"But I'll only follow you as soon as you're out of sight." A smile crooked the side of his mouth. "And that should take only about ten seconds."

Al halfheartedly tried to stare him down, but it was obvious he was going to lose this fight. Happily so, as luck would have it. He really didn't relish the thought of going alone into that misty, murky landscape. "You're a stubborn cuss, aren't you, Dodds?"

Dan nodded. "And Irish on my mother's side to boot, so you're outmatched from the start."

Al smiled fondly. "I could have already told you that." He was pleased when the pilot flushed at the unexpected praise. "Let's get going. The sooner gone, the sooner returned. And with our wayward child in tow, hopefully."

"Excuse me," Hugh interjected laconically. "But what's to stop the two of you from getting just as lost as Gideon may be?"

Dan dug into a side pocket and produced a keychain with a circular fob. He swung the fob between two fingers for all to clearly see. "I have my compass and I know how to use it."

"I'm not so crazy as to plan a long trek in this goop," Al promised. "We'll go as far as the lake, check around for prints, and see if we can raise him by calling. If we can, we'll bring him back with us." He raised an eyebrow. "Even if it means I have to deck him," he promised. "If we can't find him . . ." He shrugged unhappily. "Then we'll have to wait until this dissipates before trying something else. You three sit tight. We'll be back shortly."

"I'm counting on it, Huckstep," Lyndell said darkly, and Al knew that, at least for now, he'd been forgiven.

"You do that," he replied with a smile. "Come on, Dan."

Within a matter of steps, the campsite was lost to view. They heard the murmuring voices of the others, but the words were garbled and unclear, intonation and clarity swallowed up by the cottony stillness all around them. It was one of the eeriest experiences Al Calavicci had ever undergone and he stopped just short of rubbing the gooseflesh from his arms.

"Which way to the lake, Dan?" he asked, already turned around and confused by the fog, and eminently grateful the pilot had the foresight and intelligence to insist he come along.

"This way." Dan snagged Al's sleeve between two fingers and drew him along. "Stay close. We don't want to lose each

179

other in this murk. God, have you ever seen anything like it? It's like trying to walk through a bedsheet."

It was an apt description. Though the fog shredded apart at their approach, it just as readily closed in again at their backs, like something ominous out of high fantasy. Everything was gray, with no gradations of light to mark sky and ground, trees or rocks. This would be slow going if they traveled very far.

Al hadn't a clue how long it took them at their careful, inching progress to reach the lakeshore, but he was hugely relieved to see the water lapping gently at the wet shoals that appeared unexpectedly at his feet. It was nice to be able to focus his sight and attention on something tangible for a change, rather than just the shifting webs of fog. "Any clue where we are exactly?" he asked.

Dan peered at his compass and frowned in concentration. "Give me just a second, Gordon." He bent to examine more closely the ground underfoot, running one hand gently over the stones, as though reading them. For all Al knew, he might be.

The pilot straightened. "Yeah, I remember this spot." He pointed offshore to where Al could just barely see the slight emergence of a rock apex from the lake. "I remember seeing that stone yesterday. I was fishing just off to the left here."

Al nodded, satisfied. "In which direction is the outlet?"

"This way." Snagging his sleeve once again, Dan led him to the left, keeping always within sight of the lake and the reassurance of its visible presence. In a minute, Dan halted and pointed downward. Looking over his shoulder, Al saw a clear boot mark in the wet sand. "That's him."

"How can you tell?" he asked. "How do you know that's not from yesterday?"

Dan squatted and traced the boot print without actually touching it. "See how crisp and delineated the edges are? If this had been one of yesterday's prints, the edges would be softened and maybe already falling in. This is recent. I'm willing to bet he's close by."

"Do you think he could hear us in this fog?"

Dan shrugged. "It's worth a try, but fog produces weird acoustics. Besides, there's no guarantee the little so-and-so will answer you if he hears."

"Point well taken." Al cupped his hands around his mouth and called. "Gideon! Gideon, it's Gordon Huckstep! Where are you?" They both listened closely, their heads tilted to one side in almost perfect parody of one another. There was no response.

"Try again," Dodds suggested, moving ahead with his eyes to the ground.

Repeating the call, Al followed along, always no more than a hand's breadth from the pilot's broad back. Because of that, he almost fell over him when Dan stopped short. "What's the matter? Did you hear something?"

"No." Dan's voice sounded odd.

Al peered closely at him. "What's the problem, Dan? What's wrong?"

Dodds pointed down toward an area of sand to the right of his right boot, a patch of moist ground between them and the lakeshore's edge. Al didn't have to look too closely to know what it was, and his heart climbed up into his throat at the sight: two sets of tiny bear paw prints, complete with a flurried patch of sand where two little cubs had taken time out to tussle. The marks were sharp and clear and obviously very fresh.

Dan turned with a face blanched of all color. "We have to get out of here now," he muttered in a low, clenched voice. "We have to get back to the camp and tell the others."

"Gideon—"

"We don't have time to worry about Gideon, Gordon!" Dan didn't wait to further argue the point. He latched on to Al's coat sleeve with a hand that would tolerate no argument. Constantly checking the reading on his compass, he practically dragged the larger man back toward the campsite at the closest, safest thing to a run.

They were brought up short after only twenty paces, alarmed by a cacophony of shattering branches. Two small bear cubs tumbled out of the fog and the underbrush almost at their feet. One rolled upright onto his round little rump and looked up at the two strange creatures suddenly in view. It and the men stared at one another for several heartbeats, then it let loose a bawl of pure terror, which its litter mate instantly took up in harmony.

"Come on!" Dan shoved Al, making him run ahead despite the chance of treacherous ground underfoot. Al stumbled and caught his balance, fleeing into blankness in what he hoped was the right direction. His blood suddenly turned to ice as the baby bear's complaint was answered by a horrendous crash and a furious roar that seemed to come from every direction and made his ears ring. He stumbled backward into Dan, trying to turn and run in another direction, sheer panic taking over as a huge mass of brown fury broke from the dense fog bank and started toward them.

"Split up!" Dan yelled, and veered sharply to his right. The bear hesitated for a fraction of an instant, momentarily confused by suddenly having two quarry, then turned and plunged after him.

"*Dan!*" Al screamed. Against every intelligent cell in his body, he started after them, swearing at the bear in the voice that had made many an enlisted man go pale and wet himself. As he ran, he stooped to gather a fusillade of rocks to hurl at the bear's retreating, unconcerned bulk. In the break of mist ahead, he saw the pilot pull himself into a tree, furiously drawing himself up the trunk limb by limb like a chimpanzee.

Somewhere in the mist a rifle fired, the report crackling over the landscape. The bear hesitated and Al beaned it hard in the rump with a good-sized rock as the rifle fired again, this time definitely off to his left. The furious creature growled, reversed direction without seeming effort, and started after him.

Eyes stark with fear, Al turned and ran, sprinting desperately for what he hoped would prove to be another stand of trees. With arms and legs he could hardly feel, he clawed his way into the branches of a tall tree in a bid to get out of reach before the sow arrived.

The large-boled tree shuddered like a sapling as, roaring, the bear's solid mass thudded against its base. Al didn't dare look down. Eyes skyward, his mind null and void in the rush of adrenaline, he ordered his limbs to move, fingers to grasp, arms and legs to pull and push. He was halfway up the tree when she overtook him.

CHAPTER

FIFTEEN

There were no words to describe the pain that lanced through Al's left leg as the bear struck and tore open his flesh from knee to boot-shrouded ankle.

Life bestowed all kinds of pain. In his checkered and amazingly varied life, Al Calavicci had the not-always-fortuitous opportunity to experience most sorts at one time or another. There was the destruction of expectation and the death of dreams. There was the breaking of hearts and the breaking of vows. There was betrayal. There were the myriad sorts of physical pains to which one fell prey without too much effort. There was the pain of being stricken unexpectedly. There was everything that happened to him from the moment he fell into the hands of the Viet Cong.

None of it—not the Cong, not the disappointments, not Beth—could in any way compare to this. Try as his brain might, there were no words, there would never be any words. There couldn't be. Words to adequately describe what was happening to him didn't exist in the English language, just in the incoherency of sudden agony.

A wall of pain—blindingly, paralyzingly white, strobing red, and latticed black—slammed into his brain and sent his senses into a pinwheeling nosedive toward a suffocating but safe haven of darkness. Afraid to give in, terrified that if he did make that drop he would never again see the light of day, Al fought to retain consciousness, scrabbling after it with his mind even as his hands scrambled and tore at the limbs overhead, trying to gain purchase to pull himself out of the bear's reach. Bark abraded the skin of his hands and burrowed painfully under his fingernails. He smelled the raw, heady, copper scent of blood—*Dear God, it's my blood*—and the hot, musky, carrion scent of the mother bear's panting, roaring breath. Inside the boot, his toes were slick with something other than sweat, something warm that gathered between his toes and made them stick together.

Al could attest it was something of a truth that your life flashed before your eyes when you were close to death. In a succession so rapid that he would only clearly recall it much, much later, he remembered his parents, the Naval Academy, Beth, his years of drunkenness and despair, all the women . . . and Sam. Like all the other times, it came back to Sam Beckett. If Al had no other reason in life to live, he had Sam, and that was reason enough to grab on to life with both hands and hang on hard.

Recollection snapped him out of panic like a parent's slap, leaving him chilled to the marrow with a burning cold that had nothing to do with the local temperature. Arms stretched taut to the branch above his head and hooked around it hard, Al looked down at the bear through a haze of agony and watched detachedly as she raked his leg again with her claws. Fired by his newfound resolve, he raised his right foot and kicked the bear as hard as he could in her sensitive nose.

Blood hotter and gamier than his own spurted from the moisture-shiny orb and she roared again, this time with pain that made him glad and reinforced his will to live. He drew back his leg, ready to bestow another hard kick if she resumed the attack. There was a sudden urgent squall from one of the cubs and, in a second, the other one started in, too. Al wondered distractedly what they had gotten into, and found he didn't much care so long as it got Mama away from him for good.

It did. After what seemed an inestimably long and anguished moment, the big brown creature slid backward down the tree trunk and dropped to the ground. She peered around myopically out of small, piggish eyes, roared a baleful challenge on general terms, then struck off through the underbrush and into the fog in search of her missing twins.

Relief took away everything Al had gained. He sagged against the tree trunk, arms releasing the limb overhead and catching hard around the trunk so he wouldn't fall. Surviving a bear attack only to die from falling out of a tree was not his way to go. *You haven't survived the attack yet, buddy boy*, he felt compelled to remind himself.

Rough bark bit into the sweat-slickened skin of his face as he hugged the tree. Violent tremors shook him as shock set in. His vision grew gray at the edges, oblivion encroaching in a steadily throbbing pattern that matched the rapid tattoo of his heart and the sickening pulse-beat of his injured foot.

Did he even still have a foot? He was too frightened to look down and find out, afraid of what he might discover— or not discover—and he had no burning desire to observe shredded muscle and protruding bone, especially when it was his.

Al didn't know how long he hung there between earth and sky, scared to stay in the tree and even more frightened not to in case the bear returned (not that his escape into the tree had done him much good), but he suspected it wasn't long before the sound of voices impinged on his hearing. There were two, both male, and they sounded like they were standing right under his tree, but he couldn't be certain because his ears were beginning to ring with his effort to hang on to consciousness and not take a headlong tumble to the ground.

He thought they might be talking to him, but he couldn't make out the words at first. He didn't know if that was because whoever it was down below didn't have his voice pitched loudly enough or whether Al was having trouble paying attention. There was a lot on his mind just now. He tried hard to focus his attention beyond the wall of burning pain, but it still took him a few moments to remember he was the Gordon they were calling to, and not Al Calavicci.

"Gordon?" That was Dan Dodds, his voice pitched higher than normal with panic. Someone else was down there with him, babbling at a frantic rate, their voice shrilly pitched and as annoying as a mosquito's whine. "Shut *up*, Gideon!" Dan growled, his voice hard. "Gordon?" he called again. "Can you hear me?"

I'm coming. It took Al a minute to realize he hadn't spoken aloud. He swallowed dryly, finding it hard to work up spit, and tried again. "I'm coming down," he croaked brokenly and felt his sweat-soaked hands slide along the tree trunk's flaking bark. *Please don't let me fall,* he prayed. *Please.* He glanced down, probably not the best thing to do, but he needed to orient himself. Through a swinging break in the needled boughs (were the tree branches spinning around or was it him?), he glimpsed Dan's upturned face, skin bleached of color from fear and worry. At his right shoulder stood Gideon, fox-bright eyes darting in every direction but up at Al. A large abrasion roughly the shape of a fist colored one cheekbone. Detachedly, Al noted it was Dan who now held the gun.

Relief at hearing Gordon's voice and seeing movement in the tree made Dan's shoulders sag with gratitude. "Thank God," he breathed, squinting upward through the conifer's needles as Al continued to descend. "Christ, Gordon, that scared the shi—" He broke off, eyes widening as a red splatter the size of a quarter appeared on the nearest branch at eye level. He looked down, seeing what Al already knew was there. The soft snow around the tree trunk was patterned with a rain of crimson droplets.

"Jesus, *God!*" The rifle slid from Dan's fingers as he lunged for the first branch, feet scrabbling against the bark as he pulled himself up hand over hand to meet Al halfway with a supporting arm.

Al leaned gratefully against Dan's shoulder. Climbing with the use of two good legs could be difficult enough, and he was using only his right leg. The left, from knee to boot as he'd finally dared investigate, was a bloody tangle of mangled flesh and torn denim cloth that didn't stand up to much close scrutiny.

Below them, Gideon moaned piteously as blood continued to stain the snow, and watched as they drew nearer to the ground. Fidgeting, rocking back and forth on his feet, head tocking from side to side with the regularity of a metronome as he scanned the foggy area, he started toward the discarded gun only a few paces away.

Dan caught the motion as he looked down to check their footing. "You touch that gun again and I'll happily break every bone in your damned body," he promised levelly, his voice a low growl of warning.

Gideon's answering nod was sharp as he jerked to a halt and held his place. He wrung his hands at his sides. "What do we do?" he whined.

"What do you *think* we do?" Dan snapped, easing Al down another branch. "We get him back to camp!"

Al tried to help, but more and more he found the majority of his weight being supported by Dodds as Al "forgot" he was part of this scenario and began to drift, focusing more on voices and the scenery around him than on what was actually happening. Pain made colors *really* vivid.

"But what about the b—"

Dan's one boot tip brushed the ground. "Give me a hand here, dammit! Forget about the bear!"

Easier said than done, but Gideon leaped forward with his hands outstretched in response to the command and reached up to take Al's other arm and ease him the rest of the way to the ground. Al's head snapped back with pain and he ground a scream to death between his teeth as the lacerated foot at last touched down. Both of his legs went to water beneath him and he would have fallen onto his face if it hadn't been for Dan. The pilot caught him and carefully stretched him out on the stony ground, then moved around to kneel and elevate the leg, resting it atop his own shoulder, unmindful of the blood and smell.

The pain of Dan's raising the limb was excruciating. Al's head pressed hard against the snowy, stony ground beneath him, imprinting the shapes of several small rocks into the

187

back of his skull. Waves of dizziness and gorge-rising nausea assailed his senses and he fought hard to keep from blacking out or vomiting. He was still afraid to give in to the blackness lurking patiently at the edge of his consciousness. He didn't want that oblivion to be his last. And horking chunks meant movement, which meant more pain, and he didn't think he could handle any more pain (if such a thing was possible, and of that he wasn't altogether certain). He had never known anything could hurt so badly.

"She got me twice, Dan," was all he could think to say in his fierce bid to stay awake. The words sounded thick to his ears. He hoped he wasn't babbling incoherently and just *thinking* he was saying the words clearly.

The pilot nodded, swallowing hard before he replied. "I know, Gordon," he murmured comfortingly. "We'll take care of it, don't worry. She's gone now. You'll be okay."

Sure. And monkeys will fly out our butts. Through slitted eyes and hazy vision, Al saw him look over his shoulder at Gideon. "Are you wearing a belt?"

The fox-faced man shook his head rapidly. "No. Maybe there's something in the pack . . ." He scrabbled with both hands to swing off his shoulders the loaded backpack he carried.

"Forget the pack!" Dan ordered sharply. "Unless you stole something from the camp besides food," he added nastily. Gideon went pale and his hands stilled. He stared wide-eyed at the pilot with the guiltiest expression Al had ever seen on a human face. *And with good reason, too,* he figured, contemplating the situation through a haziness not unlike one of his former drunken fogs.

Swearing under his breath and keeping Al's leg in place with one hand, Dan loosened his own buckle with the other and impatiently yanked the length of leather free of the belt loops. Using one hand and his teeth, he slid the tongue back through the buckle to make a loop, then carefully eased it over Al's foot, up the injured leg to above the knee, and drew it snugly tight against the thigh to slow the flow of blood. Al almost bit through his own lip, but was grateful for the pain. It told him he was still awake and alive.

"I'll run and get the others!" Gideon offered, starting away.

"There isn't time!" Dan's strident tone halted the other man in his tracks so abruptly Gideon nearly fell. "Besides, you're going in the wrong direction." There was no mistaking the tone of derision and disgusted sarcasm. If Dan Dodds were the sort to hold a grudge, Gideon Daignault might have hopes of breaking free of it sometime during the next ice age. Maybe. "Just come here."

Gideon did as he was told, shamefacedly hurrying to stand before Dodds. All of the zoologist's former bravado and ill humor seemed to have deserted him. He was as meek and eager to please as a puppy.

"Kneel down," Dan ordered. "Put your arms like this." He demonstrated, holding his right arm out straight and his left bent inward at a right angle to grasp his right arm just above the elbow. "I'm going to do the same thing, only opposite, and we'll link arms like this."

Al immediately recognized one of the standard emergency carries. Dan and Gideon did it very prettily. He'd learned them all in basic training, but never had a chance to use them. Most of the time in warfare, you or a buddy were being dragged out of a bad situation by whatever appendage was most readily available to the willing hands, never mind what the carry looked like or whether or not you were comfortable. When under heavy enemy fire, semantics don't mean diddly squat.

Al jerked hard, scared to realize how close he had just come to losing consciousness. Dan continued talking, giving instructions or pointers or something to Gideon. Al didn't know for certain. His mind wandered and he stopped paying attention. *Bad move, Calavicci. Don't let me catch you doing that again or you might demerit yourself right into the grave.* God, when was the pain going to *stop*?

"You got that?" Dan asked and both men immediately nodded. He'd been speaking to Daignault, but his worried eyes were trained on Al. He'd seen the twitching spasm. Resolve settled over his features and hardened there like fast-drying cement. When he spoke, though, his tone was light and encouraging. "Then let's go. Gordon, you're going to have to help us on this one just a little bit, pal."

189

"I know what to do." Al gasped the words through clenched teeth. He was sweaty all over and felt slimy inside his clothing. The shakes had set in and he knew, like it or not and try as he may, he was not long for the conscious world.

Dan gingerly lowered the leg to compensate as Al propped himself up onto his elbows. Return of the leg to the prone position brought a renewal of pain and pressure around the tourniquet, and a further welling of blood. Al's leg felt like a giant heart, beating double time with a sickening rapidity that made his stomach roll over. Feeling snail-slow but moving as steadily as he could, Al hooked first one arm around Dan's shoulders, then the other around Gideon's. The desperate need for help was almost overruled by an unexpected upswelling of intense enmity at the zoologist's close proximity. If it hadn't been for Gideon and his blind stupidity, this would probably never have happened.

More than once in his life, Al had been willing to die for a cause or an ideal in which he believed. But he drew the line at dying because of someone else's stupidity. That alone made him feel angry enough to stay alive just for spite's sake and the chance to pay Gideon back, even if it was with nothing more than a good right cross.

Ignoring the anger for now, but mentally covering it with ash to keep it warm and alive because it kept *him* warm and alive, Al tightened his grip across the width of two sets of shoulders and ground his teeth together in readiness. "Do it," he grated.

Dan nodded, then looked across at Gideon, meeting the zoologist's eyes. Some unspoken word passed between them and they moved as one, rising unsteadily from their knees with Gordon Huckstep's prodigious weight balanced on the fragile chair of their arms.

As they rose, the leg gently shifted and lowered. Blood hammered into the foot, pulsing hard, high, and fast. Pain peaked, thresholding in a tsunami-like wave of circulation. There was a single high sound like the cry of a distant bird, and after that Al Calavicci wasn't a member of the here-and-now club anymore.

CHAPTER
SIXTEEN

Al didn't know for certain why he regained consciousness just as Gideon and Dan carried him into the camp. The look of sickening horror on Lyndell's face where she sat beside the fire made him think she might have screamed his name. It didn't matter that it wasn't *his* name (though he had sort of begun to think of himself as Gordon Huckstep and could now, finally, understand why Sam sometimes felt so intrinsically and viscerally tied to his various hosts). Her scream, if scream there had been, had done its work and he was profoundly grateful for that. Waking up meant he wasn't dead yet and he fully intended to keep it that way for as long as possible, thank you very much.

"We need a bed and we need one now!" Dan called with all the authority of an EMT as he staggered in under the shared weight of the hefty body that was now Al's. The pilot's face and eyes showed the strain of carrying the wounded man the long distance back to camp. What might have been a nice midmorning stroll for them all on a better day had turned into an arduous, terrifying trek for the two erstwhile beasts of burden as they tried to keep their passenger comfortable, while at the same time negotiating uneven, fog-bound terrain and keeping an anxious eye peeled for the possible return of the enraged sow.

An eye-flick to Al's right showed him that Gideon didn't look any better than Dan. He felt a smug, half-nasty pleasure at that pain-slashed observation. At least this time Gideon Daignault was pulling his own weight. Or Al's, rather. The mild joke might have made him laugh if he hadn't felt so much like last week's chewed-over oatmeal.

Dan was still issuing orders. "Hugh, grab my medical kit. It's in the back of the airplane. Gordon needs something for shock and infection *now*!"

"I'm on it, mate." The lanky Australian practically vaulted into the fuselage, looking for all the world like a kangaroo, and scrambled toward the back of the airplane.

Faye hauled Dan's sleeping bag out of the cockpit and hurriedly threw it onto the pile of springy boughs someone had piled near the fire to use as an impromptu seat. Lyndell hobbled along behind the older woman with her fire-poking stick under one arm to act as a crutch. "Gordon!" she cried. "Ohmigod, *Gordon*!" She reached out, wanting to touch him and obviously at a loss as to where she could do it that wouldn't cause him more pain.

Was there such a thing as more pain? Al really hoped there wasn't. He didn't need any higher attainment to shoot for. He thought maybe his eyelashes might not hurt under Lyndell's ministrations, if she was extremely careful. "Hi, Lyn," he rasped quietly. His voice sounded as if it had been dragged by a 4 x 4, naked, through a bed of gravel-growing nettles, then had pure alcohol poured into the cuts.

"What happened?" Her eyes raked Dan and Gideon, and she hobbled backward out of the way as the two men bent low to gingerly lay Al atop the sleeping bag and close to the fire.

He settled onto the soft, pine-supported bed with a sigh that grated every nerve ending. Pain hammered his temples, his leg, his groin, his back teeth, and the roots of his hair. Sinking into the down-filled material made him think of sinking into the earth. Which made him think of being buried. Which made him think of dying. Which made him pop open eyes he hadn't even realized were closed.

That was the scariest part for him right now. Not the pain,

though that was prodigious. Not the vague thoughts of what might well happen to his leg, not to mention the rest of him, if they all weren't rescued soon. What was scariest was the insidious way death had of creeping up unawares. You wouldn't even see it coming or know it was there until time ran out and you woke up dead. He had no intention of passing out again unless they made him do it, choosing to ignore for now the fact that he hadn't made the choice to pass out this last time it occurred.

"Black bear," Dan panted, answering Lyndell. He bent over with his hands on his knees as he was finally relieved of his burden. The gun, which had been balanced precariously across Al's lap during the dangerous walk back to camp, lay in the snow at the pilot's feet. Literally green in the face, Gideon crumpled to the ground beside Dan's legs, knees and elbows akimbo and all loose-jointed. "With cubs," Dodds continued. "We came upon them unexpectedly in the fog . . ."

Anything else he'd been about to say was interrupted by Hugh's reappearance. The Australian jumped down from the aircraft and hurried toward Dan with the medical kit outstretched in one hand. "Here you go, Danny! I—" He cut off in surprise as he was intercepted by Faye, who deftly snatched the kit out of his hands and began working the zipper around the case.

"What else is in here besides morphine and Tylenol with codeine?" she asked briskly in a competent tone that none of them, in their short association with the woman, had ever imagined her capable of using. "Do you have Betadine or alcohol for cleansing? Any plain Tylenol or regular aspirin?" She flipped open the top and her eyes scanned the contents for the first time. "What kind of antibiotic do you carry?" she murmured, not really asking the question as her fingers slipped dexterously across the contents.

The others stared at her with the same sense of surprised wonder that Al experienced. He had slipped far enough into a numbing shock where everything around him (except for the pain, unfortunately) was beginning to seem very far away and unattached to his person. Not a good sign, he knew, but there wasn't a blessed thing he could do about it. All he could do was lay here and observe, and there certainly was plenty to look at.

A bloom of delight spread across Hugh Bassey's features as he watched Faye's unexpectedly and obviously experienced hands turn vials to inspect them. Lyndell and Gideon looked confused, and Dan appeared to be utterly boondoggled by this abrupt turnaround in their formerly reticent compatriot. "Faye," the pilot offered gingerly, speaking in the tone of voice one uses on horses expected to spook, "what are you doing?"

"Giving Gordon something for the pain, so we can assess the damage to his leg," she replied in a clipped, clinical sort of tone. She didn't look up as she readied the injection. "I'm glad you've got powdered ampicillin, Dan. That'll get into his system much faster than the oral."

"Faye." Dan's tone was cool and competent, authoritative but not bossy. He held out his hand. "Give me the syringe."

She glanced at him, surprise quickly masked by irritation. "Why?" she asked carefully.

"Because you're a politician. An environmental lobbyist. You're not exactly Hawkeye Pierce."

"That shows how much you know," she replied lightly, ignoring his outstretched hand in favor of squatting down next to Al. Her cool, experienced palm swept the hair back off his forehead and felt his sweaty brow and cheeks. "It didn't take the fever long to set in," she murmured, mostly to herself. She raised her voice slightly. "Gordon? You still with us?"

"I'm right here, Faye," Al replied softly. He tried for a weak smile, but it was hard won. The pain was beginning to overrule what little buffer the wall of shock afforded, and battered his psychological and physical ramparts like a Viking berserker sacking a village.

"Good to hear it. Listen to me, now. I'm going to administer some morphine to dull the pain so I can examine your leg and determine the extent of damage. Are you allergic to any drugs?"

Was he? How could Al know? He shook his head. "I don't remember . . ." he started blearily. It was a good ploy, for Lyndell immediately spoke up.

194

"Nothing, Faye. I've known Gordon since I was fourteen. There's absolutely nothing his system can't tolerate."

"Somehow that doesn't surprise me." Working one-handed, Faye expertly loosened the snap and zipper on Al's jeans and shifted him gingerly to one side. She winced as he cried out in pain, but resolutely slid the waistband of his jeans down a couple of inches to get a good shot at his gluteus maximus. "Don't worry, Gordon. I know what I'm doing."

It was over and done with before Al could draw breath to form a ribald answer, if his brain could supply him with one. He barely felt the prick of the needle. That last was hardly unexpected, given the level of pain his overworked system was already trying to deal with, but he was still aware of the older woman's competence. And to think he'd considered her the weak link in their party, when it turned out to be Gideon all along. "The way you cried the first night after the crash, I didn't know you had it in you."

She looked surprised. "That wasn't me. That was Gideon. I know because I was between him and Hugh."

Somehow, the news didn't surprise Al all that much. "I guess there's more to you than meets the eye, Faye," he murmured.

She flashed him a smile that, several hours ago, he'd have bet she couldn't produce on her best day. "And don't you forget it, Gordon. Believe it or not, I was an R.N. for thirty years before giving up a real profession and becoming a politician." The smile abruptly turned apologetic and she looked up at the others. "I'm sorry it took me so long to come back to the land of the living. I feel as though I've let you down. . . ."

Hugh shook his head, eyes shining his pride in her for all the world to see. "You haven't let us down, ducks. Not at all."

She shook her head, barely acknowledging his praise with a grateful glance. "But when I saw you bringing him in like this, I . . ." One hand flipped from side to side. "Something just snapped back into place. I guess it didn't with Lyndell only because the rest of you were already taking such good care of her. You didn't need my help. With an injury this extensive"— she waved her hand at the ruined mess of Al's leg—"I just automatically took over without thinking about it."

"And it's a damned good thing," Dan declared stoutly. "Because I don't have the foggiest idea how to handle this one. What happens next?" He squatted down beside her, intent and observant. His right hand found Al's left, slack and lax atop his stomach, and squeezed it gently. The pilot's hand felt dry and clean against Al's sweaty palm.

"Next comes the antibiotic, to fight infection. We can't guess what sort of stuff was probably under that bear's claws, so we need a good, broad-spectrum antibiotic like ampicillin." She smiled. "Thanks to you, Dan, we have it."

She worked quickly, her hands moving with a practiced efficiency she obviously hadn't lost in the years since her medical career ended and her political one began. Taking the single-dose vial of powdered ampicillin out of its looped holder, she quickly mixed it with its accompanying 30cc bottle of sterile water and injected the solution into the upper right outer quadrant of Al's buttocks. He barely shifted in reaction, hardly caring if she turned his ass into a pincushion. His mind was beginning to cloud over as the morphine set to work. He knew it was the drug acting on him, but that didn't make it any easier to take. In the back of his brain was the fear it might not be the morphine at all, but something else far more insidious and terrifyingly *permanent*.

Don't let me die, he begged silently to anyone who might be listening. *Don't let me die without seeing Sam again. Just let me see Sam.*

Faye was speaking again, but he only caught the words in snatches. " . . . re-dose every eight to twelve hours . . ." " . . . get some aspirin into him, then . . ." " . . . fluids . . ." " . . . warm . . ." " . . . keep the leg elevated after we operate . . ."

That last remark roused Al from his drug-induced stupor ("drug-induced stupid" he remembered a Navy doctor having once called it). Operate? Out here in the middle of nowhere? Dear God in Heaven . . .

But he knew they had to do it. To not do it risked continued bleeding, infection, and . . . Al was no doctor. Sam was the doctor and better equipped to deal with things such as this, even if it was him to whom it had happened. Al was no good with things medical. Sam had to practically blackmail him to get him into the Project's yearly physical. And now they were going to pick through the remains of his leg somewhere out in the wilds of Canada with the nearest hospital on the dark side of the moon for all the difference it would make.

What choice did he have? He couldn't protest. Rather, he *could* if he could find a way to form a coherent sentence, but they wouldn't listen to him anyway. Besides, it would all be a moot point if they weren't soon discovered. Al didn't need Faye's expertise to tell him that. She might be able to stave off the encroachment of infection and gangrene, but she couldn't keep it at bay forever. Without rescue, sooner or later a killing infection would set in, and that would be the end of Al Calavicci. As an afterthought, he supposed someone could always lop off the offending limb with Dan's ax and then cauterize the wound with a burning brand from the fire. . . .

You've been watching too many late-night westerns, buddy-old-pal, he told himself. *What sort of bullet would you like to bite, or do you want to tough it out like the Duke?*

There was no bullet. There was nothing but the soothing haze of morphine clouding his brain with sleepiness. He felt dizzy and experienced a faint floating sensation that almost convinced him he'd risen off the sleeping bag except that through slitted eyes he still saw Dan seated above him. The pain was still there in some vague sense, but Al didn't much care about it anymore.

He couldn't see the other end of his body, but he felt the leg lifted, heard the raspy sound of tearing cloth as Dan slit the jeans leg to the thigh, felt the chilliness of cold air on hot flesh, smelled old blood with a detachment he'd never thought possible and was in no condition to remark upon, and heard the drawn intake of breath from every person there as they finally got a good look at what the she-bear had wrought.

He didn't want to know. He didn't want to look at it. He didn't want it to even have happened, *dammit*, but it had. At this moment, Al Calavicci and Gordon Huckstep were irretrievably interwoven and neither could bear to contemplate a continuation of life without a leg. Both felt less than whole psychologically on a regular basis. To have that manifest itself physically as well was too much to bear.

197

Al knew the sentiment was silly, stupid, wrong. . . . He knew it was *something*, one of these or all of them, in some level of his mind. A lot of people every day survived worse than the amputation of a limb. Hell, he thought maybe *he* had survived worse once, but he couldn't seem to recall where, when, why, or how. But amputation was for other people, not for him. Not for this new person, this AlGordon who had suddenly mixed into one, like oil into water, joined together yet apart across a seemingly minuscule void.

They were doing something to his leg. The coolness of something wet that didn't smell like water, the easing of the tourniquet that brought with it a brief, momentary renewal of pain that faded to dimness under the morphine's onslaught. Something brightly metallic caught the dim, watery sunlight. (*Sunlight?* When had the sun come out?) There was more, but none of it mattered as four sets of hands clamped firmly onto his body and held him down. Faye began to suture and Al began to scream. There was too much to feel and nothing at all, and way too much going on in AlGordon's head that was far more interesting than what happened to him here, so he thought he'd go away for a while and be back later. . . .

Friends with Lyndell since childhood and a natural friendship with her father who was better than his own and merited more understanding from his daughter than Gordon thought she gave him, especially now. Dreams of a career as a glacial geologist working with the famed Dr. E. F. Halter in Norway. Dreams dashed by a disastrous marriage to Delia, who was . . . something . . . something not right. Something gone wrong in her head, in her brain, that left her unable to function like a normal adult human being . . .

. . . something . . .

Lots of somethings, swirling so fast they could hardly be accounted for, yet Al had no doubt he was picking up on them all and that they would be there for further perusal at a later date, inside or out of Gordon Huckstep's body. Sharing this look at death, they were brothers in spirit, now, brothers in soul . . .

When Al next surfaced briefly into consciousness, his throat was sore and he thought he had been screaming, but he couldn't remember for sure. Now everything was quiet and he was too tired to open his eyes. There were no hands on his body now and he wasn't even certain for what seemed a long while that his body existed at all anymore, until tender, trembling hands wiped a cool cloth across his brow. Faintly, as from a great distance, he heard Lyndell ask, "What happened out there, Gideon? Why didn't you shoot the bear?"

The response was almost too muted to hear. "A mother with cubs? I couldn't do . . ."

Al finally, mercifully, let the arms of Morpheus take him down into the deep blackness of sleep as Lyndell Freeman heaped acrimonious vituperation on Gideon Daignault's head.

CHAPTER SEVENTEEN

Al awoke, if waking was what it could be called. It certainly didn't feel like any awakening he'd ever experienced before, but he was definitely in a form of consciousness other than that which he'd dropped into after the meatball surgery performed on his leg.

He couldn't remember opening his eyes, yet he saw with perfect clarity, his vision unfuzzed by the application of pain-numbing drugs. He couldn't feel his leg at first, couldn't feel any pain coming from the limb, and a bolt of fear shot through him, quivering his body like a windblown leaf on a twig. Hand against his thigh, reassured by the firm warmth of his own flesh through the well-worn jeans, he chanced a tentative look down the length of his body. A grateful sob caught in the back of his throat, stuffing his nose. The leg was still there! They hadn't taken it off!

It looked like hell, though, swaddled from knee to the ends of his toes in a thick wad of bandaging stained in spots by Betadine or blood, it was impossible to say which. They had to have used every inch of gauze in Dan's small medical kit to wrap the leg. What would they switch to when they needed to clean the wound?

The question didn't seem to require an answer right now.

He could wait. He tried wriggling his toes experimentally and was pleased when the end of his sock, which was all he could see of his foot, moved ever so slightly. No tendon damage, then. Good. He shifted slightly, feeling uncomfortably warm. Some of it must be the fever he had to have contracted by now as his body fought off any threat of infection. The rest was the thick mound of cloth covering him. Comprised of every spare piece of clothing, tarpaulin, and blanket in the immediate area, Al could hardly move from the weight. It was oppressive and he wanted out from under, but he couldn't seem to make even the lightest bit of cloth shift to the side.

Flames crackled to his left and he slowly turned his head in that direction. Lyndell sat between him and the fire, head and shoulders bowed in despair. Every so often a tremor shook the hand that rested ever so gently on his shoulder and he saw she had been crying.

Her concern touched Al deeply. He wanted to reassure her, to tell her it was all right, he was going to be okay, but he couldn't find the words or make himself heard if he did find them. What the hell was the matter with him, besides the obvious?

Crunching footsteps announced Dan's approach with an armload of wood for the fire. He looked better than when he and Gideon first hauled Al back to the campsite, but not by much. His beard-stubbled face was worn and haggard. Dark circles colored the heavy pouches under his eyes. He glanced at Lyndell's pale, tear-streaked face as he bent to off-load the wood onto the growing stack nearby. "How is he?"

Lyndell shook her head. Releasing Al's shoulder, she lifted her glasses with one hand and quickly swiped her red eyes with the other. "I just wish he'd wake up," she quavered. "We need to get more fluids down him. Wetting his mouth with melted snow just isn't doing the trick." She blinked at the pilot and a light of hope touched her features. "Maybe we could scavenge a little hose from the engine and get Faye to snake it down his throat so we could—" Her voice broke on an aching sob.

Lowering his rotund frame down beside Lyndell, Dan put an arm around her narrow shoulders. She immediately buried her face in his chest and began crying in earnest. "That's a good idea, Lyn, but I don't think it would work," he said gently. "And we don't want to take the risk of doing it wrong and choking him." He squeezed her shoulders. "Gordon's strong," he murmured consolingly. "He'll pull through."

I wish I could believe that, Al thought, now convinced he was watching all this through the lids of his closed eyes. Maybe he was dreaming. Maybe they weren't really having this conversation at all. Maybe *none* of this had been real.

The younger woman bit her bottom lip and cast a glance at Al. That confirmed it for him. If he'd really been awake with his eyes open, she'd have reacted. As it was, her gaze traveled over his face as though memorizing it, then she looked away. "He's so cold."

"We'll work on that," Dan promised, rising. "I'll use the rest of the tarps to make a shelter to better catch the fire's heat and keep the wind off him. If the weather stays this warm, we can all use it. It might be nice to sleep out of doors instead of inside the airplane for a change."

Old Bob's gonna start getting pretty ripe if this warm front keeps on, Al thought detachedly. *Then what do we do?*

Faye appeared in the airplane hatchway. "Good thought," she affirmed with a brisk nod, startling Al because he at first thought she was responding to his silent, internal remark. When she didn't look at him, he realized she hadn't. "And if it warms up a little more, we can strip some of this stuff off Gordon and give him a rubdown. Massaging toward the heart will improve his circulation."

"Okay," Lyndell agreed, rubbing her cold and tear-reddened nose with one hand. "Anything's better than just sitting here and sniveling."

The hell of the thing was Al knew Faye was there, *saw* her there, before she ever spoke. The airplane was behind him. He couldn't see it from where he lay with his head canted toward the fire and there had been no telltale sound to indicate someone's appearance. Even if there had been, there was no way he could have guessed it would be Faye rather than Hugh or Gideon. So how had he known?

He realized he'd known because he saw her even as he was seeing her now. Saw her with eyes that weren't Gordon Huckstep's, but were somehow his own.

Abruptly, Al was outside Gordon's hefty bulk, standing several yards away and looking back at the fire. He was not present in the corporeal sense, nor as a hologram. He felt no cold, no moisture, and no wind, but he could look down and see ... *something* ... comprising Al Calavicci, making him who he was. *Is this my soul?* he thought wonderingly, awed by the sight. *Is this my* soul?

It looked like him, but was not him. A hint of legs and hips and torso, gray and swirling, brown and whirling, intershot with sparks of colored light. The vision reminded him a little of the color-shot Leap sequence when Sam left one host and entered another, and was, at the same time, nothing like it at all. There was no sense of Leaping here, no sense that something larger was at work.

He looked at them, at Faye and Dan and Lyndell gathered near the fire, talking in quiet voices so as not to disturb his rest. In the near distance he heard the sound of an ax biting into wood with a methodic *thock-thock* sound and saw, with something other than his eyes, Gideon and Hugh hard at work hacking a tree into manageable chunks. He saw himself lying prone and unconscious beside the fire beneath seemingly enough blankets to revive the original Hudson Bay Company.

No, wait. That was *Gordon* lying there. Al stepped forward, intrigued with the opportunity to finally see his host from the outside in, rather than the other way around, and at somewhat better advantage than the reflection in the window of a downed aircraft.

It was a nice face, he decided again. Not a handsome face, certainly, but a pleasant one, for all that the jaw sagged and the fleshy features were gray and greasy looking with shock and lack of animation. Gordon's body was flaccid and unresponsive and why not? There was no one living in it right now.

That thought arrowed straight into Al's heart with a bolt of piercing fear. If he had left Gordon's body, if there was no one inside Gordon's body now, if there wasn't even a candle in the window . . .

Ohmigod. Al thought he said it aloud, but he didn't hear any words and no one in camp responded to the remark. *Am I dead?*

As though waiting for that thought, vertigo slammed into him with a vengeance, gulping up his mind and body (if he still possessed one or the other; it was too much to hope he had retained both) and taking them on the ride of their life. The scene swirled, bleeding and running together like a sidewalk chalk drawing caught in a downpour. For a moment, everything looked like the reflection in a funhouse mirror, all watery and blurry. Then all of it was gone. There was an instant of roaring black and vision came filtering in again from the edges.

This was sight as he'd never had it before. Grays and blacks and whites, some of it sharp and defined, other bits nothing more than gradations of the same. Nothing remotely like color lightened or enlivened the landscape. His head swung from side to side, feeling ponderous with weight. There was something blocky and wedge shaped down the front of his face. That couldn't be his *nose,* could it?

He shrugged. It wasn't important. His eyesight was myopic as hell and he wished he'd brought along his contact lenses. The sounds of birds came to him, and wind sighing in the branches of the tall pines on the slope above. Nothing could hurt him here. Here, as nowhere else, he was king. He breathed deeply through his nose and a floodgate opened in his mind.

It was like Saturday morning in the Strip District open-air food market in Pittsburgh! Smells of every description flooded his nostrils and made his mouth water. Air with a scent as sharp and acerbic as rubbing alcohol carried an underlying warmth and sweetness that promised the advent of spring and the return of all good things to eat with the spawning red fish only months away. Bugs had a smell, as did dirt and mold, lichens and new grass, the mice tunneling underground, the she who had come by several hours ago, and he.

He smelled like a locker room full of sweaty linebackers who hadn't showered in six months. It was great. It was *wonderful*! Al wanted to lie down and roll on himself.

He heard something, a thing that had no place in his world. Footsteps crunched through the forest, breaking dry brush and sticks underfoot without regard or concern for the noise. Whoever it was announced his or her presence like the unmindful playing of new cubs.

He turned around, lumbering about like a tugboat moving into position around a luxury liner, and saw the two things that emerged from the concealing boughs of the forest. One of them was well known beyond the instant fear-borne familiarity of something acknowledged to be dangerous and not to be trusted. Something in him knew this thing better than any other, knew it for what it was despite its outer shell. . . .

Vision flickered and wavered, briefly turning the saturnine face of the man before him, the face contorted in fear and horror, into something more recognizable. For an instant the scene turned watery, and in that moment what remained of Al inside the hulking body of the brown-furred bruin recognized the faint, unforgettable features.

Sam! The mute, internal cry resounded off the granite cliffs in a roar that numbed the brain and stilled the very air. Al felt swept along, out of control if he'd ever been *in* control, as the bear lurched to its full magnificent height and stared down at the puny individual before it. Bending the air with another cry, it raised a beefy paw over the head of the body housing Sam Beckett and brought it slashing down in a killing stroke.

And Al awoke inside Gordon's body.

"*Sam!*" he shrieked, sitting up and scrabbling at the blankets covering him, thrusting them aside and trying to get to his feet in a wave of blind terror that had him moving before he was completely lucid and aware.

"Whoa!" someone cried and suddenly there were hands on his shoulders, hands on his arms and thighs, pressing him back to the makeshift bed. "Gordon, what's the matter?"

Voices in the distance. "What's happening? What's wrong?" The sound of running feet.

"I'm not Gordon Huckstep, dammit!" Al spat viciously,

struggling futilely against restraint with all the power in him. Faye and Lyndell were a lot stronger than they looked and Dan Dodds was a veritable bulldog. "I'm Al Calavicci! I'm here from the future!"

Never divulge. Never give so much as a hint to your origins. That was the first rule of Leaping, the rule Sam deemed imperative to the success of his Leaps and his eventual return to his own time. Never let them know, no matter how much you want to, no matter how much it might make things easier for you. Never tell. Never.

But Sam couldn't have foreseen this. *This* was life or death. *Sam's* life, and nothing, not one damned thing in the entire world, not even the chance to return to his own time and his own existence, would make Al wager his friend's life. Ethics be damned, he was going to say whatever he could to make them find Sam and save his life before it was too late.

If it wasn't already forfeit. If so, he had been the one to kill him, not the bruin whose shape he'd taken on. Him. Al Calavicci. He'd been the bear, just as he was now Gordon Huckstep. He was accountable for his actions in or out of another's body and he had just killed his best friend.

He felt like a Judas.

"Sam's out there!" he cried. "He's hurt! There's another bear! A bigger bear!" He bucked hard, panting with effort. "Let me up, dammit! You don't understand! He—" A sharp prick against his skin sent him into a scathing diatribe of Faye Marlowe's lineage and the fate of her descendants. For a few more moments he fought against their restraints, railing against their stupidity, their refusal to understand that a man's life was in the balance. Then the morphine began to take effect. Still swearing, still furiously angry, he felt his body betray him, shutting down without his will, without his control, and knew with an internal cry of despair that he'd let Sam down one too many times and there was no way, now, to ever make it up to him.

But he still had to try. If Sam died here, far away from his own time, maybe there was still something Al could do to make the Leap play out the way it was supposed to. Maybe that would redeem them all.

As he stilled beneath their hands, the others exchanged looks of shock. "Who's Sam?" Dan asked, gingerly settling back on his heels, his hands ready in case Al started thrashing again.

Lyndell shook her head. "I don't have the faintest idea," she said shakily. "But I hope somebody was getting all that down because it's a great idea for a science fiction novel."

"We could retire on the royalties," Hugh Bassey commented from behind her, having run back to the site with Gideon at his heels when Al began shouting. "What do you suppose that was all about?"

"Delirium brought on by fever," Faye said brusquely, removing the thermometer she'd deftly inserted into Al's cheek the moment he stopped thrashing around. She shook it down with a hard snap of her wrist. "He's already up to one hundred five. I'm going to give him some more ampicillin." She rose to retrieve the medical kit.

"Oh, jeez . . ." Lyndell moaned, chafing one of Al's hands between both of hers, then holding it to her face. She rocked back and forth, her leg canted awkwardly beside her. "Gordon, please don't . . . *yikes!*" She yelped as his eyes suddenly flashed open, clear and fever bright and terribly, frighteningly lucid.

His fingers tightened around hers hard enough that Al felt the slender bones within the delicate sheath of flesh. She winced in pain, but he didn't release her. "Lyn—" His voice sounded like sixteen miles of bad road. "Promise me . . ."

"What?" She leaned down closer in order to hear him better. Her free hand stroked the side of his sweaty face, sliding slimily along the stubbled skin of his cheek and into his dirty hair. "Promise you what, Gordon?"

He stared hard at her, willing her to look at him, to not turn away, no matter what, and to not discount what he had to say. He didn't care that the others were there. This had to be said. He had to get through to her now while there was still a chance. "If I die—"

"Oh, Gordon, don't say that!"

"Shut up!" he ordered, startling her to silence with his vehemence. "*If I die,*" he resumed, grating it out between clenched teeth, "or even if I don't, you find your old man

207

and you make peace with him, you hear me? You just make peace with him."

"I can't!" she wailed, tears coming to her eyes. She was a child again, hurt and frightened by a father's confusing distance and a friend's pain. A rose of discomfort stained each of her cheeks.

Al hung on harder, both to consciousness and to her, driving the bones of his hand into Lyndell's, not caring if he broke each and every one of her fingers in the effort to make her pay attention. She was going to understand him, *really* understand him, if it was the last thing he did on this earth. Sam would not die for no reason at all.

"You *can* and you *will*," he stressed, fighting the morphine, fighting the drug's desire to put the pain and the Leap and Sam's death and all of it far behind him. He wanted the pain. He deserved the pain for letting down the only man he had ever felt pleasure and honor in calling his friend. "You live and you find your dad and you make the stupid son of a bitch see reason. Do you hear me? You make him realize death isn't a good enough reason to cut himself off from the rest of the world. You make him realize the time he's losing by being so stupid. You make him realize that sometimes you only get one chance to tell someone you love them. And if he won't listen, you tell him again. And again. And you don't take no for an answer no matter what he says or does. You *don't*." He couldn't stress it hard enough. "And if he still doesn't listen, you tell him to stay out of my way on the other side, because I'll knock him on his ass if I see him."

The morphine finally won out as he'd known it would. Sleep smeared over him, blurring his vision as his eyes settled closed. The pain in his leg, as well as the pain in the depths of his heart, receded to the horizon to await the inrush of the tide when he next awoke. He never saw the look of resolve settle over Lyndell Freeman's features as his hand went limp around hers and slipped away.

He roused once, briefly, while the others were eating dinner. Eyes closed, he listened sleepily to a low-toned argument between voices he was too tired to identify. Someone wanted to pack up and attempt hiking out. Someone else asked how they were going to get Lyndell, not to mention Gordon, off the mountain in one piece? There was only one gun, another stressed. What about bears? It went on and on, around and around, and only served to annoy them and lull Al back into sleep without the others even knowing he'd been awake.

When he rose to consciousness again, it was full night. He was still outside, snug within the confines of Dan's shelter with the fire before him and the others cuddled around him for warmth. A mild breeze smelling of an awakened earth tossed the pine boughs overhead, making them sigh with pleasure.

He lay there for a long while, staring at nothing. The eerie call of a far-off wolf made Lyndell shift beside him, turning over and grunting softly as her injured leg flexed and relaxed. Beyond her, Gideon's rust-colored hair was all that protruded from beneath his blanket. Somewhere else, Hugh or Dan snored gustily, sounding as though they were coming down with a cold.

Al stared into the darkness, taking it all in, cataloging it all in his mind—the woods, the wind, the smells, the friends around him—so he would never forget it. Because he knew, as sure as he knew anything in this life, that Gordon Huckstep was dying . . . and taking Al with him.

CHAPTER
EIGHTEEN

Sam didn't have the energy to utter more than a quiet "damn" when he emerged into the morning air from the tent he shared with Eric.

The night's light snowfall had piled fluffy hillocks against the sides of the tents, along their shock-corded domes, and across the snowmobile seats. Sometime while they slept the weather turned, warming, and now the snow was a collection of soggy lumps working its bone-chilling wetness into everything it touched.

Tom, kneeling by the fire to feed it rejuvenating pieces of kindling, smiled slightly, one side of his mouth crooking upward. "Good morning, Philip. That's not putting it quite so eloquently as Kris did when she saw it, but it's nicely succinct and to the point."

The Leaper smiled in response. "You mean my response or hers?"

"Both."

Sam briefly chuckled and shook his head. He could just imagine Gunn's opinion of the morning and was surprised he hadn't heard her blowing off steam. "Where is she?"

Tom, intent on the fire, his tail of hair a dark streak down the middle of his back, cocked a thumb over one shoulder in a vague direction. "Ladies' room. And she wanted to make a phone call to see how the others are doing."

Sam nodded. Kris had been adamant about checking in with her people at set intervals during each day, in order to keep abreast of who was searching where and what, if anything, had been found. So far, everyone had come up empty-handed, but there was something to be said about no news being good news. At least no one had found any bodies yet, either.

Hands on his hips, Sam turned in a slow circle to survey their camping area. There wasn't much to see. The entire expanse was socked in with a fog as thick as sheep's fleece. Not only could he not see the stand of trees where he and Kris had their "discussion" the night before, he could barely make out the terrain just a few feet beyond their tents. "Won't she get lost in this?"

"Kris?" Tom asked, surprised, then nodded. "Oh, you mean my remark about teaching her to use a compass. That's an old joke between us. She took a survival course of mine when she first moved up here and had a dickens of a time learning to read a compass. I'm still not certain she can do it, but she's never needed to. The woman has an innate sense of where she is at any given moment in any sort of terrain. Hell, I've taken her out blindfolded so she wouldn't know where we were going, then taken off the cloth and let her go. She's found her way back each and every time. It must be the native blood in her," he added with a grin. He shook his head, mouth pulling down in false sadness. "I guess this means I'll never be able to get rid of her."

"If you do, someone else will snap her up," Sam warned.

"And don't I know it," the woodsman replied with utter conviction.

Sam gestured one hand at the surrounding wall of mist. "All the same, this must have put her in a charming mood."

"It doesn't take much," Tom chuckled, duck-walking from the fire to his backpack and removing what he needed to make breakfast. Last night's Stroganoff had been unsalvageable, thanks to Eric's tumble over the cliff and Sam's neglecting to take the food off the fire before rushing to the rescue. By the time they returned to camp they were all too tired to do much more than throw out the charred remains and have a cup of coffee and a few handfuls of the ever-present trail food called gorp. Sam felt the lack this morning. He was *hungry*.

"Seriously, Philip," Greycloak continued, "you don't need to worry about this stuff." Again the thumb-jab over his shoulder, this time at the fog. "I've got a good feeling this'll burn off by midmorning."

The Leaper looked up toward the sky he couldn't see. "You let us sleep in this morning, didn't you?"

"We all needed it," was the truthful response. Tom's dark eyes met Sam's briefly before he returned his attention to preparing breakfast. The Leaper smiled to himself. He and Eric were the ones who had needed it. He was certain Greycloak could go several days on very little sleep or food without showing much strain, and he was reasonably certain Kris had the same ability. Not so for Philip Payne, and doubly that for Eric Freeman.

"How are you feeling, anyway?" Tom gave the batter he was mixing a few more brisk stirs with the spoon and set about readying the griddle for pancakes with a piece of salt pork.

Sam's mouth watered in anticipation of a stack. "Okay," he confirmed. He rubbed the back of his neck. "Bruised as hell from the fall, but other than that I'm fine."

"Glad to hear it." That was Kris, returning from her foray into the murky morning, stepping out of the mist like the Lady of the Lake at Avalon. She walked with a decidedly jaunty step and her look was chipper and refreshed, her cheeks pink with the morning's chill. In her left hand swung the radio she used to contact her home base.

"Anything new?" Sam asked, giving the radio a nod.

"Very little," she replied, straddling one of the snowmobiles and settling onto the seat with a sigh. "Nothing much beyond the weather report. No one's seen or heard anything and, weather-wise, everyone's had the same bad run of luck we have. If the clouds aren't low, it's snowing. If it's not snowing it's foggy or the clouds are low. Rich Selikoff called and said they haven't been able to get a chopper in the air since we

212

left, but that he thinks today might actually be the day if the weather holds, so keep your fingers crossed. Even Canadian Helicopters over in Williams Lake hasn't been able to get their 204s and 206s off the ground, and they're essential if we're going to comb that area adequately."

"What's over that way?" Sam asked, smiling his thanks as he reached to accept the cup of coffee Tom offered.

"Bowron Lake Park for starters," the woodsman replied. "About one hundred twenty kilometers northeast of Williams Lake as the crow flies."

"Plus a good stretch of territory that includes Cariboo Mountain, Mount Stevenson, Mount Watt, Mount Perseus, and Big Timothy," Kris added, rattling them off on her fingers like the names of old and dear friends. "Of that batch, Perseus is the highest at twenty-five thousand and thirty-seven feet. Not that height means anything. Plenty of aircraft have gone into hillsides hardly bigger than a barn."

Sam nodded, remembering, just offhand, the number of rock and roll singers who had died in such accidents. Buddy Holly, Ritchie Valens, Stevie Ray Vaughan . . . Tom's voice brought him out of his reverie.

"Plus there's Quesnel Lake and the North Arm," the woodsman added after a moment's thought. "That's a pretty vast stretch of area, just like Kris said. The folks at Williams Lake will want to check that out thoroughly as well. If the aircraft's pilot was worth anything at all, he may have tried to set them down near water. That's provided he could see where he was going and didn't fly straight into the side of the mountain."

"What a charming thought." The sourly delivered remark came from Eric, who, slowly and with obvious pain, crawled out of the tent to join them. Sam stepped forward to offer a helpful hand and Eric irritably waved him away, determined to do it all on his own.

Tom made a face, patently annoyed with himself for the indelicate remark. "I apologize, Mr. Freeman. I spoke out of line."

"Save it for someone who cares." Bent and hobbling like a man three times his age, Eric shuffled in a tight circle, taking in the lack of scenery around them. "Son of a bitch," he swore, voice tight with emotion. "Son of a bitch. We're never going to find that goddamn plane."

"Hey, don't let this stuff worry you," Sam said, trying for an upbeat, optimistic approach. "Tom says it should all burn off by midmorning. That means the air search can finally begin."

Eric gave them a long, slow look designed specifically for the things one finds under rocks. "And who gave him that pertinent piece of information?" he asked snidely. "The Great Spirit?" Hands jammed into his jeans pockets, he stiffly walked away from them to the farthest edge of the camp and stood just inside where he would have disappeared from view altogether. His shoulders were hunched almost to his ears and his slender back was rigid and tense, thrumming like a taut bowstring.

Sam made to apologize and Tom held up his hand, silencing him. "Don't, Philip. I deserved that. I don't know what I was thinking to make such a stupid, thoughtless remark in his hearing." He thought a moment, then nodded. "Yes, I do. I wasn't thinking much at all, obviously. He had every right to say what he did."

Sam thought about arguing, but the expression in Greycloak's eyes told him it would be futile and a waste of precious time. Instead, he hunkered down beside Tom, the fire in front of him and Freeman in plain view. "Those places you mentioned," he began, keeping his voice low and conversational, pitched so it would carry to Tom and Kris, but not to Eric. "Williams Lake and Mount Watt and the others. They wouldn't be located to the west by any chance, would they?"

Kris and Tom stared at each other, eyes wide. Some bit of communication passed silently between them before they both turned toward Sam. Kris's face split with a grin and she slapped Greycloak soundly on the shoulder. "You owe me ten bucks, pal." She leaned forward, forearms propped across her knees. "You're thinking of the animals, aren't you?" she asked pointedly. "The ones on the necklaces and the ones out here that have contacted us."

Hearing it couched in just that way made it sound eminently silly to Sam Beckett's ears, but he forged ahead bravely anyway. They had nothing to lose and possibly everything to gain.

"Yes," he replied, deciding honesty and forthrightness were the better part of valor. "I think He Who Sees knew what he was talking about. It's just too weird that two of the animals he mentioned have made themselves known to us in very strange ways." He waited a minute, hoping one of them would finish the thought for him because, despite this new belief stirring in his breast, he was still a scientist at heart, as was Philip Payne, and some of this was just a little hard for either of them to accept at face value.

He sighed when it became apparent they weren't going to help him out, that they wanted to hear him say it himself before committing themselves to what all this implied. "They seem to be pointing us in the same direction. To the west."

Kris gusted a huge sigh and grinned triumphantly at Tom. "See? I *told* you he noticed!"

"Someday I'll learn to appreciate that you're never wrong," Greycloak replied dryly. He dug into his back pocket, pulled out his wallet, and produced a ten-dollar bill, which he handed over to her, bowing low over their briefly joined hands. Pocketing the wallet, Tom leaned toward Sam. "Kris and I had a long talk about this. Those wolf cries we heard came from the west, from an area where we haven't had any wolf sign in a long while. The elk that visited you and Eric came in from the north, but left by the west and the track he dug in the ground ran east to west."

They stared avidly at one another. The excitement between them was a palpable electricity that raised the hair on Sam's arms. "We're all nuts, you know that? This is stupid."

Tom and Kris nodded avidly in reply, eyes intense and wide with excitement, hounds at the slip just waiting to be loosed. "Things out here often are," Greycloak confirmed quietly. "There's a different set of laws at work out here, laws that have absolutely nothing to do with how mankind has come to use their minds."

Feeling giddy, feeling foolish and suddenly, illogically *right*, Sam nodded. He learned a long time ago to follow this sort of hunch right to its end. "Then to hell with what everyone else thinks. Let's do it."

Kris clapped a hand over her mouth to keep from shouting aloud with glee, but her eyes over her muffling hand told him all he needed to know. For his part, Tom smiled with quiet satisfaction and bonged his wooden spoon against the side of the frying pan. "Breakfast is served."

The meal was eaten mostly in silence. Eric's foul mood was unabated and precluded any but the most cursory of conversation. Sam guessed it was comprised of equal parts frustration, worry, and poor health, so he could hardly blame the man for his ill-tempered growling. In truth, he found he was beginning to understand the geologist a little better than he'd ever thought possible and that compassion, rather than irritation, was now the mainstay of his emotions about Eric Freeman.

With breakfast over, it didn't take them long to strike camp and start back onto the trail. Through it all, Eric remained stonily silent, doing as he was bidden, responding if he was spoken to, and no more than that. Tom led the way this time, being the better tracker through such slow going as afforded by the fog-bound, moisture-heavy snow. Eric followed him with Sam behind, and Kris brought up the rear.

As the morning progressed, the sun did, indeed, put in an appearance, bathing them all in the pleasurable warmth of its watery light. The fog began burning off, separating into loose, slow-moving strands that shredded apart at the snowmobiles' passing like gossamer mozzarella. Before another hour passed, the way was crystal clear before them with a sky of purest azure overhead. There was no doubt in Sam's mind: today the choppers would fly. With luck on their side, today the aircraft would be found and everyone (God willing) would be alive and safe.

I'm coming, Al, he thought as he tooled his machine along behind Eric's, his eyes alternately on the geologist's back and then flicking ahead to Tom and the view beyond his shoulders. *I'm coming, buddy. Hang on.*

They stopped shortly after noon to rest and eat, and allow Kris the opportunity to check in with the other searchers. While Tom placidly set about getting together their quick lunch, Sam volunteered himself and Eric to walk down to a nearby stream to refill their canteens. Tom gratefully accepted the offer, then sent a commiserating look Sam's way when Eric ill-humoredly picked up two of the round receptacles and started through the bushes alone, not even waiting for him. Sam ran to catch up and made a jocular showing of puffing and blowing at the geologist's heels.

"If you're out of shape, Dr. Payne, I suggest you take some of your own advice," Eric said frostily, no teasing tone to the words.

Sam let it go. There was nothing to be gained in carrying on a pointless argument with the contentious individual. At this point in the game, Eric would have been snotty about Christmas. He felt he had every right and Sam highly doubted there was anything he could do to change the older man's mind.

He came out of the woods at Eric's heels, head sunk in thought, brooding. As far as he could tell, he'd made no advances in his attempt to get through to Freeman, to change his attitudes about death and, more important, about life and his daughter. How could you talk to someone who already had himself nailed up and buried six feet under?

Eric paused at the stream's edge and slowly, carefully, knelt to fill the first canteen. Head bent, watching his thin hands with their bony knuckles work loose the cap, his face obscured by the fall of his longish hair, he spoke quietly. "We're heading west, aren't we?"

Something leaped in Sam's chest, doing a quick somersault for luck. "Yes," he replied carefully, guardedly, knowing this was uneven terrain on which to tread carefully. With Freeman, you never knew where the tar pits would be.

"Because of the animals." He still hadn't looked up, just bent slightly at the waist to hold the lip of the canteen under the rush of crystalline water.

Another slow nod. "Yes," Sam confirmed, and winced, waiting for the eruption.

It didn't come, at least not with the fanfare and fireworks Sam had come to expect. Freeman merely shook his head from side to side. Strands of baby-fine white hair drifted around his chiseled features as he capped the first canteen, set it aside, and reached for the second resting beside his right knee. "Jesus Christ. I can't believe you three are giving in to that old man's mumbo-jumbo. Them, maybe." He jerked his head back toward where Tom and Kris patiently awaited their return. "But you, Philip? I never thought I'd see the day."

"So you keep telling me," Sam replied dryly, keeping his voice low because he knew getting into a shouting match with Freeman would be futile and do absolutely nothing to further his cause. "What other choice do we have, Eric? This makes as much sense as continuing to search the way we have."

"Sure it does," Eric nodded, his voice gently sarcastic. "It makes a whole lot of sense to break off from a disciplined, gridlike search pattern to go lollygagging around the mountains of British Columbia because we think the *animals* are telling us which way to go. Oh, yeah, Philip, it makes a whole lot of sense."

"Okay, so I admit it sounds a little weird—" Sam stepped gingerly down to the small stream and knelt beside Freeman in the soggy snow to fill the two canteens he'd brought.

" 'A little weird'," Eric echoed, and shook his head wonderingly. "This is really the blind leading the blind."

Sam sat back on his heels, the canteens temporarily forgotten. "Where's the harm, Eric, really? We haven't had any success searching this way, and neither has anyone else. Today is the first day the choppers will be able to get off the ground. They have a lot of territory to cover. You know as well as I do that time is running out. Where's the harm in believing a little in magic? Where's the harm in trusting the life around you?"

Eric's chin lifted. His pale eyes blazed with such intense ferocity that Sam's voice stilled in his throat. "Where's the harm?" Freeman asked, his voice tight and tense. "The harm is because it's all a fallacy. Believing in life is an enticement dangled in our faces like a donkey's carrot. When we dare try to nibble at the treat, it's yanked out of reach."

"People have fought leukemia before and won the battle," Sam stressed. "What makes you think you can't?"

"Philip—"

218

"You don't even have a clue as to how many years you might have left, Eric." Sam was surprised at the intense emotions rising within him. A fierce anger burned in his chest. "How can you just toss away the future, *any* amount of the future, now that it's become threatened? You should be grabbing with both hands for what you can get and hanging on to it with all the strength you have. How can you alienate Lyndell when you both need each other the most right now? Don't you love her anymore?"

Eric's look was black, but in the depths of his eyes Sam saw something breaking apart. "I'm looking for her, aren't I?" the geologist rasped. There were tears in his voice, tears he did not dare, or have the personal strength, to shed.

"That doesn't answer my question," Sam pressed, certain he was finally on to something. He lifted his head, blond hair touseling in the freshening breeze, and froze with his eyes widening in fear as for the first time he saw the grizzly on the same side of the stream, but further down the bank. He must have made a sound, some tiny little sound, because Eric turned in that direction and froze on a hissing intake of breath.

The animal was magnificent, greater in stature and in the sheer immense *power* of its presence than anything Sam had ever before experienced. A prominent, muscular hump bulked over the massive shoulders and sloping back. Even from where they sat they could see the creature's long, curved claws. Its color was a deep, rusty cinnamon with a whitish tipping that gave the fur its overall grizzled appearance. Sam guessed the enormous beast easily weighed between nine hundred and one thousand pounds. It was a bulking mass of raw, elemental power.

It raised its head and looked directly at them.

Panic churned in Sam's gut, panic that had nothing whatsoever to do with Sam Beckett's reaction to this animal's presence. It took every ounce of willpower he possessed to not move, canteen still in hand, mud and snow soaking through the knees of his snowmobile suit. He heard the whiny exhalation through his nose and drew a breath with forced, silent slowness through his mouth.

"Son of a bitch," Eric mantra'd under his breath, fists knotted on his knees, eyes unblinking on the approaching bruin. "Son of a bitch, son of a bitch, son of a . . ."

The image of another bear abruptly superimposed itself over the scene, startling Sam with its intensity. Instinctively, he knew that something of Philip Payne, some little memory dormant in the body Sam borrowed, had awakened and was clamoring for attention.

The image was so strong that Sam had to stifle the impulse to rub his eyes. Fog-shrouded green mountains in the American summer of 1973. A sudden, snarling ursine face. He was running, branches slapping his face, drawing blood, then came the heavy power of a black-pawed blow. . . .

The chill breeze that touched his face was rank with bear and Sam suddenly clicked back to the here and now, overriding Philip Payne's fear. His heart pounded so loudly in his ears that he was certain the bear could hear it, too. The sound of fear. Beside him, Eric was silent and rigid, fists still on his knees, poised for flight if Sam but said the word or made the wrong move.

Blinking myopically, looking for all the world as though it needed a good pair of bifocals, the bear started toward them, grunting softly with its head swinging ponderously. Sam stared mutely at the advancing animal and felt cold dread prickle across his shoulders. *Downwind,* he thought. *We're downwind.* Not that it was going to do them any good in a few more moments. Strength held him still when everything in Payne's body shrieked for flight. Mere heartbeats had elapsed since they caught the bear's attention. Still it approached unhurriedly, checking logs and mounds of dirt on the way, but steadily headed in their direction.

Not knowing why, only knowing he felt the compulsion and trusted in it to guide him rightly as it always had, Sam's hand dived into his shirtfront and grasped the medallion He Who Sees had given him, pulling it into the light. He was not aware of his body—Philip Payne's body—wailing for escape. He was only aware of his clenched fist and the symbolized bear-faced medallion hanging from it.

The live incarnation halted not quite three feet away, hulking on brown-furred haunches, bass noises coming from somewhere deep inside. It smelled rank and rancid, old meat and fur cooped up for a long time, but the gamey breath was oddly sweet like meat just turning bad. The blunt-snouted head slowly stretched forward—it amazed Sam how far the bear's neck could stretch—until the black nose nearly touched the medallion. A snuffle, a rush of warm bear breath over Sam's cold knuckles, and the bear sank back, its bright brown eyes boring into the man's unblinking blue ones.

Then there was only a blur of movement as the bear reared, one paw rising and swinging high. Nerves screamed inside Sam, but their frenzied message never reached his brain as the bear's entire body mass moved behind the downward motion of the paw and swept across the stony soil inches from Sam's snow-soaked knees.

Just as quickly, the massive muscles relaxed. The bear snorted and turned from the men, lumbering away with its rolling gait as though Sam and Eric had proved to be logs disappointingly empty of larva. The beast splashed across the icy stream, clambered up the far bank, and vanished into the woods.

"Philip! Eric!"

Through the ringing in his ears, Sam heard Kris's and Tom's alarmed cries. Still, he could not move. He remained on his knees, aware of Eric so still and silent beside him, staring at the break in the tree line where the bear had disappeared, with He Who Sees's medallion still clutched in his rigidly outstretched arm. A hand—warm and competent and strong—suddenly grasped his shoulder, turning him with more roughness than was probably intended. In a single explosive rush, control of his body returned. His hand tingled as though his life were flooding back into him from the icon. He sank limply back, just barely resisting the urge to curl into a fetal position as Tom caught his shoulders and eased him back onto his rump.

The woodsman was rattling on in a panicked litany of mixed French, English, and some native language as his hands raced over Sam's body, checking for injury. Beside them, Kris was doing the same with an oddly unresponsive Freeman.

"It sounds very pretty, Tom," Sam heard himself say testily, still not certain he was altogether back where he needed to be. "But I can't understand a word you're saying."

Tom swore. "Sorry. But when we heard the bear—"

Sam grabbed his wrist, cutting him off. "You *heard* the bear?" he echoed dazedly.

Kris nodded frantically, her hands gently slapping Eric's pale cheeks. "It roared twice. We . . ."

Sam didn't hear the rest of what she said. He shook his head slightly, confused. Was *that* why his ears were ringing? How could one's ears hear something without the mind comprehending? Silly question. All one need do to answer it was check out any of a half dozen college students on any given day. He ran his hands over his face, feeling like he had awakened from a particularly odd nightmare.

"Are you both all right?" Kris asked worriedly. "I can't find any marks, but—"

"We're fine," Eric answered her, speaking for the first time since the bear's approach. "Although why is beyond my understanding." He looked at Sam then, meeting his eyes with a long, measured gaze. "It seems somehow disrespectful not to be freaking out right about now."

The remark, delivered in such a placid manner, made Sam laugh, and laughter seemed to finally get his blood moving. He got his legs under him and clambered awkwardly to his feet. He bent to brush snow and muddy gravel from his knees and paused, seeing for the first time what lay imprinted in the mud by his feet. "What do you make of this?" he asked, pointing with one finger at the slashing cuts marking the earth where the bear had raked it with his claws just in front of Sam's knees.

"Who has a compass handy?" Tom asked quietly, fetching into his back pocket to produce a map on which he'd already drawn a couple of penciled lines.

"Who needs one?" Kris asked, her arms folded tightly across her chest now that she wasn't busy checking Eric for injuries. Her gray eyes had darkened almost to black. "That's as true west as you can get."

"Are you sure?" Tom stressed, dark eyes intense.

She snorted at him and her head jerked in a nod so sharp he could have cut paper on it. "I'm sure."

They all paused suddenly, waiting, none of them brave enough, suddenly, to say what needed to be said. Someone could have pointed out how ridiculous it was to assume three random encounters with wild animals could somehow reveal the location of a downed airplane, but no one did. One by one, the eyes of three rose and turned toward the fourth. Silently, they watched him and Sam couldn't begin to guess what the view looked like from the geologist's vantage point.

The silence dragged on interminably, until finally Eric shrugged and said, "What?" in a whispered tone that didn't sound at all like him.

"It's daft," Sam said quietly. "You already think we're nuts . . ."

"I'm not sure I think that anymore." The geologist wavered suddenly on his feet and Kris caught his arm before he sat down hard. Carefully, she and Sam lowered him to the ground. When Sam knelt to examine him, Eric slapped his hands away. "I'm all right, Philip. It's not the leukemia." He stared at the stream, at the rippling glint of sunlight on the water, then looked back at them. "I saw something when the bear was here." He licked his lips, looking confused and afraid. "I saw something I shouldn't be able to see, but I saw it."

"What, Eric?" Tom asked quietly.

Eric looked around at them all, judging their expressions, obviously fearing he would be laughed at. After all they had been through, Sam wondered how he could even consider the notion. "Due west, you've all been saying." He shook his head. "This is stupid . . ."

"Let us be the judge of that," Kris encouraged, and actually awarded him with the first smile she'd given him since their initial meeting.

To Sam's surprise, he actually returned it. "I saw two bodies of water converging to form a Y. One arm of the Y is crooked, like this." He drew it in the dirt between his legs. "There are mountains between the arms of the water. I saw a valley, a

223

small valley, separated from a lake by a stand of trees. The lake has a gravel shore. It—"

"*Jeeezus,*" Tom breathed. "They're on Watt."

"Where?" The query burst sharply out of Eric. "You mean I saw something that actually *exists*?"

"That you did, my friend!" Greycloak nearly crowed with delight. He reached over and one-arm-hugged Kris. "If we're going to take all this craziness on faith, it has to be. The only piece of water like that is Quesnel Lake and the North Arm. Mount Watt sits right between the far ends of the two arms, and I swear to God I've fished that lake you described."

"Then what are we waiting for?" Sam asked.

"Hold on," Kris ordered, releasing the woodsman. "There's some bitchy terrain between us and there. We'd never make it on the snowmobiles."

"Then what—"

She was already up and running back toward their tiny camp. "Williams Lake is in range!" she called back over her shoulder. "I'll have to cash in some favors and make up some story for my theory, but let me handle that. You guys prefer 204s or 206s as your limousine?"

Simple as it was, it took the men a moment to understand what she was getting at, then they were running after her up the slope.

CHAPTER
NINETEEN

Sam held a tight rein on his sense of triumph as the two 204s hove into sight, their rotors ratcheting loudly to break the natural silence. Those pilots' beliefs in the downed airplane's whereabouts were based on nothing but a story fabricated by Kris based upon the strangest set of circumstances he could recall (and he could recall quite a few). Though it was difficult not to feel elation, he tried hard to keep it at bay. There was still the actual crash to find, and the survivors, if any. If this proved to be another wild-goose chase, or if Al had already died . . .

He waited with the others at the tree line until the helicopters settled into the brown meadow-grass near where they'd called their lunchtime halt. At a wave from the cockpit, they abandoned their snowmobiles and ran to scramble aboard the nearest chopper. The noise was so intense they could do little more than nod their greetings to the pilot. Kris yelled something that was taken away by the wind, but whatever it was, the pilot gave her a thumbs-up that made her grin from ear to ear.

Sam snagged her sleeve as she passed and pulled her down between him and Eric. "What's the good word?" he yelled into her ear to be heard as the noise increased and the choppers rose skyward.

"They sent one of the bush pilots out as soon as they heard from me."

"And?" Eric prompted eagerly.

"*And*"—she practically jumped up and down in her seat— "the airplane is exactly where we said it would be. And they saw survivors."

"Thank God," the geologist murmured, and leaned back with his eyes shut. "Thank God."

Sam smiled tightly, glad someone had survived the crash and feeling just slightly guilty for his hope that the survivors were the *right* survivors.

He looked out the small, low window to his right. The view of snow-whitened crags and areas of dense coniferous trees was outstanding and one he wished he could better enjoy. After a while, water glinted in the distance. "What's that?" he called, pointing.

"North Arm," Tom supplied, his face split by an enormous grin. "We're nearly there." He crossed his legs atop a box, as at ease in a helicopter as he was in the forest.

Sam stared at the box, reading for the first time the stenciled lettering MEDICAL SUPPLIES across one side. It was right, of course, and logical, but the sight froze the blood in his veins and he caught himself praying again.

The choppers circled Mount Watt, watching closely, and then someone let out a cry. "There they are! I see them!" There was a mad rush to the windows. Sam peered out and down . . . and caught his breath painfully. The plane lay like a butchered bird, surrounded by crushed trees and flattened vegetation, with its wings nothing more than rubble some distance behind it.

There was movement below. Someone was running about and waving at them. Eric drew a deep, shuddering breath. "That's Dan Dodds, the pilot. I'd recognize that ratty baseball cap anywhere."

More figures emerged from the wreckage and waved frantically. The copter dipped once in salute to let them know they were seen, then began its vertical descent. The rotors of both choppers had barely slowed before Eric and Sam were out and running toward the plane with the others not far behind. Sam's eyes raked the assembled passengers. Which one was Gordon Huckstep? Which one was Al? Would he even be able to tell? Could they see each other the way Al, as a hologram, could see Sam in his new skin?

Dan met them first, swinging the taller geologist into a hug that probably bruised every rib he had. "*Eric!* I don't think I've ever been so glad—" The others converged, babbling excitedly, drowning him out and making themselves impossible to understand. An older blonde woman wiped her eyes while a red-haired man cried openly.

Sam nodded, trying to listen, trying to pay attention, and hardly able. He watched Eric, whose eyes scanned the group, searching frantically for someone he did not find. Sam's heart chilled and ice slithered in his guts like snakes. What if Lyndell were already dead, and Al along with her? What if they'd never survived the crash? What if—

"Dad?"

Eric spun, staring at the wreckage and the forlorn figure rising from beside the fire. She looked tiny and frail to Sam's eyes, a wisp of a young woman with too-big eyes in a dirty and scratched face, hobbling forward a few steps on a makeshift crutch and then holding out one arm imploringly. "Dad?"

Tears spilled from Eric's eyes as he rushed to sweep his daughter into his arms.

Sam turned aside, unwilling to intrude on this private moment. Seeing them together like this, he had no doubt he and Al had somehow managed to successfully do their jobs. Al . . .

Sam cleared his throat and turned to the nearest person, a lanky individual standing a good four inches taller than Philip Payne's six foot one. "Gordon Huckstep. Is he . . .?"

"Over by the fire." The Australian's accent was twangy on Sam's ear. "He's in bad shape, mate. There was a bear. We—" Movement near the choppers caught his eyes and he took a deep breath. "Thank God you brought medical supplies. We've got to get him out of here." He pushed past Sam to offer help to the pilots.

Sam turned away. If they took Al before he saw him . . . He ran ahead, pushing around the others to reach the man lying prone beside the fire.

Once Gordon Huckstep had been a big man. Many would still think him so, but Sam saw where the flesh had begun sinking away from his bones, leaving a flat, unanimated look to his sweaty features.

Sam slammed onto his knees beside the man he knew was Al. A kind of weighty war was going on inside his thin, tired body. Relief over having accomplished the Leap and reunited the Freemans was draining him of the adrenaline that had sustained him for the past few days. At the same time, dread filled him with its own chilly mass. He reached for a beefy hand and found it limp and frighteningly clammy. He bent low and put his mouth to the man's ear. "Al?" he hissed, whispering, hoping no one would overhear and question what he was doing. "Al, it's Sam. Open your eyes, pal. It's me."

To his surprise, the eyes did open, focusing immediately onto his face. More surprising yet was that when they did, Sam was able to see *Al*, not Gordon. It was as though the physical connection of eyesight fortified the weakening bond between host and Leaper. It didn't take much to see this was bad, very bad. Unless something were done soon, Gordon Huckstep might very well die.

"Sam?" His voice was a hoarse, incredulous croak and sounded nothing at all like Al. "Ohmigod, *Sam . . .*"

"I'm here, buddy."

"I'm not dreaming?"

Sam nearly laughed with relief. "No. I'm really here."

"Thank God." The look of rapt wonder Al trained on Sam's face shifted to their joined hands and both felt the realization simultaneously. For the first time in more years than they cared to count, they were actually touching. Granted, it was through the auspices of two unsuspecting individuals, but Sam would take what he could get and thought Al probably felt exactly the same.

"I knew you'd get here in time, Sam. I just knew it. I've

228

been trying to hang on, but I'm hurt so bad . . ." He grimaced in a brief spasm of pain.

"I know, Al," Sam whispered, his own voice hoarse with emotion. Movement caught the corner of his eye and he looked up. The medics were there with the stretcher. For an irrational instant, Sam wanted to rail at them, tell them to get back and leave them alone, give them some peace and some time to talk. There was never enough time. . . .

But that was selfish as well as stupid. Gordon needed to be tended to and they were the ones best qualified to do the job. He watched with a critical eye as they strapped him into the stretcher, then followed along behind them as they put him in the chopper. The others were climbing in, too, dividing themselves between the two aircraft, more than obviously ready to go home. Kris and Tom waved at him from the other chopper and he raised his hand in salute. There would be time to thank them later. Now, there was Al. There was still something that needed saying.

He clambered into the helicopter and snagged a seat right beside the stretcher. Eric and Lyndell were coming now, at a much slower pace given her injury, but that meant he would have to make this quick.

Sam leaned over and took Al's hand. "Al? You still there?"

"Where else would I be?" he asked. His eyes were shut now, but Sam could still faintly see Al within Gordon's shell.

Sam smiled. That sounded like the Al he knew. Suddenly, he knew Gordon would be okay. He couldn't be otherwise, having carried Al Calavicci around inside of him for the past few days. "You mean the world to me, Al. I just want you to know that." He squeezed the hand gently.

Fingers tightened minutely around his own and those eyes were open again, boring into his with an intensity of emotion that might have been embarrassing were it not so honest. "Same here, pal."

"I—" Whatever Sam was about to say got cut off as the rotors kicked in loudly and the helicopter lifted skyward. There was no way to talk over the deafening sound, so he settled back and contented himself with leaving one hand on Al's shoulder.

229

He glanced out the window beyond Al's prone body. The sun made a blinding panorama off the snow-covered ground below, shining as brightly as the thankful triumph in Sam's heart and as brightly as the coruscating colors that surrounded him momentarily as he, and Al, Leaped.

EPILOGUE

On the balcony circling the main building of the Quantum Leap Project, Al Calavicci leaned against the wrought-iron railing and stared at the night sky and the breathtaking panorama of stars. Granted, that sounded like something out of a cheap public relations campaign, but he found himself fascinated with the night sky and the out-of-doors since his safe return from British Columbia.

Some things change you forever, he thought, and drew deeply on the cigar held loosely between two fingers of his right hand.

He'd been busy the past twenty-four hours since his return, checking up on history himself rather than have Ziggy do it. The Freemans reunited and remained close until Eric's death in 1995. Lyndell was still alive, still a photographer, and residing in California. Gordon Huckstep survived his mauling and presently taught geology in Toronto. Al was giving serious thought to a visit to that part of the world, just to see his former host face-to-face. Dan Dodds had died in an airplane crash in 1988 and Gideon Daignault committed suicide in the winter of 1986. Hugh Bassey and Faye Marlowe married three months after their ordeal. Faye died seven years later of breast cancer and Hugh now lived and worked in Arizona. Philip Payne still practiced medicine and was a neighbor of Lyndell's.

The medical department had insisted that Al undergo a thorough psychological profile to reassure themselves that he was still the same old Al Calavicci. He'd managed to get through it, knowing it was a lie and that he'd never be the same old Al Calavicci again. Something had left its mark upon him, and if that was the case with only one Leap, what would Sam be like when he was finally allowed to return home? Would anything of the old Sam Beckett remain, or would he be an utter stranger?

"Admiral Calavicci?" Gooshie called from inside. "We've located Dr. Beckett. You're wanted in the Imaging Chamber."

Al drew one final time on the cigar, released the smoke on a long, slow sigh, and pitched the butt over the railing. Turning, he started inside. He was limping slightly, favoring his left foot. It wasn't injured, but often felt as though it somehow should be, a holdover from his days as Gordon Huckstep.

His eyes tracked to the Imaging Chamber, open and glowing and ready for him. He straightened his shoulders and the peacock hues of his jacket caught the light and fed it back to the machine. "I'm coming, Sam," he said softly. "And one of these days I'm bringing you home with me. I promise." Head high, he stepped over the threshold and the doors sighed shut behind him.